The Sting of the Scorpion

COLOPHON

This book was typeset in ITC Novarese Medium,
11 point on 14 point leading,
with chapter titles set in 18 point ITC Novarese Bold Italic.

The unusual combination of using roman capitals with the italic lower case is a tribute to the ancient original style when italic types were first used. At that time italic capitals had yet to be designed, so the roman capitals were the only ones available.

The typeface was designed by Aldo Novarese in 1978 and released through the International Typeface Corporation (ITC). The designer was born in 1920 in Pontestura in the Monferrato region of Italy. He began his typographic career at the age of sixteen working for the leading font foundry of Nebiolo in Turin. Novarese was imprisoned in 1939 for protesting against Mussolini's fascista dictatorship's involvement in the European war, but was kept from hard labor because he had won a medal in a juvenile art competition in 1938.

Following the war he returned to Nebiolo and became art director in 1952. He stayed at Nebiolo until 1975 when he became a freelance typeface designer, and continued working until his death in 1995. His final typeface, *Agra Nadianne*, one of forty-one, was completed just before his death.

The Sting of the Scorpion

By

KARL BRECKENRIDGE

with

LINDA PATRUCCO

Jack Bacon & Company
Reno, Nevada
2006

A *note to readers*:

The text that follows was composed during a six-week period in the summer of 1993, then left to lie in repose in a box as 244 typed, double-spaced pages. A MacIntosh disc of the work was laid to rest into the box with the printed manuscript.

In 2006 while planning a journey to Petaluma, Calif. with a friend, the writer mentioned that he'd written a novel in 1993 that took place in Petaluma, and that neither he nor anyone else had laid eyes on it since. She read the novel, enjoyed it, and suggested that it should be published. The MacIntosh disc would not open, even on a contemporary Mac, so it was necessary to retype the entire novel. Her help in editing, organizing the graphics and keystroking the original manuscript into a Word document, was immeasurable.

What follows is that original text, with no significant changes save for correction of some grammar and style errors. The red Mazda Miata curiously appears in the original text. The decision was reached to leave the writer's 1993 idiom intact. e.g. "…the Apple QuickTake camera," which would become simply "a digital" by 2006.

This might be the first novel published in America wherein the author honestly did not remember how the story ended…

All photographs were taken by the authors in Petaluma, 2006
Cover and interior graphics and design by Jim Richards

ISBN 0930083-29-6

Printed in the United States of America
by RR Donnelley

Jack Bacon & Company
516 South Virginia Street
Reno, Nevada 89501

www.JackBacon.com

A *midsummer daydream...*

A light rain streaked the windscreen of the Navy jet as it popped below the low cloud line, and the floodlit deck of the *Antietam* appeared off the pilot's left shoulder. The landing gear fell from the fuselage as the left wing dropped and the sleek plane started a long U-turn that would put its course parallel to the carrier's for a controlled crash onto its rain-soaked deck. The tailhook that lowered with the landing gear would snatch one of the cables stretched across the deck and jerk the plane to a neck-snapping halt, then roll it backwards a foot or two before it came to rest.

But the landing gear's drag against the night air failed to curb the plane's speed as its nose dropped toward the ocean. The pilot instinctively shoved the joystick harder to his left and stood on one rudder pedal, his left knee now locked straight. The weight of his body bore down on his ejection seat. The plane's arc began to carry it across the carrier's wake through the water, beyond the glide slope. The pilot dropped the wing further, and shoved the throttle forward to build up steam in case he had to make a second try, which was beginning to look like a damn good possibility. Waiting until the inevitable "wave-off" to firewall the engine would be too late – he'd splash into Santa Rosa Bay like a big orange-and-white penguin. The plane was still gaining speed, and the racket from the screaming turbine and the airflow over the landing gear rose to an ear-splitting pitch in the cockpit.

With the plane now cutting through the air on its side he had to look almost straight up through his canopy to find the carrier, and only slightly to his left. "Jackrabbit" strobe lights raced the length of the carrier's deck, quickly from stern to bow, to aid his approach. Then he glanced down at his instruments, but the white markings on the black dials were blurred.

He could barely read the climb/dive indicator, but could tell it was pointing way down, and that his airspeed needle was pointing too far up. And the increased gravity on his fanny hadn't let up by one pound.

What the hell's the matter with this bird?

He craned his helmet back into the headrest, struggling to focus on the carrier deck, now almost level with him as the plane continued its tight knife-edge turn. He thought he saw the floodlit landing signal officer on the aft corner of the carrier waving his murky paddles rapidly *climb, climb*. An urgent *go around! go around!* rattled through his earphones.

Then the carrier's deck lights went out – the LSO's paddles disappeared, the jackrabbits on the deck went dark, the red lights in the carrier's superstructure were pitch black. He held the turn and looked down at his instrument panel. It too was dark.

Now only two hundred feet off the black water, he raced through a tight turn with the engine on high-fire at twice the plane's touchdown speed. With a ton of bricks on his butt and a carrier five blocks long out there somewhere in front of him, the full gravity of his predicament set in:

Brent Douglas had gone blinder than a bat.

❖   ❖   ❖

Many years later on a cloudy Monday morning, Brent parked his Explorer in front of the thriving real estate brokerage business he managed. He paused for a moment to look with greater interest than most Realtors might, at two megasonic Air Force F-15 Eagles as they lazed overhead, side-by-side, probably transients in no hurry to the air guard base at the north end of the little valley.

I should be driving one of those torches instead of running this office.

Brent was a daydreamer, a wool-gatherer; a weaver of soliloquies about a life more exciting than real estate, woven occasionally in an airplane's cockpit but more often as mental vignettes about a life of espionage, taking over where Maxwell Smart left off behind a bamboo curtain or a shoji screen in a rural oriental bathhouse with an indigenous lass or two. He had fantasized thus since his childhood in this valley, and swore to write, someday, a tale of international suspense. And, could he only type, he may well have already finished it.

But he remained a roguish sort in spite of his ground-bound career, tall and slim for a man in his mid-forties and popular with all in the little valley town where he lived, alone; adept, if off-the-wall in the pursuit of his real estate endeavors, and as honest as the day was long. Most in his office were glad that he *couldn't* type – they knew that if the man reduced some of his labyrinthine plots to the printed word, he'd command clinical observation when his thoughts departed from his co-workers for digestion by the profane world outside.

❖   ❖   ❖

The myopic pilot keyed his mike and hollered *your airplane!* and raised both hands over his shoulders. He saw the joystick snap to the center as the plane's wings leveled. The throttle handle by his left hand slid back toward him and the engine noise died immediately. He heard the landing gear start to retract. As his eyesight returned from the total blackness to a dull blur he saw his left wing shoot by the red lights on the carrier's radar array.

"How much longer were you going to let me fly this crate?" Brent asked Sandy McCollum, the instructor-pilot in the seat behind him.

"About another two seconds would have been it," Sandy replied laconically, his usual ice-water tone of voice slightly shaken. "What were you looking at, Brent? You goddam near flew us into the carrier."

Brent explained his vision loss as Sandy pointed the little trainer toward the Navy's sprawling air training station at Pensacola, a few dozen miles across Santa Rosa Bay. Then he asked Sandy, "Why didn't the thing slow down?"

"You forgot to lower the flaps with the landing gear, sailor."

Oh.

Score one to first-time night-carrier-landing jitters.

Few pilots ever won their wings without forgetting the gear or the flaps at least once in the terror of a high-speed night carrier landing in the rain, but the Navy medical review board was less charitable about Brent's vision – an unusual case of the human eyeball distorting under high gravity loads – his during the tight turn toward the carrier – with no image focusing on the retinas. The board called it an early blessing in disguise – the "Gs" in a big, ballsy Phantom II fighter-bomber would have put a hell of a lot more load on his peepers than the little Buckeye trainer did, without Sandy in the aft seat ready to take the stick.

Brent was relegated to the flight engineer's seat on a four-engine

Lockheed P-3 Orion, an aging turboprop subchaser offering proof-positive that if enough power could be hooked to a boxcar, it too could fly. On the up-side, Brent spent most of his next nine years where the subchasers were based, within 25 miles of his home. But life aboard the lethargic Orions was not steeped in the high excitement he recognized as his destiny.

Brent's P-3 Orion

Lockheed P-3 Orion

He had ample time between missions to finish his degree at nearby State University, and left the Navy to become a land surveyor's field technician. He very soon learned that there was more money to be made by selling dirt than by pounding brass stakes into it all day in the heat, and he began studying real estate in the evenings. He passed the state broker's test his first time around.

❖   ❖   ❖

Brent stood in the parking lot, and watched the F-15s start to let down into the guard base. He fumbled with the office key in his hand, wondering for the thousandth time whether he might have become a latter-day Francis Gary Powers, his space-age stealth flying camera brought down by a death ray from a satellite circling Venus, taken hostage by an alien orbiter, one hand now gripping the strychnine tablet sewn into his tattered flight suit, the other clutching the ravishing Klingon princess locked in the small cell with him on the orbiter, promising him anything, *anything* he wanted in return for employing his unbelievable bravery and limitless skills to emancipate her. That might have been just a typical day in his life had he just remembered to extend the damn flaps on the Buckeye like he'd done a dozen times on dry land before that rainy Florida night over Santa Rosa Bay.

The two Eagles dropped out of sight behind the low hill just north of the little farming town, and Brent turned toward the office to unlock the door. He would learn in the next five days that a client about to visit the office would make his recurring daydream of high espionage aboard the alien orbiter seem like a quiet walk in the park.

CHAPTER ONE

Monday morning: The week begins...

Brent Douglas crooked the morning paper under his arm and turned his key in the stiff deadbolt – nothing. *Damn*, he thought to himself, *we've been in this joint for four days and I still can't get it right...* He turned it hard the other way and pulled the French door open, peeling the yellow Post-it from the beveled glass: You're front door was unlocked at 2:15 this morning. Janitor

You're, he thought. *No doubt an English major.* He flipped the coffee pot *on* and walked back to his office off the entry lobby of the new building. His sparse office was still in a state of evolving décor that bugged him when he walked into it – his old office had been likened to Rio Verde's longest ongoing garage sale, and he wore that comparison like a badge of honor. The most he'd had time to restore from his old office so far in four days was the bountiful Miss April, displaying her ample blossoms over a leafy bower in South Bay Title's ill-advised *Twelve Girls of Escrow* 1986 calendar, now tacked over his credenza. That calendar proved to be a disastrous marketing ploy that South Bay would like to have to do over again. He had toyed with hanging one of his favorite artifacts alongside Miss April, a parchment scroll in an Olde English font, possibly off a Gutenberg press,

> She offered him honour,
> He honoured her offer,
> And the rest of the night
> It was honour and offer

There was an attribution on the parchment to King James, whom Brent knew had made some contribution to the Bible, and the text seemed somewhat relevant to real estate. He liked it. It lasted three days in the old office before the firm's owner's wife told him that either it went or he went, and only after lengthy consideration, it went. Home. But now it was back, a thumbtack away from the attention it deserved. On his floor, waiting to go somewhere in the new building, was a foot-high brass ship's bell, mounted on a plaque with some asinine inscription about a Calvinistic work ethic – taken from either a Realtor magazine or a fortune cookie. And, he had salvaged the old ceiling fan, taken from Fundas' Fountain after the office sold the fountain's building in the 1950s. The brass fan housing had long since tarnished to black and the turn-of-the-century motor ground like a Waring blender full of walnuts whenever it was running. Brent had grabbed the old fan and the bell just before the moving vans backed in last Tuesday.

Brent plopped his Reeboks on his desk and stared at the firm's old

The Old Chapel/Office

office across the parking lot. The old place had character, even though it was just a surplus World War II Army chapel moved onto the lot after the war, added on to, brick-facia'd, re-gabled, shuttered, cedar-shaked, and finished off with a clock in the former belfry over a *Time to Buy* sign dreamed up by one of the firm's founding fathers' genius wives. The clock, not unlike the founding fathers' wives, seldom worked, and had stuck years ago at 7:16. The clock tower was later incorporated into the firm's advertising, properly depicting the time at 7:16.

That was an office for selling real estate. Were Sam Spade a first-time home buyer, Dashiell Hammett would have portrayed him visiting this old chapel-turned-office with a clock that was right twice a day.

❖ ❖ ❖

Brent smirked as he stared out the window, at his image of Sam Spade visiting a real estate office. Why in the world would Sam Spade ever come anywhere near a real estate office? Sam was cloaked in a sense of mystery, a man who did his best work in the shadows. Hammett himself could explore the sum total of the shadowy experiences of the million people in the real estate business and still have one hell of a time coming up with one decent plot for a novel – real estate is about as boring as it gets.

He'd heard rumors of guys in the business that did have some hairy tales to tell. Like the commercial agent who was recruited by the DEA when they were trying to close the net on a band of druggies in West Palm Beach. The local DEA and FBI agents needed a foil who could talk to a white collar perp about trust deeds as fast as they could talk about Uzi rifles and wireless bugs. That Realtor, according to the rumor, had never so much as fired a .22 pistol in his life, but wound up in a classy beachfront hotel suite wearing a Kevlar bulletproof vest under his blazer portraying a mob bean-counter, greeting five drug dealers at the door and answering their questions about laundering money through the local real estate market for 45 minutes.

Legend has it that the sting was going famously until one of the seven narcs behind a two-way mirror into the adjoining room got his videocam too close to the glass. One of the bad guys saw the dull flicker of the *record* lamp and all hell broke loose. Mr. Realtor hit the deck, taking a round in the vest and another in his ankle on the way down, and the whole operation went into the tank. The three bad guys that survived the firefight went to jail, made bail in six hours and the real estate agent took an extended vacation out of town, courtesy of the U.S. Government while affairs settled down locally. He returned to town with a new hairstyle, a slight limp and wears Ray-Bans when in public. He looks over his shoulder constantly.

And the taxpayers bought him a new blazer, without the 9-millimeter vent under one armpit.

Brent laughed. *Why can't I get plugged into an operation like that?*

The smile suddenly departed from Brent Douglas' face: *While that Realtor was doing all that, I was probably sitting in the old building working on a goddam appraisal.*

For free....

He looked at his wristwatch. 7:30. Coffee's probably perked.

Brent picked up his Garfield cup and started toward the break room beyond the four long rows of cubicles, six desks to a row in the open "bull pen" area of the new office. As he was admiring the view outside through the eucalyptus trees bordering the parking lot to the main street of Rio Verde across the Sequoia River, he saw a turn light blinking behind a piece of yellow cellophane taped to the fender of a faded green Pacer. This broad-butted mobile relic of the early 1970s was delivering Brent's preëminent management nightmare to the workplace – 230 pounds of amorphous flesh in a 100-pound sack, piled 70 inches above the ground, cloaked in the same polyester trousers it wore last Friday, a graying white long-sleeved shirt probably from Tuesday, Thursday's necktie, scuffed black shoes with brown laces, a cellular phone stuck into the frayed back pocket – a self-propelled unmade bed. The name on the nightmare's real estate license read *Dave Nichols*; the other agents in the firm who he'd tried to screw, which was all 20 of them, had their own favorite sobriquets for Dave, all uncomplimentary and most never too well-concealed.

7:30 a.m. Christ – what's he doing here this early? This is my time to myself.

The break room in the new building had a 1950s-diner motif – subdued lighting, neon soda pop signs, a replica Wurlitzer jukebox and four honest-to-God leatherette booths with chrome trim. The floor was a checkerboard black-and-white tile, the clock had the cobalt-blue neon rim that people living in the cold war era were convinced was nuclear and would therefore make them sterile. A movie poster of James Dean sprawled across the hood of a jet-black '49 Merc coupe hung beside a Hires' root beer sign. All that the employee lounge lacked was the Fonz.

He filled Garfield and started the morning routine he'd fallen into when he hung his license with the company eight years before. He liked the solitude of the office before the crowd arrived, and out of the goodness of his heart, made coffee and got the place up and running. And as is the reward of those who do favors long enough, he became taken for granted. On the rare day when he wasn't the first through the office door in the morning, he'd catch hell from everybody if they had to face an empty coffee pot. That thought brought another smirk to his face, and he thought of the pilots of the two F-15s, by now both taxiing onto the hardstand of the guard base south of Rio Verde. It was for damn sure nobody would bug them about forgetting to make the coffee.

They didn't forget to drop their flaps in flight school, either.

He turned on the CD player and heard Eric Clapton tuning up his acoustic guitar through the overhead speakers throughout the office. Edith Fischer would spend half her day reloading the carousel with new tunes.

Nichols was at his desk, a phone already jammed to his ear. He loved selling over the phone and scrunched his pale face with the perpetual five-o'clock shadow into a sardonic grin while he talked and punched the keyboard of his terminal with his grimy fingers. Somewhere in the little valley an early-rising homebuyer was getting the prelude to the Dave Nichols treatment. But, like the treatment he gave all the other buyers, and the end runs around sanity and ethics that he took at his fellow agents in the office, this present conversation too would lack the smoking gun that would finally give Brent license to disregard the welfare of the fish downstream on the Sequoia River and float the son of a bitch out to sea for once and for all. Already hot from just having to be associated in the same office with him, Brent slammed his cup down and stared out the window.

People like Nichols made it lonely at the top, if Brent was in fact at the top. Day-to-day, maybe; but the firm's two owners, while they seldom darkened the office's door, outranked him, and both their society wives yanked *their* chains. One of these fine ladies thought that Dave Nichols was the greatest thing since night baseball, and every time Brent tried to send Dave packing, she pulled her *de facto* rank. But Brent, in his own mind, knew that the years he had spent orchestrating one feat of espionage after another for the book he planned on writing, had prepared him mentally for one day soon, if not canning Dave or floating him out to the blue Pacific, at least making Nichols' life more miserable than it already was.

The fact that the firm's two owners could have even built this company into the dominant real estate office in the four little towns like Rio Verde, all in a 10-mile radius, was somewhat of an enigma. The towns, plus the farms in the rolling hills intervening them, were now being "gentrified," as the big-city reporters called it, by the rich and famous whose cars had been shot with a spraypaint can once too often in the big city an hour away. A decrepit old clapboard house with a peaked green shingle roof, surrounded by a big covered porch right out of The Birds – filmed in the Rio Verde valley – a sway-back barn and a split-rail fence enclosing 10 acres, and a curved-top galvanized rural mailbox as big as a doghouse welded to a vintage John Deere tractor parked at the two-lane county road, could fetch 300 grand from the fed-up couple in the Mercedes with a stub over the radiator where the three-pointed star was last night. And there were dozens of these homes, probably a hundred in the two counties the office served, not counting some commercial land over the hills to the east, with some office parks being built and bedroom cities to staff them springing up. His office's business was hot right now. Real estate competition would surely arrive, along with the clients in Mercedes followed by those who would spraypaint them, but for now, he ran the big he-bull office in the valley.

The founding fathers never saw this coming – they opened the office when the little John Deere was still bright green and yellow, pulling a feed-wagon to the small herd of Holsteins in the back side of the 10 acres. The barn was then the newest barn in the valley, built right after World War II when lumber again became available. One of them probably sold the little farm for $20,000 back then.

And Brent, sitting in his Reebok-elevated comfort at his desk and knowing that the fetching eight-o'clock shift would soon be making her grand arrival, wondered how either of these gentlemen could have held together a simple VA escrow that would have surely taken as long as 30 days to close in the late '40s, given their collective personalities, panache, and aptitude for the real estate business.

He really knew little of either one of them, aside from their shared abysmal choices of love interest and deep desire to spend time outside the office, which in retrospect was probably the linchpin of Brent's success and tenure. Brent came aboard as a broker/salesman the same morning that Chernobyl blew. The founders were even then only occasional visitors to the old chapel/office he held so dear. The sales manager at that time had been an escrow officer in her former life who held that all home-buyers should be flogged it they didn't pay cash-to-loan. Predictably, she crashed and burned; the founders visited the office, convening behind the only door in the chapel that would lock, while looking for a manager. Four days later, as the agents watched and waited, white smoke curled from the chimney and they walked out and anointed Brent as their replacement manager. *You'll do fine, son. No more beating the bushes all over town – you can sit here all day while the others do the work and just help them along.*

Thanks a lot…

❖   ❖   ❖

Brent was asked one day at a Toastmaster luncheon how Horton Landau and Oliver W. Holmes ever, *ever*, came together and succeeded so well given the widely-held civic perception that Horton was a suave and polished critic of the arts, music and fine local wine, and a fanatic for detail, whose wife shared his cultural prowess and whose children were well-established professionals – a physician son and a barrister daughter. Oliver was a boorish pain in the ass who conducted his personal life like a manic-depressive and once scratched his neck with a salad fork on the dais at a black-tie Chamber of Commerce gala, but was nevertheless considered charming by his spoiled bride of 44 years. Mercifully, they bore no offspring. Neither Horton nor O.W. demonstrated any great knowledge or commitment to the fine art of real estate brokerage. Brent was once asked about this in the bright beam of another club luncheon amongst the pillars of the community, and the new lackey of the firm felt obligated to respond with something deeper than "It's a damn mystery to me, too…"

He stood glistening at the podium, 300 civic eyeballs upon him, and related that in their youth, they were both fugitives from their native Austria – Landau reputed to be from the royal family – separately pursuing illicit commerce deep in China before her borders closed to Westerners. They sat together one afternoon idly sipping Slings in the otherwise-deserted Long Bar of the Raffles Hotel in Singapore while Horton fumbled a matchbook cover touting *Get Rich Quick in Real Estate*, pitching a real estate school offering instruc-tions in English, Malay and Mandarin. They enrolled together, but one night Horton's sarong became caught in the spokes of a rickshaw and it was torn from him, leaving him in the teeming downtown streets wearing naught but white boxer shorts imprinted with red fire engines. This, in the local culture, was an insult and an outrage to the indigenous people, clearly a precursor to further crimes against nature.

Brent was on a roll.

Horton, dressed, and Ollie, a vision in Jockey and American LaFrance, were pursued but dove into a nearby river and were swept to sea, to be picked up 20 hours later by a Liberian tramp steamer. Three weeks later they would be, only by a sheer twist of fate, aboard the first foreign ship to sail under the new Golden Gate Bridge.

He liked that line.

Together, he continued, they greased cable cars by day and continued their real estate studies by night. When their cherished real estate school diplomas arrived from Singapore, they started taking the test for state licensure, which in those prewar years was offered over eight weeks as a tear-out-and-mail-in exam in the San Francisco *Chronicle* Sunday funnies. They passed.

Christ, Brent thought as he looked out at the luncheon gathering, somber as judges and eager to hear more of the Horatio Alger origins of their fellow businessmen. The tenor of fear rose in his throat. *They're soaking this up like sponges — now what do I do?*

Wrap it up. Anyway, that's how my brokers came to be in the business; right after the war Landau & Holmes was formed as a brokerage company.

And I'm outa here.

❖   ❖   ❖

Brent slurped the last of his coffee and smiled, still wondering how 150 grown men and women could buy the specter of the boring founding fathers bobbing out to sea, one in his skivvies, then both passing a state test sandwiched between Dick Tracy and the Katzenjammer Kids. Curiously, and perhaps fortuitously, the yarn never got back to the Merchants of Singapore themselves.

8:12 a.m. The eight o'clock shift had arrived, right on time, in a manner of speaking. The attractive receptionist with the fiery red hair and big emerald eyes uncurled her lengthy and durable legs from behind the wheel of her Celica, hit the ground with both of them already running and burst into the office, modeling this morning a tight sleeveless Kelly green turtleneck and a skort, sewn from a pattern suggestive of Desert Storm meeting Rorschach. Katy's long hair was always creative, her attire always impeccable but nothing about her could be considered normal. Brent grinned as she hustled into the office, as if a little celerity on her part could turn back the big clock over the canopy by 12 minutes.

For some reason vaguely related to a St. Patrick's Day celebration several years ago that would have scared the IRA into submission, Brent ever after recalled William Butler Yeats' words from his *Easter* 1916 when Kathleen O'Rourke wore green:

> *Now, and in time to be, whenever green is worn,*
> *Is changed, changed endlessly, a Terrible Beauty is born*

Katy, the Terrible Beauty. A beauty, unquestionably; terrible in the sense of terribly interesting, terribly exciting, terribly unpredictable, terribly frustrating, but a terribly good pal. He was her biggest fan, but to let her know that would be lethal.

She knew it anyway, but let him think whatever he wanted. The affection ran both ways.

"Hi, Brent. Boy, do I have some good news!"

I can hardly wait, Brent thought as he slid his Reeboks off the desk and resigned himself to the fact that his daily rendezvous with serenity was over. "Good morning to you, gorgeous," glancing at his wristwatch. "Glad you could join us."

8:13 a.m. Kate was at her post behind the two-receptionist counter in the lobby, and Dave Nichols was still stoking his pigeon-for-the-day on the phone. Day had begun at Landau & Holmes. Or, at Homes and Land, as everyone except Landau and Holmes referred to the firm.

CHAPTER TWO

Later Monday morning: A client for Dave...

The phone panel in front of Katy chirped, and she touched a button.

"Good morning, Landau and Holmes Realty." Her brow furrowed as she pulled the headset mike nearer her mouth and listened for a moment. "Can you hold? I'll get an agent on the line." Dave Nichols perked his ears, making a motion toward picking up his phone. Katy unplugged her headset and walked into Brent's office.

"This man wants to know about our standard commission. Can you take it?"

Just great, Brent thought. *Eight-fifteen on a Monday morning and a stealth bomber from the* FTC *is checking us out. Again.*

"I got it."

He collected his thoughts for a moment before he picked up his line. It's a given in the business that the Federal Trade Commission has a nasty perversion against real estate agents coming even close to insinuation that there's any standard or statutory percentage of commission the business. And they've spent every day since the Magna Carta was signed on the grassy meadow in Runnymede in 1215 A.D. playing this goddam game over the phone, hoping some agent will screw up and admit it so they can haul the agent into a courtroom and play the recording and jump up and make an example out of him.

"Good morning, this is Brent Douglas, may I help you?"

The sound over the wire sounded like a call he once received from London – static and howling, with a slight echo – probably the recorder. "Yes I'm thinking of selling my home and I'm wondering what the standard rate of sales commission is in your area."

Your area. *Gimme a break – at least say* our *area and make this a challenge.*

"Let me pull my door closed. *Pause.* "It's so nice and warm out this morn-ing I had the door open and couldn't hear you over the traffic." *See if he goes for that.*

"It is a beautiful day, isn't it?" *Bingo. It's cool and should rain by noon. Where is this guy?* "Anyway, I've heard there's a standard rate I'll probably have to pay as a commission and just wondered what it might be?"

Brent told him that there was, by law, no standard commission; that commissions were negotiable between the broker and the seller, and that this office usually evaluated the task involved in selling a home, how much advertising it might take, how long it might be on the market and a few other factors, in determining what the commission would be. He glanced down to see if his nose had grown any longer or whether Geppetto was walking through the front doors.

The voice said, "A friend told me that you *usually* charged six per cent. Is that your usual rate? What do you *generally* charge? And isn't it *customarily* 10 per cent for vacant land?"

Christ. Usual – general – customary. He left out "market" – that'll be next. What's it going to take to get rid of this doorknob? "Why don't we make an appointment to come out and see your home, and I'll be able to give you a better idea then? May we do that today?"

"Well, commissions in your, er, our market, seem to run about six per cent, according to the other brokers I've interviewed – do you think you'll be in that range?" *Bullcrap. The business is competitive, but when we get one of these ringers, we burn up the phone to every other office in the valley to warn them.*

Brent was growing weary of this line. He debated giving the call to Dave Nichols, telemarketer *extraordinaire*, knowing that Dave could unwit-tingly drive a saint to drink. But he was fearful that Dave, not known for passing up a listing opportunity over small impediments like the FTC and two-to-five at Club Fed, would probably screw up and admit that L&H usually, customarily, generally charged right around six per cent, yessir. Back to the ringer:

"You'll probably like to know that our office has no fixed, standard, usual, general or market commission. And you may also be interested in knowing that if your home is nice enough on a high-traffic street in an upscale neighborhood, that we have a program to pay *you* six per cent or more just for letting us put an L&H sign on it – think that over and get back to me!" He slammed the phone down, lamenting that the new Asian phones don't slam with the authority of the old Western Electric jobs, and he walked out of his office for some more coffee.

❖   ❖   ❖

"Good call, Brent?" Katy had the headband embedded under her hair again, the earpiece apparently proximate to her ear and the mike peeking out from where it belonged. It would probably stay there until she walked away from her desk, as she had done on at least three occasions in the past four days, without unplugging the cord from the phone.

"Not good, but *great*, Katy." He raised his voice subtly, and watched Nichols' expression out of the corner of his eye. "Microsoft. Human relations department. Hush-hush stuff. Six key executives in an advance party transferring down from Seattle, a bunch more following." Katy's look was dumbfounded, but Brent winked at her and kept talking. "That one call could bag me two million in sales in the next six months." Katy spun around to hide a grin, and Brent saw Mr. Nichols flinch, the flinch of a man who kissed, say, $120,000 at the nonstandard, non-statutory six per cent rate, goodbye, due to Katy's caprice of giving the call to Brent and not to him.

"Good for you, Brent. They're a huge outfit – you'll make a bundle on that call." He trailed off to the break room to refill his coffee cup, and noticed a few more agents starting to pull into the parking lot.

❖   ❖   ❖

Only 9:00 a.m. A receptionist had arrived, promising great news to be forthcoming, no doubt involving some exploitation of a chassis honed to the consistency of granite by a mania for ærobics and weird food, or of a pretty face, a bright smile and a mane of red hair, always fetching. The news would not be of a cerebral nature, nor would he ask to learn of it, but he knew that learn of it he would before the sun next set over L&H. A federal investigator had made an inquiry, albeit one that would get tossed out of most courts on the basis of entrapment, but the key words remained *federal* and *inquiry*, and Brent had essentially told him to stick it, just before he hung up on him. Like a cat, his lives were finite; last month another bozo, this one distaff, with another scratch phone and an unsure perception of the local weather feigned a foreign accent emulating the parentage of a Cockney marrying a Samoan, and snaked Brent into a dialogue about Homes & Land's probability of having a listing in "her" part of Rio Verde. Seeing a fast trip coming into the land of racial discrimination, having not started his first cup of coffee, and feeling general frustration at the impending prospect of being uprooted from his chapel/office into the new edifice being completed across the lot, he told her that Homes & Land had no listings on the third ring of Saturn where her people probably congregated, but the Prudential California office across the street could probably help her. The phone he slammed then was from good ol' Western Electric, and it felt good.

But he just *had* to quit hanging up on federal regulators.

Ah, but the perfection of letting Dave Nichols twist in the wind over missing what he thought was a floor call from the personnel department of a Fortune 500 icon, now that was sweet, and Brent debated over how long to keep it afloat.

The phones were getting brisk now, and a few more agents were drifting in. Most realty agents hit it pretty hard during the weekend, and few among them are driven by any compelling work ethic to hit the ground running on a Monday morning. And thanks to the new Centrex system, agents could give their clients an internal number. If the agent was out, VoiceMail would pick up a call and record a message.

Brent always sensed that VoiceMail was invented just for the real estate industry a former agent who grew tired of his fellow workers poring through his little pink telephone message slips, filled out in longhand by a receptionist and put into a message slot for all the world, or at least for an agent lurking around the receptionist like a vulture to snoop at.

VoiceMail brought that to a grinding halt – agents dialed a code, known only to themselves and God, to retrieve their "mail." They could then erase it or store it. When the former agent finished inventing Voice-Mail he invented the car phone, also for the real estate industry.

"Dave's acting strange," Katy said. "He scares me sometimes."

"So what else is new?" Brent reasoned. "Dave's squirrellier than usual because he thinks I jumped three years' worth of commissions on that nothing call from the FTC. He's hot because I took the call and he hasn't figured out how he can do me out of it yet. And he'll probably wrap you up into it too. In the meantime, zip it about the call I took over the 'standard' commission. I'm going to have some fun with him when I get my thoughts together."

"I don't know about any call that you're talking about," Katy said, "but if this stunt works, treat yourself to typing lessons with the imaginary commission, write your novel, and retire from real estate."

❖   ❖   ❖

A new face had joined the office a few weeks ago – a sharp one, new to the office from across the bay, where she had a fairly active residential following but gave it up to follow her husband who had opened up a CPA practice a couple of miles down the road in Fairfax. Liz Claymore had impressed Brent in her interview because she seemed to have a life, and Brent had heard of a recent sale she made in her former office. A gnarly seller rejected her buyer clients' cash offer. She told the sellers that on second thought, her buyer had offered too much money for a home with no formal dining room and that furthermore she didn't feel like putting up with the wife's crap through a 30-day escrow, and good night, thank you very much. The sellers begged for the offer the following morning.

Brent saw a kindred spirit in this smallish fireball and hired her on the spot.

Katy ambled into Brent's office in her high-top beige Keds, a sturdy creature wide of hip and narrow of waist bearing one of Brent's weaknesses, at least in the morning: a maple bar, a big gooey one. "Compliments of First Bay Title, Skipper. I rescued it from Hathaway for you."

"You're too good to me. I'll walk an extra mile at lunchtime."

"No you won't. You'll drink one less beer after work. The phones have been busy."

"Seven new listings," Brent replied. "Automatic 28 calls, guaranteed. Douglas' Rule."

"This ought to be good. Tell me about Douglas' Rule."

"Douglas' Rule says that when our *For Sale* sign goes up on a home, the sign will bring four calls to you, Katy. From the neighbor on either side and the neighbor across the street. Lead-pipe cinch. Some will want to know what we think about the neighborhood, all will want to know how much they're asking, a few will ask why the sellers are moving. A good time for us not to say that they're moving because they're fed up with the neighbor carrying on with the cable TV guy during the day."

"You're rottener that I thought. You *wouldn't!*"

"I *did.* Bored as hell, back in the old chapel a few years ago. Don't know yet who we had on the phone, but we lost the listing 45 minutes later. Might have been the cable guy."

That's three calls. What's the fourth?"

"The sellers, bright eyes, or at least their friends that they put up to it. What's the place really like? Is it priced right? Are the sellers hard to work with? How much work has to be done to it?

Brent had pushed and pushed this rule in office meetings – for the first few days a sign's on a listing or the ad's in the paper, don't say a damn word to anyone that you wouldn't say into a recorder, because you might be.

❖　　❖　　❖

Brent saw Patricia Benham glide past his window.

"Hey, Patsy, got a minute for ol' Brent?" The slim tanned figure with the elegant jaw line and A-line auburn coif slowed to a stop and pirouetted slowly, as a model on a runway might, so that Brent would not have to rush to take in the entire vista of her crisp white knee-length shirtdress from a variety of angles. It was a pleasant vista and they both knew it.

Patsy and he had been together for many years, he thought four, she said five. While they didn't wear their love on their sleeves, the office crew knew they were an item, or beyond whatever plateau follows item status. They were popular in the non-realty Rio Verde social scene, likened to a municipal Barbie and Ken, albeit with a hint of crow's feet around their four brown eyes.

"For you, always." Few of her minutes away from the office were without 'ol Brent. "Nice hair. Been hangin' ten with the chicks from Malibu?"

Brent knew the season was upon him when he would begin to hear the smartass comments about his straw-blonde hair, so unusual on a 45-year old guy and what bottle is the straw coming out of and do you use it on your mustache too?

"I need your help. Which lady friend of yours looks the most like she works for Microsoft? I need a Microsoft lady."

"Have you been mixing your prescriptions again? What's a Microsoft lady look like? What are you up to now, Brent?"

"She looks like you. She's tall, she's beautiful, but she's businesslike, she's guarded, she's austere, she packs a briefcase and plays an HP-19 calculator with her eyes closed, she drives a rented car and she's in town to get even with Nichols for every goddam crooked stunt he's ever pulled on us."

"I like it. I think everybody in the office would like it. His former clients would like it, and most agents in the valley would love it. The weenie jumped a call of mine and done me out of a million-dollar office building sale three years ago."

"I think you might have mentioned that once or twice back then, in conjunction with small arms fire. Who do you know?"

"Except for working the calculator, my sister. The car's easy, and she can be as cold a whore's heart. It's a family trait. Where's this going?"

"Nichols moseyed in at the crack of 7:30 and busted up my solitude, then Katy gave me a floor call that he thought he should have got. I let him think the caller was a Microsoft advance man setting up showings for six bigshots that are moving to town, with the rest of their department in tow next year. Now I'd like to see him make a dozen showing appointments in corners of the valley he hasn't seen since his youth."

"And my baby sister has to drive all over the valley in that piece-of-crap Pacer of his?" Brent grimaced. Few, if any, real estate agents have voluntarily driven Pacers since the Watergate era.

"No. She has to come into the office with a map and some addresses of homes and ask for videotapes. About three days' worth of driving should get them all onto a couple of cartridges. In a few more days he can scout out a few more industrial sites, and all her inquiries about rail service, a strip with a short runway, local labor demographics and a new 30-inch gas main to the sites, and we won't see him for a week. She doesn't even need a business card – she can play cutesy and keep her client 'confidential.' He'll sell himself on the rest."

"Jesus, you play rough, for a guy. I'll call sis and we'll add some girl-stuff that'll even scare *you*. How'd you come up with Microsoft?"

Brent pointed at the new computer on his next, next to his shoes.

"Oh. I'm surprised sis isn't working for Reebok. Dinner?"

"Little early for me, Patsy. How 'bout we wait 'til seven?"

CHAPTER THREE

The Monday matinee...

Brent nosed his Explorer into the parking space marked with a crisp white MANAGER on the new jet-black asphalt, beside the MR HOLMES and MR LANDAU spaces. While he was speculating how long it might be until some nitwit added and S to both MRs in recognition of the two women who would forever occupy them, he noted the SALESMAN OF THE MONTH space to his right, and wondered how any idiot in politically-correct 1994 could conceivably use sales*man* in conjunction with anything to do with the real estate business.

He found that a two- or three-mile walk at noon was balm for managers. While others stuffed themselves on power lunches with clients and fended off pleading buyers over their cellular phones in pricey restaurants, he was happy to walk the mile-long shoreline of one of the reservoirs outside of town. Over the years he had made nodding acquaintances with nameless friends with nameless faces on the path, and come to memorize the location of abandoned hardware of the old railroad that once paralleled the water and the reeds where the Great Blue Heron stalked *her* power lunch. He lost himself with tunes from a twelve-buck tape player, and frequently couldn't remember whether he'd walked two or three laps without looking at his watch. This was his power lunch, and he'd enjoyed it almost daily. Let Katy and Nichols and the rest of his band of charges unleash whatever annoyances they wanted to visit upon him this afternoon – they now had a refreshed man to deal with.

Holly Harris pulled in along the row of cars, a vision of girl-next-door in her little fire engine red Chrysler LeBaron, the ragtop folded. As was his custom whenever Holly was gliding from place to place, he watched her, and it became apparent that he was in her sights also. "Hey, Skipper," she hailed in a voice belying her small stature. "Got a minute?"

He loved it when the crew called him "Skipper," a moniker he acquired the day 11 of the agents from the office took a friend-of-somebody's 42-foot yawl from the Sequoia River out on the bay. Brent was no stranger to blue water, as John Denver might say, but he had no idea that the shadow in the fog off Angel Island that he thought was another small island was a Navy ship. And not just any ship, but the *Missouri*, laying at anchor awaiting her farewell appearance during the upcoming Fleet Week celebration. Next Saturday the fleet would steam under the Golden Gate Bridge then past her, each ship in the flotilla striking its colors momentarily to the *Missouri's* company, assembled in tropical whites along her railing and three turrets, who would accept this tribute to the historic ship's final voyage. The fog lifted for a moment, revealing the *Silverheels* to be on a collision course with the grey battleship. Brent, a former sailor to whom the black BB 63 on the side of the starboard bow should have meant something beside *Boston Braves*, asserted the age-old right of the master of a vessel under sail to right-of-way over a powered vessel, in this case a ship powered but with steam down, held fast by two 40,000 pound anchors right smack where it had been for three days and would remain for four more. He hailed her skipper, eight stories over the bay, with a Radio Shack loudspeaker and demanded that he get her the hell off the *Silverheels'* tack. The distance closed to a few hundred yards and the fog lowered.

The mighty *Mo's* launches came alongside with boarding ladders at about the same instant that two helicopters with depth charges arrived over the yawl, blowing food, drinks and everything else that wasn't bolted down from hell to breakfast with their rotor wash. Above the noise most of the Realtors heard the command *everyone face down on the deck, now!* and gladly complied, only a few in tears. One sailor commanded Brent to turn to and release his sheets to spill the wind and bring the craft to a halt. When asked who the master was, the crew pointed in unison at Brent. He was roughly cuffed and escorted to a launch, where within 10 minutes he convinced the assorted SEALS, marines, Secret Service suits and God Almighty that they really weren't the Greenpeace activists who had shot their mouths off in the *Chronicle* that morning about blockading an ominous war machine that surely used baby seals for target practice. And furthermore that the fine agents of Landau & Holmes Realty, loyal Americans all, weren't really PO'ed in the least about the awesome arsenal of nuclear weaponry 150 yards away, nor out to make an issue of it.

Everybody unracked their AR-15 rifles, made friends and played nice, and the Chinooks retracted their .50-calibers from the cargo doors and thumped off above the fog belt. One sailor videotaped the L&H assault team as they arose from their prone positions and probably later sent the videocartridge off to the FBI. Brent noticed that he lingered a moment longer on Holly, and thought he saw the zoom lens twist...

Thereafter, he was known as "Skipper," guardian of the seas, arbiter of the seafaring man's right-of-way, the mild-mannered real estate sales manager who once sailed In Harm's Way. Curiously, L&H was never again offered the use of the *Silverheels*. Horton Landau hated the "Skipper" nickname, which suited Brent just fine. And somehow, as if a good-hearted sailor wanted to make the whole thing end on a high note for the crew of the hapless yawl, a brand-new blue Navy baseball cap embroidered with U.S.S. MISSOURI BB-63 in gold was mysteriously left on board the *Silverheels*. The cap was now displayed on the brass coat rack in Brent's new office – a reminder of a prominent, if terrifying, chapter in office's memory.

[*2006 note: The BB-63 would be decommissioned after Fleet Week and towed to Pearl Harbor to become a permanent memorial alongside the* Arizona.]

❖   ❖   ❖

"Talk to me, you rosy-cheeked siren of the deep," he hollered back to Holly. Holly had achieved widespread, if temporal, acclaim in the five bay area counties when the Navy released an official photo of the incident to the *Chronicle* depicting two helmeted sailors checking out Holly's cute little butt in her red-and-white striped shorts, high in the air over a Coleman ice chest where she landed in her haste to hit the *Silverheels'* deck. "Want to go for another sail?"

"Leave my cheeks out of this," she said, recalling the picture. "And, no. Never. What I need is a partner. Got a showing appointment with Norman Bates tonight out in West Valley. Can you do it?"

"No, but lemme think." He remembered his dinner with Patsy. "I'll get somebody – if I can't, I'll bring Patsy and we can hang out while you show the place. Let me work it out, and I'll talk to you later in the afternoon."

Norman Bates was an apocryphal buyer, inspired by the innkeeper's son in Hitchcock's *Psycho*, feared by agents and managers around the nation. There was an element of callers who were somehow always able to get the fairer flowers of a real estate office on the phone, then set up in a listing that was usually vacant or off the beaten path, or both – and often after hours.

No one ever knew if Norman was going to bring Mrs. B, or could they ever be too sure how he found *that* agent or why he'd set up a showing for *that* listing, when it wasn't remotely like what he called about. Canny agents just had a feeling about Normans, and Holly had one about hers.

Offices worked together on this problem and usually bounced around contrived *nomme de kooks* and telephone approaches with each other if a flake was working an area. Brent had laid down some pretty stringent guidelines on remote or evening showings. The policy was that nobody goes alone, particularly in the evening, if the listing is vacant or the sellers won't be home. Nobody goes out in a client's car. And if Norman is coming to the office in the evening, another agent will be close by. If a second agent can't be found, blow the appointment – it's as simple as that.

In the same vein with the Norman Bates of the world was the car-sign issue that Brent fought and won shortly after he became the sales manager. One night he saw Lydia Wainscroft, one of L&H's comelier agents, buzzing about town in her Continental with not only an L&H clocktower magnetic sign on the door, but a smaller one proclaiming *call Lydia Wainscroft* and (707) KL5-1539 for all the testosterone-charged world to see. The sign came off the car the next day, amid plaintive cries of T*hey all do it in LA and Vegas*. But from that day forward they didn't do it in Rio Verde. He regarded magnetic car signs with the same fondness as he did polyester suits and one founding father's wife's Giorgio perfume. A sign that told the world not only where the lass works during the day is bad enough, but including her name and phone number was asking for trouble.

Christ – what are they thinking about? Half of them pack revolvers and Mace so they'll feel safe, then they fight me on a stunt like this…

Like few other aspects of his life as it pertains to real estate, Brent was serious about the agent-security issue. All this started in the dark ages before cellphones. Some of the ladies thought that some slack could be cut if they had a phone. Brent replied that phones were only deadly when thrown at short range. The rules stand.

Holly would have an escort tonight.

❖   ❖   ❖

Brent sat in the break room working on some kind of mystery meat sandwich while he called his VoiceMail from the wall phone next to the booth. *Thank you for calling, please enter your code now.* He had given himself the nickname SCORPION for an entry code but somehow it lost something continental and intimidating when dialed as 72677466 – Double-Oh-Seven it wasn't.

SCORPION had a call.

"Mr. Douglas, my name is Jane Doeman and I'm in town researching some amenities to the area and its environs. Your name has been given to me and I would like to speak with you. Please return my call at area code 7-zero-7 number KLondike 5-2139 and I will be paged. Thank you." Beep.

The voice was inhuman. Deep, throaty, like Kitty in *Gunsmoke* wearing Darth Vader's helmet. And the text sounded like a computer – *7 zero 7? environs?* Who was this person? Ah-ha – he remembered the ringer of his own invention set in motion to annoy Dave Nichols.

But why did Patsy's sister call me? Is this already underway? I haven't even doped it out yet.

Patsy's sister must have fouled it up – that call should have been to Nichols. He'd return the call in a while and get "Doeman" back on track.

The deep and mysterious Katy appeared in the break room's doorway, now wearing, over her terrorist fatigues, a vest of gold lamé in the front and shiny red satin in the back. Three lucky yellow Post-its adhered to the lamé on the gentle swell of her left lapel.

"Surprise!"

"You're right, I'm surprised. I thought we paid you, with your little partner, a vast sum to answer the phone up front, and to my surprise, you're in here. Who's Jane Doeman?"

"I know no Doe, man. Why?"

"Never mind." *Ms. Doeman didn't come through the switchboard – she obviously has my inside VoiceMail number. How'd she get that?* "Would this be the surprise you mentioned this morning before I had my eyes truly open?"

Katy giggled. "Yes!"

"And would this have anything to do with wearing a vest with whatever color that is and those, whatever you call them?"

"The color's butterscotch and the things are a skort. Aren't you going to ask me?"

"No. Beat it."

"That's no fair. Soon you're going to see me on TV and tell everybody you know me."

"You're taking Marlon Perkins' place?"

Katy did a little sis-boom-bah, shot a can-can kick, and then yanked the Post-its off her vest, exposing the official NFL 49er oval logo. "No. I'm going to be a 49er cheerleader. In fact, I am one. I won in an audition."

Brent collapsed his head into his hands, vaguely recalling that the 'Niners had three away games in a row and three Monday night games this fall, two on the road. "That's lovely. Just lovely. I'm happy for you, but I can see a hell of a lot of time gone from here." He looked at the buff upper torso and the buns of steel and tacitly pictured a late fourth quarter of a playoff game, 'Niners four points down, ball on the five, fourth and short, Rathman on the bench with a pulled hamstring and 55,000 people in Candlestick shouting *Katy, Katy* in unison. The cheerleader pulls a Lycra uniform over her muscular legs, tucks her red mane under the golden helmet, pats a few fannies in the huddle, takes the handoff from Young, and with a monstrous second effort breaks the plane with the ball for a TD, dragging Lawrence Taylor along with her. The conversion is meaningless; she's carried from the field, signs a multiyear contract and tells L&H to stuff it. Taylor retires, in pain and humiliation.

"Only a few afternoons a week for a few months. Can you hear me?" Brent snapped back to reality, if this encounter could be called that, and stared into her big teary green eyes and weeping little face. "You're mad, aren't you?"

Lydia Wainscroft walked into the break room, and Brent called her over. "Lydia, a wondrous thing has happened to Katy. She's going to tell you all about it." Lydia led the ecstatic, sobbing, jubilant, repentant and contrite receptionist to the winners' locker room. She looked at the pitiful creature in the clothes of many colors, and then back at Brent.

"You're going to owe me big-time for this."

Brent checked Felicia, now the solo receptionist, and saw that in her usual unflappable style she could cover calls alone for a few minutes while her compadre resurrected her life, and he turned without further adieu to review the ads scheduled to go to the local paper.

Real estate ad-writers are the masters and mistresses of overstatement and hyperbole, and at the top of the list was Hap Durst, ad writer supreme, whose *laissez-faire* attitude made Brent appear committed by comparison. Hap in real life drove DC-10s for Delta Airlines on some God-awful schedule that allowed him loose on the real estate community for days on end. During these layovers at home he often picked up a sale, usually to an airliner-type migrating to the area to join the legion of airmen and attendants who live in the valley and keep a couple of vans available for a daily round-trip to and from the airport an hour away. The Photo-of-the-Week in the local paper one week was of eight three- and four-stripers, commanders of multimillion-dollar DC-10s, 747s and Airbuses bearing upwards of 250 souls to their world-wide ventures, staring at a flat tire on their ancient Ford Club Wagon and declaring a Mayday.

They all probably bought their homes and mini-ranches from Hap…

❖   ❖   ❖

Opus the Penguin-screensaver started waddling across Brent's computer screen and he realized that he must have been staring at it mindlessly for at least five minutes or Opus wouldn't be waddling. Brent needed a break from ads, and wandered out into the bullpen like a tall blonde bird-of-prey in Reeboks, circling around for a while and finally pouncing on Pete Stephens, innocently seated in his little cubicle. Pete was trying to make sense out of a home inspection report, a document generated by wannabe structural engineers to give a homebuyer a dozen good reasons to weasel out of a contract and lower an offering price. Pete was a rakish dude, a hell of a lister but couldn't sell a home if he tried, which he didn't. He hated buyers. Brent admired that in a person.

"Peter, my friend, how have you been? It's been so long since I've seen you! You're looking well!"

"I've been fine. It's been since ten this morning in the break room, and I look like one of my pre-war listings has a cracked driveway. Imagine that, cracked after only 50 short years. What the hell do you want?"

Brent sensed a defensive posture. "I bring the opportunity of a lifetime for you; a beautiful woman in a boss car, a drive in the country – what could be nicer?

"*Murphy Brown* and Pete Stephens, alone in my condo, a six-pack of Bud and no real estate."

"Murphy's a re-run. Frank buys a toupee, Jim Dial gets an earring and Miles touches Corky inappropriately. You've seen it. It pales next to my offer."

Pete threw down the report. "Who needs a hired gun? Norman back in town?"

"Maybe. Holly got the call, and needs you tonight. West Valley. Can you cover her? I'd appreciate it."

"You got it. She'd do the same for me if I were going to West Valley to meet a crazed person wanting to have her way with me until dawn."

"In your dreams, stud." Brent wandered back toward his office. He stared at the note with Jane Doeman KLondike 5-2139 and decided to face the music. He pressed the keypad and heard a whiny voice "Five two one three nine, good afternoon."

No clue there.

"Hi, I'm Brent Douglas from Landau & Holmes Realty, returning Jane Doeman's call."

"One moment, please." Click. Music. Click. "Miz Doeman is unavailable. She will meet you at your office at 11:00 tomorrow morning and would like to look at your MLS quarterly review supplement for home sales in this area for the past six months, and condo and townhouse rental amounts and absorption rates for the same period. If you have any information about the local school district, zoning and regional transit routes, that will probably come up in your first meeting. Thank you for calling her back, Mr. Douglas." Click.

What the hell was all that about? Doeman's gopher just set an appointment in my own office and gave me a homework assignment.

But she called the wrong agent – all this was meant for Nichols, not me.

Brent autodialed Patsy's number. She was home.

"Your sister's crossed up. She just tied me up at eleven tomorrow and gave me two hours' computer work through an interpreter that sounds like Peter Lorre. I can tell she's going to sink her teeth into this, but for Christ's sake, get her on the right page – Nichols is back in the conference room setting the hook into two clients. Tell her to get to him before he takes off. And how'd she get a KLondike number? I thought she lived across the bay."

"Let's see, this would be Brent, wouldn't it? I'm fine, thank you for asking, and before our discussion of subterfuge begins, first things first. We have a date tonight, do we not? Dinner, wasn't it? I've selected a little garment that will knock your socks off, and I don't plan on having Peter Lorre screw it up."

"Peter screwed up tomorrow. Tonight's clear – I'll pick you up at seven. We had a little scare with Holly. She made a weird appointment out in the West Valley, but I tore Pete away from Murphy Brown to ride shotgun with her. We're clear."

"You mean hunkish Pete and demure little Holly? That's like leaving Colonel Sanders to guard the chickens. Those two could embarrass Norman if they both needed their horns trimmed on the same night. Speaking of which, I've got a Toastmasters meeting at oh-dark-thirty tomorrow morning so we can't be out all night."

"I'll nudge you at daybreak. What about your sister?"

"I didn't expect her to be with us."

"I mean about straightening her out on the scam on Nichols."

Patsy was quiet for a moment.

"I called her house but I missed her. She's out of town until Sunday…"

CHAPTER FOUR

Tuesday morning: Another new client arrives...

Brent wheeled his Explorer past the shaded redwood townhouses he'd called home for the past four years, for the short drive on the two-lane county road to the office. Rio Verde's narrow main street was lined with two-story Mediterranean Villa or Italianate buildings, many with classic iron front trim, retail stores with striped awnings and rich gold-leaf lettering on the second-story office windows. Dates centered on the ornate parapets dated the building to the 1910s and '20s. Diagonal parking was still permitted by the grassy median, set with giant oak and eucalyptus trees planted when the street was still a path for horse-drawn carts delivering grain to the four-story brick McNear's Mill across the Sequoia River. The mill had been turned into a boutique mall, a nice one. An antique Baldwin locomotive came to its final stop in a triangular park with cast-iron benches. The loco was maintained by the towns' firemen, a traditional duty they gladly inherited from the old volunteer department. Across the street from the park was the pride of Rio Verde, the Alhambra, an immaculately-restored theater in the Egyptian architecture popularized during the era of the early motion pictures. The exterior of the building and the art-deco ticket booth, with the large covered lobby lit by a gazillion lamp bulbs in the ceiling and pre-war movie posters in display cabinets had been seen in a number of movies and TV commercials.

Downtown Rio Verde

Past the park, he turned left onto the D Street Bridge, a classic old iron drawbridge built to allow the *Steamer Gold* access from the bay up the river to the mill every morning at eight o'clock. A promenade ringed the turning basin for the *Gold*, where the small turn-of-the-century coastal freighter could belay her hawsers to the cribbing and winch herself around for the voyage back down the river with a cargo of feed. Patsy and he liked to walk along the gas-lit promenade in the evening – he harbored a smirk-provoking fantasy that across this river and at this very moment, Patsy was being called upon by the head Toastmaster to deliver a three-minute extemporaneous dissertation of her most pleasurable recent experience. Embodied in this fantasy was his hope that she could keep a straight face and lie like a rug.

This was the first clear morning since the move, and the first daybreak that the bright sun bathed the dark green fascia and trim against the white walls of the new L&H building.

Job One for Mr. Douglas this morning seemed to be, by 11:00, assembling a potpourri of facts vaguely relating to home prices and rental rates in the valley, with an overview of bus lines and school district info, for the mysterious Jane Doeman of KLondike 5-2139. Most of this would be in his computer somewhere, but the bus line? One bus roamed the whole valley, twice a day, except for the commute line to the ferryboat park-and-walk. He booted up his computer terminal.

Why me? Twenty-one agents in this store and Jane Doeman finds me.

❖   ❖   ❖

Felicia Cochran parked her impeccable black Ford Granada in the spot Brent assigned to her. She liked the vintage Granada coupe because it had the longest doors in modern automotive history, and she could swing her wheelchair from behind the front seat and transfer into it in one controlled swoop. She wound up in the bright fuchsia chair – Hot Wheels, as she called it – when a daydreaming motorist rear-ended her bicycle on one of the narrow county roads up the river six years ago. Recovery and rehab took her out of college for two years, during which she spent most of her waking moments learning computerese. She came to L&H after she was graduated from State University three years ago with dual degrees in Black Studies and Information Science. Brent called her a receptionist; in reality she was the guru of the office's computer system and had spent most of the last four months getting it upgraded for the move to the new building. And unlike her partner, the inimitable Katy, she hit the deck religiously at eight bells on their every-other-morning early shift. She stopped in his doorway.

"Hiyo, Skipper." She was an alumna of the attack on the *Missouri.* "How's the coffee situation?"

"Mine or yours? Mine's empty, but I read Ann Landers daily and I know the national havoc wreaked by secretaries asked to make a coffee run."

She grabbed his cup. "You're going to work for it. There are two boxes of copy paper from Office Depot in the trunk of my car."

Brent logged on to the computer with his LOGON code and started pulling up the median price home sales in the valley in the past six months.

Brent heard Felicia, still the only other human in the building, coming around the corner.

Felicia set his coffee cup on his desk. "Thanks, gorgeous. I heard the CD stop and start. Who might this group be?"

"Just arrived yesterday – 'Crash Test Dummies.' You like them?"

"Yeah, sounds like about six old groups I can recognize, all playing at once. Be good for mid-afternoon when all the world's asleep." He thought about the Nichols adventure. "I'm going to be getting a call from a lady code-named *Falcon.* When she calls, tell her I've been called out of town unexpectedly and my right-hand man, Mr. Dave Nichols, is going to be handling her account. Then track his fat, er, track him down, page him if necessary, but make damn sure he gets her message if he's not in the office."

"You're giving an account to that cretin without him having to steal it? What'd you and Patsy smoke last night?"

Brent was surprised. "How do you know that I wasn't working hard, very hard, last night, until very late?"

With a smile out of a Pepsodent ad, Felicia said, "Unless there's two green Eddie Bauer wagons with 6 PCT personalized plates in this burg, you were at the Green Mill Inn last night when we drove past, and Patsy's the only woman I know who'd go out with you."

Touché. The 6 PCT was a little in-your-face statement to the FTC about their fixed-commission mania. "OK, so we were hungry."

"Now to the issue at hand: Why are you giving Nichols a lead? Is Patsy a party to this stunt?"

"It's complicated, beyond your comprehension. We're going to try to put a thousand miles on his Pacer, if there's that many left in it. Falcon is Patsy's sister, in disguise as an advance man for a big company moving some people here."

"And *Falcon* perpetuates your fantasy to do for real estate what Ian Fleming did for sex and martinis? Is *Falcon* her VoiceMail code too, *Scorpion*?"

"How do you know about *Scorpion*?" His access code was a secret, protected by the software.

The long fingers with read enameled nails and a heavy carved gold wedding band played a few notes in the air like an arpeggio on a Hammond. "These fingers know DOS, Scorpion. But I don't know you." She spun around to leave.

"Nice not talking to you, Felicia."

Brent killed Wiley Coyote the screensaver with his space bar and brought *HouseNet* to life. He typed the date and *Client: Jane Doeman* in a field that would appear on all the final output.

He picked three target home prices, then started searching for some sold homes. He introduced a swimming pool and pasturage available on the property. The computer printed a list, and Brent opened an area map with a number keyed to each sale, and the computer printed a side-street for each home on the list. This took some time.

If Katy still loved him, she'd have saved him a maple bar. He sat down in the break room under the *Hire's Root Beer,* 5¢ neon sign. Katy still loved him. She brought the maple bar. "Thanks, Irish, and sis-boom-bah. You're a sweetie. Got me any tickets on the fifty yet?" He strolled back to his office.

He found a presentation folder with the L&H 7:16 clocktower on the cover and started to assemble the package. He punched the reception-ists' comline: "If either one of you hear from Holly or Pete, I want to know what happened last night with that Norman Bates showing out in West Valley."

Katy keyed her phone, "I saw Holly jogging this morning and she looked pretty happy, although that may not mean much about the show-ing." She giggled to herself. She had also seen Patsy in the 7-11, and she wasn't exactly dismayed by life herself.

"Something a little more definitive would be nice. I want to light up the MLS computer network if there's a weirdo loose."

Tom Yarbrough walked across the lobby to Brent's office. Tom was the *de facto* second-in-command of the good ship L&H, by an unwritten and unstated consensus of the staff, Brent, and Tom. Brent wasn't sure if Landau or Holmes knew. Or cared.

"I saw Pete this morning and he said it was a no-show, but they did a see a guy that looked like Einstein in an old bronze El Camino drive by a couple of times, looking up the driveway on both passes. They couldn't see the plates, but they looked dark red, like Arizona's."

"Did you turn all that in to the MLS network?"

"Yeah. The description of the car and Einstein and the pitch he gave Holly on the phone. It should be on the screen by now."

Brent cleared his screen and brought up the NEW LOGON window. It was there: AGENT WARNING, followed by all of Tom's dope – this window appeared the first time any agent in the valley turned on the MLS program.

"Looks good, Tom. Thanks!"

❖   ❖   ❖

9:30 a.m. Mouse in hand, Brent clicked out of the ARCHIVE window into the CURRENT LISTING and started his journey through homes for sale in the valley. He added school districts and ran a list by elementary, junior and high schools, cross-referencing to swimming pools and separated condos from single family homes. The stack of paper in his printer tray had grown, and while the computer sorted out all the data on the current listings he grabbed the sales information and started punching it to assemble into the presentation folder.

Is this what agents do all day now? A rekindled appreciation for his management status began to glow within him.

Condo and townhouse rental rates, the lady said. Most of his stuff would have to come from the newspaper and could go completely into the tank by the time Doeman's entourage of executives arrived here. If that's really why she's here.

As Butch asked Sundance, "Who are these guys....?"

He located all that he could and entered them on the growing map. Then he started the laborious task he had taught many times in junior college classes but never yet done once in his life, of adding index tabs in a profusion of colors and captions to the side margins of the pages. *Eyewash*, he thought, for the cryptic Ms. Doeman…

Next, as he watched the clock climb inexorably toward the big One-One O'Clock, he fumbled with Doeman's *absorption rate* request. Where the hell did she come up with that? – that's CCIM lingo. Brent was a Certified Commercial and Investment Manager candidate years ago until he crunched enough numbers about nebulous data that he became convinced that it stood for Can't Close I Miscalculated. One night after three margaritas he offered a bunch of CCIMs his own overview of their acronym. His meteoric ascension to their lofty professional plateau ended that night by mutual assent.

Wowee – what's that in the parking lot?

A woman – no, a goddess delivered unto earth by a late-model plain-vanilla GM sedan. She landed on long slim legs within shimmering fannyhose, a shapeless bod and the tightest blonde chignon he'd ever seen, all wrapped and delivered in a fitted two-piece black linen business suit. She pulled a briefcase, not just any briefcase but a Halliburton stainless steel case from the white Buick Regal, tucked a cellphone into the handbag that matched her low leather heels, checked her Rolex against the clock over the entry and strode like a Valkyrie into the Homes & Land lobby.

Felicia and Katy were dumbstruck as she took command of the room, with the look of ice on fire in her blue-grey eyes. These receptionists were seldom intimidated – this was indeed a happening. She even made Brent squirm. He looked at the Buick – it had the barcode of a rental in the back window. *Falcon is here, in the building!*

Katy looked at the In/Out board. Nichols was Out. The three women now at the reception desk, all beauties in their own way, each cracked not a smile as Felicia wrote down a number on a Post-it and handed it to the Falcon, who then stepped into the phone nook adjoining the reception lobby. Felicia and Katy stared at each other and quietly tended to their business. Brent was worried. *They both know who Falcon really is. Why the shell shock? Something's wrong…*

Brent paged the receptionists' desk and told them to kill the speakerphone. "What's going on?"

Felicia spoke into her boom mike in a low voice. "This better wait," and clicked dead. The hour was nearing eleven.

The wraith in black linen stepped from the phone nook, pocketed the Post-it, and handed a note to Felicia. She took some office brochures from the dispensers, nodded coolly at the receptionists and the floor agents. She paused on the way to the open front doorway and looked at Brent through his window, holding his eyes captive with her huge grey ones until that instant when a long glance becomes a short stare. She continued her walk, more like a glide, to the parking lot. She entered the Buick gracefully in a sequence of rotations, twists and bends of her rump and long legs, like the circuitous motion of a 747's four main landing gears up and into the wheel wells. She backed the car out, holding her cell phone to her ear as she drove away, never once looking back toward the office.

The visit was short, her beauty captivating. A taxi drove in just as the Buick drove out toward the D Street Bridge. The squat passenger's jet-black close-cropped hair barely rose above the headrest. Brent looked at the clock – eleven straight up.

Nuts! Doeman?

Brent started for the reception desk to find out what the hell the theatrics with the Falcon were all about when the taxi's passenger lumbered in. Brent was at the front desk when she arrived, a short figure in a lightweight denim jacket-and-skirt set that accentuated her squarish butt and the calves that could pull a plow. She was devoid of any cosmetics or jewelry save for a black Casio watch on her wrist and pair of thick-lensed tortoise-shell specs.

"My name is Doeman, Jane Doeman." *Would that be like Bond, James Bond; shaken, not stirred?* "I'm here to see Brett Douglas."

Brent extended his hand, hoping to get it back intact. "Hi, I'm Douglas. B*r*e*nt* Douglas," the emphasis apparent. "Let's go in my office. Would you like some coffee?"

"I never touch it. My body is a temple and I worship it daily." Brent watched the pebble grain flat shoes propel this temple into this office and aim it where it might land in a chair. Brent looked at the pilot and co-pilot in the receptionist station, neither concealing a wry smile. Brent winced and closed his office door.

Jane Doeman was one beat ahead of Brent on almost every document he had generated, as if she had watched him prepare it. He offered her the impressive L&H VIP presentation jacket with her name on the cover and an inch of sales, listings, maps, demographics, an overview of the firm and of himself, and a computer-generated appendix of the resources used to verify the information. She promptly pulled the Acco fastener open and tossed the Mylar clocktower jacket into his trashcan, complaining that it wasn't recyclable. She shoved everything on his desk onto one corner, plopped her briefcase on top of his and started "Harrumphing" and marking the hell out of every document with a selection of bilious Day-Glo markers that she tucked in her bra between uses. Her fingers flew across her huge TI pocket calculator and she constantly made notes in shorthand in a spiral notebook. Brent knew Gregg – whatever shorthand she used wasn't Gregg. He didn't rule out extraterrestrial.

An hour later his presentation was in shambles and her only interests were those he hadn't prepared for. She proposed to read what was left of his presentation at leisure that evening then moved the discussion to diversity in the local workplaces, typical places of worship, smoke-free restaurants, the probability of bike paths in the community, air quality, a free press and the municipal commitment to dolphin-free tuna. Brent's collective knowledge of these matters was zilch, and it showed.

It was already 12:40 – how time flies when you're having fun. Felicia, the early bird today, was at lunch and the staff was starting to drift back in after the MLS meeting and a tour of new listings in the valley. Lydia was on floor duty, alone during the slow lunch hour. But Brent, who would by now have done two laps and most of an Elton John tape around the reservoir, was hostage to a five-one gorilla in denim. "We'll resume this tomorrow at one your time. I'll have some specific homes to explore then." *Your time? Where was she from?* "I have a microwave uplink reserved for 20 GMT on Friday. I'll scan and transmit then. Can you give me a disc of everything we have by then in UNIX?"

GMT? *Microwave link? UNIX? Jesus – they call me a frustrated Ludlum – this broad would scare the Scorpion!*

"I'll ask our receptionist about converting our DOS to UNIX. She's out for lunch, but if anyone can, she can." He thought about the GMT bit. Greenwich Mean Time was eight hours ahead of local time, if his Navy recollection was right, which it usually wasn't, thanks to the Daylight or Standard time correction. That'd be noon here, Thursday. He had visions of ending his real estate career, years hence, with Doeman still tearing up his office like an ape throwing straw around its cage while he waited for her first client to arrive.

Who was she, Sundance?

Doeman looked at him, a strange look, the soulful look a yearling doe lying near death on the Interstate gives the driver of the car that just ran over her, as if to say, "I'm sorry for demolishing your Lexus..."

"I'd like to take you to lunch for your trouble so far this morning."

Brent, large and long of body, distracted by *amour* during what would have been his normal 7 AM feeding and now ready to eat the ass out of a grizzly bear at this late hour, looked well past the external visage of the hostess, now with three pencils in her hair, half the TI calculator spilling out of her left breast pocket, a Kleenex under her Casio strap and dye from various marking pens all over the underside of both sleeves and one knee. A more recently-fed man might have passed. But Brent accepted.

"We're out of here. Any preference, or do you want the local boy to pick?" He caught Katy's attention, pointed to his mouth, then at his watch with one finger held up, then slid his finger from left to right and held up two fingers, indicating to the well-trained receptionist, in sequence, nourishment, one hour, slide my In/Out guy to back-at-two-o'clock. She nodded an OK followed by disgust. The six-three Brent and the four-thirteen Jane walked out, passing Felicia as she rumbled back in over the tile walkway from her lunch hour.

Felicia looked at Katy: "Are Yogi and BooBoo buying a house...?"

CHAPTER FIVE

Tuesday afternoon: A discouraging word...

The odd couple walked through the parking lot, and as Brent's' usual luck would have it, the fair Patricia Benham, fresh from starting the day with a bang, then off to the Toastmasters breakfast and on to an agent open house at one of her better listings, drove into the L&H parking lot. Brent looked at her, paled slightly, and waved. The fair Patricia feigned sun in her eye and ignored the couple on the path to the Explorer. Or so thought Brent.

In truth, Patsy watched her manager in the Taurus' side-view mirror, moving the mirror slightly to keep the pair in view, and picked up her phone as a guise to remain in the car for a while longer. She watched Brent open the same passenger door of the wagon that he had so cavalierly opened for her last evening at the Green Mill Inn, and then watched his short luncheon date back up to the seat. Patsy caught the look that Jane and Brent gave each other when it became apparent that the majority of Jane's rear, an area difficult to define, was well below the level of the Explorer's seat. She then turned to face the wagon, pulled her skirt up well past mid-thigh and stepped up onto the door jamb with one foot, then the other. She fell forward putting one hand on the steering wheel and the other on the headrest, and for reasons unknown to Brent, Patsy and the half of the office staff that were probably watching, leaned almost over to the driver's side, bare white thighs framing a full denim moon, then fell with a half-twist into the leather seat. Mary Lou Retton she wasn't, and Brent looked forward with exuberance to the prospect of her going through these gymnastics all over again after lunch. Brent looked at Patsy, still sitting in her car talking on her phone, and could only hope that she might have a shred of understanding of what he was going through with this woman. She did. She was an agent, and agents take clients as the come when multiple escrows beckon.

❖   ❖   ❖

Time to face the music, big guy.

"I know a little brasserie a few minutes up the county road that's got a great sandwich menu and a salad bar, with a nice view up the river," Brent offered, leaving out the dark-and-usually-deserted-at-lunch part.

"Actually," Jane countered, "I found a place last night when I got into town that I'd like to go back to. It's called the *Heron*, I think it is?"

"The *Blue Heron*? Right downtown by the bridge?" *Yikes. It's a wannabe '60s health food pad.* Brent got lassoed into the Heron just once since it opened in the early 1970s and had avoided it ever since. *Wabbit food. Weirdo cooks in tie-dye shirts. Sitar music. Earth mother waitresses in chambray shirts and string-straight ponytails down to their butts with eight bracelets per arm, skirts to their ankles and little hexagonal glasses. Graying men with pukka shell necklaces and macramé book bags reminiscing fondly about the Summer of Love with others too young to remember it. How does this woman seem to know exactly what drives me nuts? From CCIM lingo to the no-nukes café.*

"I know right where it is – there's usually parking in front." *They can all watch me unload you.* She had removed most of the pencils, the calculator and the Kleenex, stored the coke bottle specs and was trying to do something with her hair.

The unloading went painlessly. In full view of the Heron, she swung her thighs toward the sidewalk and displayed more flesh than the patrons of the Blue Heron had seen since the place opened, pushed off, and landed on the high curb, still standing. She fit right in with the noon crowd, a montage of latter day fugitives from a Lovin' Spoonful album jacket. And all apparently able to take time well past two o'clock from their positions as CEOs and neurosurgeons and Pulitzer journalists to discuss ways to further the lot of the spotted owl. "Hi, Jane, welcome back!" came a voice from a fugitive of the 60s flipping tofu on a griddle. "Who's your friend?"

Brent's natural-fabric clothes were scrutinized, and acceptable to most save for one six-foot-six hundred-seventy pound balding gent in a Stones tank top and fake Birkenstocks, a peace symbol dangling from his scrawny neck. He pointed at Brent's belt with a talon finger and told the villagers that an animal died to keep this man's pants up. Brent told him to go check out the Explorer – a whole herd died for the seats and dash.

Brent pulled out a chair for Jane, who stood on her tiptoes and backed in with a grunt.

"I'd like to talk to you about closing agents," she said as a vacant face with an apron and a grey ponytail under a red bandana brought a glass of water and a menu. Brent picked up on the *closing agent* reference, an East-of-the-Rockies variant of the more-familiar West Coast appellation *escrow officer*. "Do you know one you can trust?"

"I don't know one I *can't* trust," Brent responded truthfully. "Why do you ask?"

"We're getting to the point where I have to start getting specific about what I'm here about. The privacy of my clients is paramount. If I could, I'd close the escrow ten counties away to maintain their privacy."

Escrows. plural...

Brent took that as a good sign. She could close them ten counties away, actually, but why do the title work here, then ship the escrows to the other end of the state, drive everybody in the loop nuts, raise Ma Bell and FedEx' stock, then send it all back here to the county seat to record the deeds? *Plural.* "Our escrow officers are OK. As you know, when the deeds record, they're public record, as are the revenue stamps that reveal the sale prices."

The waitcreature looked their way, and she looked him off. She was still all business. She absent-mindedly pulled two Hi-Liters from the dark crevice between her lapels while they talked. Brent had misplaced his tape dispenser while they were working in his office and he debated the wisdom of having her check for it next time she reached down there.

She continued, "How about if we record to a fictitious name?"

"Convince the title insurors and you can record to Mickey Mouse for all I care." Brent was getting testy. The only things worse than having the lunch delayed by this palaver might be having it actually arrive. He knew that if he ever did get out of here, then reload and unload Jane, that he was going to make about three trips past Burger King's drive-through window. "What's the problem with recording in the actual name of the buyers?"

"As I said, my clients are coming here for privacy. Can your local closers conceal that an escrow has been opened on certain properties, until they close?"

"That they can do." The waiter showed up again – time to face the music. "I'll have what might have been a dead animal last Sunday, garçon, and a copy of the wine list." People in the adjacent tables glared, and the waiter pointed at the menu. This was a mean crowd. "Bring me the toast with the cup of honey, and a bowl of soup. Jane?"

Jane asked if the baby tomatoes were fresh then ordered the tomato and wild rice salad with the toasted sunflower seed dressing on the side.

The waiter glared once more at Brent and took their menus; Brent glared back, and turned to Jane. "How do you propose to handle the earnest money deposits and transfer closing funds into the escrows? Those details tend to bring others in the community, like the bankers, in on the secrets."

"My clients will be closing their purchases with bearer drafts drawn upon my government. I will handle their earnest money on my Visa card. I have power-of-attorney for them."

Good, Brent thought. That shouldn't draw too much attention. How do I disclose a Visa deposit to a seller? How do I clear it through our trust account? And we get government bearer instruments all the time, even in the World Series pool.

Did she say my *government?*

"Did you say *the* government, or *my* government?" Whose government is buying these homes?"

"A government with friendly relations with the United States."

Great. That narrows it down to 160 nations and some parts of Texas.

"You'll be told when it is necessary."

Luncheon was served.

"If my clients want to see the homes before they open an escrow, it will be necessary for their inspectors to view the listings first. Is that a problem?"

"No. What kind of inspectors?" He had visions of men in black overcoats and porkpie hats climbing around the listing scanning for the kind of bugs that the pest-control guys wouldn't be looking for.

"These are child care specialists from their country, looking after the welfare of the buyers' children's safety. They may want to drive the neighborhoods, see the schools and look at the homes thoroughly before the clients open an escrow."

Jane just skipped a couple of steps in the Yankee home buying ritual. Most buyers want to see a home, in Brent's opinion, and then they make an insulting offer, answered by an insulting counteroffer from the sellers, both sides pick up their marbles and it's over. The buyers come back a day later, the agent offers to replace the busted garage door opener that touched off the whole dustup, the buyers make a new offer and the sellers change one thing just to hack them off one more time before opening escrow. Jane's got to learn how we operate. Going from child-care inspectors directly to an open escrow would deprive Brent of the satisfaction of justifying his commission. His conscience would probably make him give it back to the sellers.

Yeah. And Dr. Spock will supervise the "child-care" specialists

It was beginning to dawn on Brent that he was into some heavy traffic with this cookie, a foreign government was apparently involved and that the settlers new to our shores were not about to be featured in the LifeStyle section of the Sunday paper. *Scorpion's* intrigue was great fun on a VoiceMail code but the reality of this international lunch was becoming unsettling. On the bright side, it took his attention away from the surprise soup that was still festering in the bowl in front of him. "What kind of work do your clients do?"

"They're all retired businessmen."

Oh.

Willie Nelson brought the check and a fresh snarl for Brent. The man was obviously not in this for the tips. Jane put a Visa card on the tray, cleverly concealing the name area with her pudgy thumb until Willie returned to pick it up. He thanked her for lunch. The card and the slip returned. She quickly hid the card, signed the slip and made a note in her weird shorthand on the receipt stub. Then, unbelievably, she drained the last of the water from her glass and exuded a belch that rivaled Mean Joe Greene filming the award-winning Coke commercial. Brent was embarrassed, but few in the restaurant gave her a glance.

His adrenalin pumped as they walked back to 6 PCT, knowing that the time was at hand to demonstrate to the townsfolk on the sidewalk and the guys in Carl's Barbershop the finer points of entering an Explorer. She let no one down – Brent opened the door and she basically fell face first across the driver's seat with the usual display of denim and limb. She pulled herself to a kneel and did the now-famous Doeman twist, akin to the eponymous skater's Lutz or the airman's Immelmann, where the surname of the move's original performer defined the acrobatics for those who followed.

Heading for the office, he told her he had an appointment to keep, but to check with Felicia, who by now would have this morning's presentation converted onto a computer disc. Then Felicia would drop her at her motel.

Brent stopped in front of the entry canopy; she opened her own door, swung sideways and half-fell onto the sidewalk. She said she'd see him at one tomorrow, and slammed the door.

Brent kept his appointment, the one at Burger King.

❖   ❖   ❖

2:15 p.m. Brent, nourished by a Wubble Dopper, a chocolate shake and a box of fries that he held high out the window as he passed by the Blue Heron and laid on the horn, strode back into the office. Donna Macgregor and Rafé Morales were both on the hot desk phones – he could hear Rafé speaking to a client in Spanish. Katy and Felicia were like pilot and co-pilot, side-by-side behind a glass screen in front of the reception counter, and Brent noted an apple-size gold 49er helmet, no doubt procured by the Niner's newest and sturdiest cheerleader. Closer inspection revealed that the helmet was atop a jersey with a number 16 and supported by two little white cleats. Brent pushed the helmet down and it hopped about ten times until it fell onto Felicia's phone console. "Must have been a long walk to Kansas City. Let's leave Montana on the bench. Mrs. Landau's orders: 'Thou shalt not trash the new office. At least until after the open house.'"

Katy was crushed. "You're no fun."

"It hasn't been a fun morning. Lunch was worse."

"Given your flair for the absolute, I suppose it was the worst lunch you ever had?"

"No. Food was served at the worst lunch I ever had. Anything I should know about going on?"

"Patsy was looking for you after lunch. Not a happy camper, I might add. You took another woman to lunch. Not much else going on."

"Good. Keep it that way."

Brent closed his door, and noticed that the ads were done and transmitted to the paper. He turned to the office meeting tomorrow morning.

Office meetings, like almost every other function management can dream up that would normally be considered obligatory behavior in most employer/employee environments, were largely voluntary in nature in most real estate offices across the land. A quirky thing about the real estate industry is that the agents are independent contractors to a firm, not employees. Why the IRS ever went for that was an eternal mystery to Brent.

Independent contractors, to enjoy the IRS' blessing, must be independent, and a movement toward anything *mandatory* – as in mandatory office meetings – threatens that status. Or a dress code. He recalled the morning he told Katy to use her bean before she wore a skirt *that* short to the office again, and she countered that Lydia's was shorter than mine and why don't you say something to her? The plain truth is that he could tell Katy, as an employee, to straighten up, but Lydia had the God-given right to look as trashy as she wanted to because she was an IC. Fair? Hell, no, but again, Brent didn't get the big bucks for nothing.

Almost forgot – the Falcon *was here!* He bolted for the receptionists. Katy was talking on the phone. He turned to Felicia. "Tell me about the Falcon! What was that little visit all about?"

"Don't think the lady was the Falcon, big guy. Came in looking for Nichols. She apparently got his number off the *For Sale* sign on his Pacer."

The faded sign had been on Dave's back window for three years.

"What did she want to see him about?"

"She wanted to buy it."

"*What*? BS. That lady? She had class. What the hell would she want his Pacer for?"

"She said she collects them. No accounting for some people's taste."

Incredible. Brent gets Jane, Dave gets the Falcon. Patsy's miffed. He shook his head and walked back into his office. His back hurt – he missed his noon walk. His morning was shot, the double whopper was double-teaming him, his lunch date had embarrassed him, she's working for a bunch of terrorists and she's coming in tomorrow at one to do it all over again. Three days shy of 46 years old and not a bright spot on his horizon.

The agenda for the office meeting was shaping up to a short one – the usual "needs and wants" – real estate notions still just a gleam in the eye of a buyer or seller, usually a precursor to a more formal attempt to list or buy. Then the housekeeping items: Lock the front door. Turn out the lights. Move your little magnetic In/Out man when you leave and return; it saves Katy and Felicia some heartburn and may make you a commission and have you heard this before? Don't park in the customers' spaces. Brent's list was starting to look like a page from *Everything I Need To Know About Real Estate I Learned in Kindergarten*. Share. Be nice to each other. Nap. Flush.

Thank you, Robert Fulghum.

The guest speaker however was drawn from L&H's own ranks. Rafé Morales was a local boy, whose grandfather once traced the family's roots in the valley back to the time of the Spanish land grant that created the *Puebla* that was now the major city across the bay. Rio Verde took its name from the Spanish *Green River*.

Rafé won his junior college degree in urban zoning and had been an abstractor for a Rio Verde title insurance company. It was there that Brent met him in a class he was teaching and took him on as a protégé.

Brent was light-years ahead of most managers in matters of welcoming the growing Hispanic population into the mainstream of home ownership. His motivation was crystallized by an escrow with Hispanic buyers that went to hell in a hand basket, and the parties were ready to skin the buyers' lender over issues creating the perception of discrimination.

The lenders weren't really guilty of anything but insensitivity. Under Brent's closer scrutiny it became apparent the lender didn't have a facility with Hispanic surnames and got the credit reports all screwed up and nobody could put together what was really a husband-and-wife, enjoying joint-tenancy under the laws of the state.

Title insurors went thought the same rigamarole in running their research. And credit reporting agencies weren't faring any better – a couple's clean credit history often looked like the bottom of a birdcage. All this bothered Brent – a good transaction had been blown and there was not real culprit to blame.

Another element of the dilemma was the language problem incurred by non-Spanish-speaking agent representing an Hispanic buyer or seller. He'd had trouble with clients whose mother-tongue was English – how could he expect to do a credible job of counseling a Spanish-speaking client?

Following his crashed transaction with the Mexican couple, he became more annoyed than he usually was with the whole real estate industry. The multicultural issue ought to rank up at the top as a concern, if anybody were thinking straight.

Brent recruited Rafé into real estate, meeting at the End of the Beginning, a watering hole across from the junior college. Rafé enabled Brent to champion the minority-client dilemma, and tomorrow Rafé was the featured speaker at the office meeting, not for the first time.

Felicia came into Brent's office with a glass of lemonade. "Patsy called in while you were brooding, Skipper. Said if you can tear yourself away from your newest client that you're invited to be on her deck in your cook play-suit tomorrow after work. She'll bring the steak, brews, and propane, and something else that I didn't catch." She grinned.

"I think I know what the *something else* is. Anything else going on now? Phones look busy."

"Oh, Jane Doeman called. Her laptop computer is giving her trouble – something in the phone link. She wants to have her head office send something here, but I told her ours would be going until midnight on month-end stuff before I could open a window for her modem. My home PC is a lower baud but it's OK with me if they transmit it to me and I can download it into her laptop. Is that OK with you? She's your client."

"Felicia Rae Cochran, I have told you before that talk like that is neither comprehended nor tolerated in my office and is a firing offense. I'm sorry. We'll miss you terribly. Goodbye."

"It's been nice. I'll share my maple bars with another person now. What'd I say that caused it? *Baud*? *Modem*? *Download*?"

"No. *Jane Doeman*. And I don't care if you want to receive her data at home and make her a *disc*, do you dweebs call them? In fact, if you make two, I can see what they sent her. Since she's working off material I gave her, that doesn't trouble me. She'll know damn well that I'm getting it anyway."

"I'm a simple fun-loving girl trying to make my way in the world get-ting pulled into a dark hole of espionage by a pencil-pusher who calls himself the Scorpion, a fashion model with legs up to her quit-that who wants to buy a trashed '70 Pacer, a fireplug in denim that takes shorthand in Cyrillic, in an office that occasionally reminds me of the Galactic Café in *Star Wars*. What happened to the days when bosses just oppressed secretaries by having them bring them coffee and calling them *sweetie*?

"It's the nineties, Felicia. New rules. Thanks for the lemonade. And, lest I forget, for getting the ads done. By the way, pay close attention to Rafé tomorrow morning. You're doing the same pitch at Better Homes in Fairfax next week." She turned to leave, but Brent suddenly stopped her.

"Hold it. What'd you say about *Cyrillic*? You said something about Cyrillic and shorthand. What's that all about?"

Felicia spun around and stopped. "Her shorthand was in Cyrillic."

"She's Greek?"

"No, Mr. Geography Major, she takes shorthand in the language common to areas of Russia, or whatever they call that land mass now. Where she's from, I have no idea, but I wish she'd go back there before you put yourself in the booby hatch. Wherever she's from, their women get into cars funny."

"How do you now about Russian shorthand?"

"The majority of the world uses it. Gregg came later. A friend of mine in college showed me – it's easier to learn, because their language is so difficult." Felicia again turned for the door.

Brent walked out behind her, and gave her a pat on the shoulder as he headed for the break room. "Thanks, pal."

❖   ❖   ❖

4:10 p.m. The hour had grown late. Katy was gone to her first cheerleading practice. Only three weeks remained until the first preseason game with the Raiders, a Sunday afternoon at the Coliseum. No job interruption there.

The bull pen and the break room were almost deserted – late afternoons in real estate offices were not busy times. Jeff Terrell was alone in the break room, awaiting a five-o'clock client. Seeing Jeff, a thought came back to Brent that he had flashed on during the dismal luncheon patter.

"Jeff, you told me years ago that you sold a house to a guy who never looked at the house past a photograph, never asked about financing and basically came out of the wild blue yonder, closed escrow, and went right back to the wild blue and stayed there."

"Yeah. I never proved it, and was about half afraid to pursue it, but my wife put the pieces together. She figured that he was a government-relocated witness that had put some heavy-hitter clear across the country into the slammer by turning state's evidence in return for immunity from prosecution, and for health reasons was relocated to here with a new home, face, name, car, Social, birth certificate and life story. And his family got papers to create continuity with the town they said they came from, which wasn't the town they came from."

"How did he find you?" Brent asked.

"Actually, *he* didn't. A guy about as transparent as the buyer came to town first with a satchel full of requirements for a home. I got him on a blind floor call. He alluded to cash and a short escrow. Then he started getting demanding about who was going to handle the escrow and how confidentiality could be handled. And then a team came to the listing he settled on and shot some videos. The home entered into escrow, and the buyer never even saw his home until he moved in with his family. When the home was vacated by the sellers, a pest-control inspector I had never seen before came out and checked the home with some kind of electronic diathermy gadget I'd never heard of before. Marcia said they were looking for bugging devices – I told her she read too much."

Brent thought about lunch and allowed that Marcia Terrell could write her own book about Doeman.

"What *did* they find?"

"I don't know," Jeff said. "I never went into the listing after the escrow opened."

"How did he pay for the house?"

Jeff shrugged his broad shoulders. "Who knows? It closed at Bay City Title, but some officer who had come in from LA to take Gwen's desk while she was on vacation did the escrow instructions and the deed. Funds were wired in from another Bay City branch, so nobody in Rio Verde ever saw a check or a draft. Strange. Bucks notwithstanding, I wished I'd never heard of him. Any of them. He drove my family crazy."

"How's that?"

"From the day I met them, I felt like I was being watched. The guy they sent to look on his behalf was from another planet, like a machine. He was hyper on confidentiality, and one night he showed up at a soft-ball game I was pitching with the videocam and filmed the crowd and me, but never the game. Never said a word to anybody. I got a few strange calls during and after the sale, from people passing themselves off as appraisers or moving van company reps, trying to find out about the sale. I felt like I was being tested."

"Was that over when the escrow closed?"

"I got strange calls for about a year. I never talked to the buyer, only saw him once when our kids played Little League together. Another guy was at the park with a videocam again, still on me. It still gives me the creeps. The cars driving by our house and the late-night calls, always checking, checking, checking, will I talk about the escrow? It almost broke up our marriage. I always felt that the buyer saw me as the weak link in the chain, and would just as soon I be pushing up daisies somewhere. And I probably wouldn't be his first victim. On the other hand, I knew people were looking for *him*, and I still have visions of somebody named Guido with a violin case shoving bamboo shoots under my fingernails to find out where the witness bought his home."

"How long ago was that?"

"A couple of years, maybe. But I never felt like it was over. Still don't. They're not nice people, and they know there are some bad dudes out there with a bounty on them. People who cross them, or pose a threat to their cover, or who they even *think* may give them away, go to sleep with the fish. I wish I'd never met him." He looked into the bull pen, where Felicia was leading Jeff's clients into the conference room. "Got to go. See ya in the morning."

Brent sat, alone, in the break room, and thought about lunch. *Fictitious deeds. Privacy. Bearer drafts from my government. Child-care specialists.*

He multiplied Jeff's perceived peril by a factor of three. Three witnesses' safety for the cost of one aging broker. Not a bad trade for this type of clientele. Brent didn't feel real good, and wasn't sure an hour's walk on the reservoir would make him feel any better. He was concerned. He hadn't been scared of much in his life, and he wondered if this is how it felt.

He walked out to his own office and shut down his terminal. As he walked by Felicia, she did a double-take.

"You add a new dimension to *white* man, man. You OK?"

"Long day. Maybe not. I'll tell you about it tomorrow after the meeting, maybe out on the millpond away from this place. Let the janitor close it up – let's go home."

She followed him out the front doors, and let them close. "You're worrying me, Skipper…"

Brent looked inside every car left in the lot before he cranked his own up. He watched Felicia until her backup lights lit, then drove out toward the reservoir.

CHAPTER SIX

Tuesday evening: The end of a perfect day...

The walk around the reservoir did little good save to burn off the last calorie of a gut-bomb Double Whopper. Brent saw Doeman under every rock and behind every tree.

The prospect of dinner now was appealing. He prepared himself philosophically for the awesome responsibility of barbecuing two steaks tomorrow night with Patsy. A fine night on her comfortable patio, in a heavily wooded section of older homes with a view of the lights of the town from her redwood hot tub, music on the deck and her special lo-cal dessert later. He called her real estate line: "Hi, this is Patricia Benha..." He hung up and speed-dialed her unlisted number: "Hi, this KL5-1539. Please say your name and stay on the line..." Beep. "This is Brent, Brent, Brent calling Patsy. Come in, Patsy 1-2-3-4-5-4-3-2-1..." No answer. She was out. Or sitting there mad – but why? God knows agents all go to lunch with clients, and Doeman was a client.

He slumped low in his La-Z-Boy, and clicked on the tube. The Giants were on. He looked out the window over his deck to the view up the river, flowing between the low rolling green hills. Breathtaking at sunset – why couldn't he get with the program? He should have been out on the deck. The Cards were cleaning the Giants' clock – little interest there. He fiddled around with his ukulele, and then laid it back down. He had a new Grisham, but the attention span of a gnat.

What the hell had he got himself into? He thought what Jeff said: *I'm sorry I ever heard of them – they've screwed up my whole life.*

Murder? Drugs? Espionage? My government, she said. Counter-espionage types, defused by the Soviet détente? Who might have a bounty out on the homebuyers? Their former Russian handlers? The Mafia? Maybe the Pol Pot regime. The Ayatollah. That was it, the Ayatollah, looking for that guy Rushdie who wrote the book that pissed the Ayatollah off. *Rushdie*? Sure. Rushdie was buying a home in Rio Verde and was going to write articles for the *Christian Science Monitor* and fax them to Boston. That's it.

You're losing it, buddy.

He snapped himself back, looked at the river, the top of the ninth in Busch Stadium, his uke, Grisham's *Chamber* and an 11 x 14 photo of Patsy in a thick oak frame on the wall group between his study and the dining area. He took the picture one night when they were driving down the Oregon coast. She was standing ankle-deep in the Pacific Ocean; arms outspread, holding a big floppy hat. And grinning. The deserted beach was known appropriately as Sunset Beach, where during only a few weeks of summer the setting sun exactly bisects the two cliffs forming the inlet to the bay.

Patsy was wearing a pair of faded blue 501 Levis that accentuated her long legs and shapely little fanny. She had knotted Brent's old long-sleeved Sears work shirt that she lived in on that trip above her tiny waist. Her hair was still long, below her shoulders, and the sun turned her auburn hair to an eerie diaphanous glow in the photo. He wished he'd taken a few more shots, but none would have been more effective.

Or made her look more beautiful...

To hell with it. I'm going to bed.

And so he did. At 9:38 on a Tuesday evening, Brent Douglas went upstairs to his bed, his earliest solo retirement since the third grade.

There was a saying about "good" tired and "bad" tired that Brent often recalled on evenings like this, and this evening redefined any "bad" tired he'd ever known. The expression was taken from an old Harry Chapin album that he'd played a hundred times until he found it on a CD, and played it a hundred times more.

Chapin was the best of the best when it came to songs of protest, humor, or folk, often in the same song. He was well on the way to raising a million dollars for the nation's fight against hunger when he died at 38, too young, in a traffic mishap in 1981. He defined good tired as the tired you feel when you solve, or don't solve, your own problems in the course of a day. Bad tired is when you solve, or not, somebody else's.

Brent was bad tired.

He fought off demons with fat little ringless fingers on a calculator, soup with eyeballs floating in it, CCIMs forcing him to fill out internal-rate-of-return financial tables, and a big greasy child-care technician in a black suit with an eye patch and an Uzi, crying out in the night *Vere did they buy zere houses, Douglas? Ve haf vays of making you talk…*

It was a hot night, and still. And he was bad tired. But sleep finally came.

❖　　❖　　❖

11:22 p.m. Clad in nothing but this morning's Old Spice and lying on top of the sheets, he heard a phone ringing and passed it off as just another demon. But the demon didn't give up, and he finally shook the cobwebs and dove for the phone on his nightstand. Patsy? This phone was unlisted – his published line only rang downstairs.

In a groggy voice: "Hello?"

"Brent, this is Jane Doeman. I'm working on your file and am having some trouble with some of the categories in the MLS listing printouts." The line had an echo. A recorder? He thought about what Jeff had told him this afternoon – it seemed like weeks ago:

From the moment I met them I felt like I was being watched. I got strange calls for about a year.

He wondered how she got this number.

"Like what?"

"G-F-A and R-O-D-G-M. They're in all six listings I've picked out for tomorrow and I want to know what they are."

"At 11:30 at night?" He looked at his alarm clock. Close enough. She was beginning to annoy him and he didn't give a damn if she knew it or not. Then he thought better of what Jeff had said: *They're not nice people.* "Actually I'm glad you caught me – I was just turning in."

"So what do they mean?"

"G-F-A is gas-fired forced-air – the furnace. The others are the kitchen appliances included in the sale. Range – oven – dishwasher – garbage disposal – microwave oven. OK?"

"That's fine. I'm told by my office that Felicia got the transmission loaded onto her computer at home, but she's out. Please tell her I'll pick it up when I see you at one tomorrow. I would like it on a high-density floppy. Thank you."

Click.

Had Brent been even semi-conscious or sane at this moment, he would have remembered a passage from the Manchurian Candidate, postulating that the human mind is merciful – when it goes into overload, it shuts down into unconsciousness. Or in Brent's overloaded case, sleep.

And sleep he did. He didn't hear the car in the lane in front of his condo start, and then idle down the forested road.

CHAPTER SEVEN

Wednesday morning: The office meeting...

The Scorpion, an awesome force whose name is spoken only in a whisper, if spoken at all, in the darkened bistros and walk-up flats where intrigue is orchestrated, assumed for today the persona of a mild-mannered pencil-pusher for a real estate firm, and strode toward the lobby of the office, vowing to kick butt and take names should a caped invader named Jane threaten to despoil this gorgeous day that he had seized. He saw himself reflected in the glass door, and thought, what mortal would mess with this tall, muscular figure in a brand-new heliotrope-striped shirt with a flowered tie to match, if they knew what was good for them?

Most of them, the pencil-pusher within him responded. So what if his unlisted phone was tapped and a gnome wants to feed him rabbit food and buy three houses with box tops? So what if Jeff Terrell's paranoid wife thinks the bad guys would like to vaporize his clients and that his clients would like to vaporize *him* right after they close escrow? So what? This is mere child's play in a day for the Scorpion.

But not necessarily in the day of Brent Douglas. The Scorpion frame of mind, however, might get him through the meeting. He liked office meetings and arrived at the office a little later that usual. The receptionists took weekly turns at opening the office on meeting days and made extra urns of coffee.

Per his standing instructions, whoever opened Wednesday put on a disc from a rack of music reserved for office meetings to pep up the atmosphere. This morning Katy was the early bird and started *Gaité Parisienne*. Brent was anxiously awaiting the can-can passage, wondering if today would be the inevitable day that the uninhibited Irishwoman in mattress-ticking bib-overall shorts would kick one stout calf to her forehead without bending her knee, as she was wont to do in moments of exuberance at social occasions. This was not a social occasion. The crew continued to drift in. Patsy arrived, in a loose cotton sleeveless print dress and a straw hat with a periwinkle band that matched the dress. He wouldn't mind looking at that little outfit up to and past barbecue time tonight.

"Steaks tonight, I'm led to believe? I'm ready." Brent watched for a signal – he hadn't seen her since his lunch date with Jane.

"You look like you're ready for the undertaker. You wear yourself out helping your new client in and out of the wagon? Did she get a booster seat at the Blue Heron?"

"This is past the mildly-amusing state. Frankly, I'm shook, but I'd just as soon the whole crew didn't know. The only things spookier than her customers are the people looking for them."

"What's all that mean?" Patsy said, noting that Brent, the can-do, roll-up-his-sleeves manager with the strong personality and sense of self-assurance was showing some ugly feet of clay.

"It means I'm not bulletproof and I'm not in control, and I don't like it but I don't know how to stop it." He glanced past Patsy's wide hat brim. *Christ – it's Horton Landau. What the hell's he doing here?* "Just what I needed – here's Landau. What's next?"

"Look at the bright side, Skipper. He could have brought his wife. Happy day, if I miss you. See you about five-thirty."

"I'll bring my toothbrush and duckie slippers."

"Your duckie slippers are already there, but your spunk is encouraging. See ya."

An unseen hand squelched the music and Katy's likelihood of terpsichore in the workplace, which, given the presence of the stodgy founding father in their midst, was just as well. Eighteen of 21 agents were present or accounted for, not a bad number at all. All could sense that Brent was uncharacteristically strained. He stood in an area that was visible to most of the bull pen, where agents' side chairs had been pulled from their cubicles into a semicircle.

"OK, boys and girls, we're here for a meeting, so let's go to work. I'd like to welcome you all to the first meeting in our beautiful new office, and ask one of the men who made it possible to offer a few remarks."

Damn few, with any luck.

"Please welcome Horton Landau, the man who put the Land in Homes and Land." Brent began applauding and was joined by a few agents, somewhat weakly. And he winced. Horton Landau hated the Homes and Land appellation. Eyes rolled and looked to the ceiling around the semicircle, and a few looked at their wristwatches.

Horton was natty this morning in a yellow Macgregor knit golf shirt tucked into a pair of orange plaid pants that looked like they might have once been seat covers in a Volkswagen beetle. A jaunty little cap topped his smallish head and a full coif of a store-bought toupee reminiscent of salt-and-pepper road kill. And long sideburns – his wife liked sideburns. His pants rode high atop the upper slope of his pot belly. He was, *in toto*, a polyester vision of a geriatric dirt merchant in the third trimester of a long gestation period. He gave Brent a stern look, no doubt for the homes and land gaffe, and then he spoke.

And he spoke, and he spoke.

He paid for the room, so I guess he can talk in it if he wants to.

Brent gazed around the main room, at the high ceilings with the exposed rafters and the Victorian warehouse porcelain lamp reflectors. Dead-center in the room, a three-inch brass rod was suspended from the peak of the ceiling, for right now a wire harness dangling out of it. Brent had engineered this – the fly fan moved from Fundas' Fountain downtown to the old chapel/office in 1957 was being rebuilt with a twentieth-century motor, the huge ornate brass motor housing was being polished, and the five mahogany fan blades were being stripped, refinished and gilded to match the original grain. This was Brent's brainstorm, conjured up one liquid night with a bunch of the boys and a girl or two in The End of the Beginning,

Fundas' Fan.

a watering hole across the bridge frequented by the office staff. The eight agents present thought the restoration would be a splendid gesture, a gift to the founding fathers who had treated them so well. Eight hangovers, nine hundred dollars and seven weeks later, possibly even by next weekend; the splendid gesture would once again rotate in silent grandeur at the end of the brass rod.

Horton spoke of real estate vis-à-vis the Truman administration, when he launched the firm. The agents' minds drifted. Liz Claymore, at her first office meeting with L&H, wondered if this was the norm, or possibly the most exciting meeting ever, the meetings to follow to be dull by comparison. Edith Fisher, sitting low behind a cubicle, worked a crossword puzzle. Pete Stephens looked at Holly Harris' knees, and then some, and thought fondly of their evening non-showing appointment. Actually, they had set an appointment of their own tonight to critique their professional activities of Monday evening last. And Tuesday morning early.

Brent drifted with his crew and for one of the longest stretches in the last 18 waking hours he thought little of the net he'd been drawn into. Rafé Morales was waiting in the wings with his presentation, the primary motivation for the good turnout at the meeting. Felicia had set up the videocam on a tripod and sat next to it, waiting to capture Rafé's maiden voyage. Brent wandered up to Katy's desk, and saw that the phones were quiet. "How long will he go on?" she asked in a muffled voice. Brent shrugged and walked away.

He looked at his watch, hoping for the old geezer to get the message.

❖   ❖   ❖

He didn't. As Horton detailed the firm into the Reagan years, Brent thought about his nocturnal call from Doeman. What was she doing working at that hour? *All six listings I've picked out for tomorrow*, she had said – did she want to go see them today? It would be a damn sight easier if she'd call now instead of marching her tail in here at one o'clock and announcing the contenders. Or did she just want to see if I was home? And the recorder if it was one. Why would she tape her own call?

It hit him. S*he* wouldn't. Somebody else would tape them *both*! Whoever was looking for the buyers dropped the tap on his phone. Nothing else made any sense. She called on his unlisted line. Why not the office line? Was it tapped too?

He walked up to Katy: "Call my house on my business number and see if sounds tinny or beeps or something when the recorder answers. I'll be back in a few."

"OK, Skipper, but our lines here are tinny too so it may not prove anything – the whole switchboard sounds like it's piped through an echo chamber. I'll let you know."

Christ. They've got to our office board too? Doeman, or the others?

He looked at the parking lot. Wonder of wonders, it was Hap Durst, actually paying homage to his earthly friends at a Wednesday office meeting. This was a rarity, as he was usually out on a lofty mission for Delta Airlines during the week. "Morning, Captain. The flight surgeon finally declare you too old to play in a DC-10?"

"Negative, boss. But if he looked into your peepers he'd probably pull your Explorer ticket. You OK? You look like 40 miles of hard highway."

"Thanks. Just what I wanted to hear. Been a little busy."

Katy buttonholed Hap as he walked through the lobby. "Remember your little magnetic man, Captain, from your last visit through here? I know it's been a while, but if you move the little guy on the *Durst* line to IN, I might be able to help you make a couple grand while I sit here drawing my pittance."

A crude DS had been inked onto Hap's little magnetic man, following his recent ascension to hero-ranking in the local papers when bells and horns started going off on the dashboard of his comfy DC-10, forty thousand feet over the cold Atlantic Ocean. His center engine had overheated and shut itself down. The remaining two were ringing bells so he powered them back also. The overall assessment of the situation by the flight crew was that the craft would turn itself into a lawn dart long before they made Dallas, so they parked it into the waiting arms of the Atlanta fire department. Hap and his crew were lauded as heroes for making the urgent descent without alarming the passengers.

Felicia pinned the newspaper's account of his Immaculate Descension on the bulletin board, and in an unguarded moment in the crowded break room she referred to him as *Dead Stick*. It took the nickname only two days to travel the length and breadth of Rio Verde, and a day longer to reach the aircrew lounge at the international airport across the bay. Henceforth he was known as that, often shortened to the *Stick*, sometimes DS, or while aloft, *Delta Sierra*. And Felicia was known, by the Stick, as *Mud*. Retribution followed, and it wasn't over yet.

❖ ❖ ❖

Horton was through the Bush [41] years as they related to L&H, nearing Bill Clinton's haircut on the tarmac at LAX. Brent walked across the room, showing all that he was about to take charge. He motioned to Rafé and

Felicia to warm his vocal chords and her videocam. Horton got the message and wrapped up his diatribe, thanked the dazed audience profusely for their time, wished them well, they clapped, he left.

Brent walked back to the apex of the semicircle, unsmiling, and suggested that everybody get a coffee refill before Rafé's segment of the meeting. They reconvened, and Brent called Rafé out. The camera was rolling.

Rafé's presentation was flawless, and his fellow agents let him know with a round applause, and Jeff spoke for all, in his best third-base-coach voice, *Gracias!* Brent stepped out again and made a final announcement: "That's it, folks. As those of you who were conscious might have noted, we had an early interruption and my executive decision is to dump the agenda. Meeting's adjourned. Thanks."

The agents looked at each other, and he could tell they were concerned about him. The collective look asked *what's bothering the boss?* A long-standing tradition had been skipped, the Sergeant Esterhaus "Oh, and let's be careful out there." Brent had the Blues, and they weren't of the Hill Street variety this morning.

❖   ❖   ❖

9:50 a.m. The crew drifted out. Many poked their heads into his office, where he had planted his shoes on the desk while he stared out the shadeless window, to offer conciliatory "hang in there" or "if I can help, call me..."

The under-running "what's wrong with Brent?" thing was beginning to drive him as buggy as Doeman and her antics and adversaries were. He walked out of his office and asked Felicia if she wanted some fresh air. She unplugged her headset and followed alongside him across the parking lot and over the bridge, onto the turning basin promenade to some benches.

"I had to get out of that joint before I lost it. Tell me about the transmission from Doeman's head-shed. She had the courtesy to call on my unlisted number last night 11:30, asked me some BS about six listings, and said the transmission to you had been made."

"I got it. It came in about 8:30 and I downloaded it onto a disc for your one o'clock meet. How did she get your inside number?"

"Who the hell knows? The information she has is uncanny."

"This is bothering you more than anything I've ever known before. What do you think is going on? Is she more than just an abrasive jerk looking for some homes for clients, like a corporate relocating service?"

"No. It's bigger than that – I keep getting pieces of the puzzle – you gave me one. The shorthand. She talks about a foreign government. Secret escrows. Scratchy phone lines. I think she's trying to find some homes for relocated government witnesses – I don't even know which government. And Jeff's wife says they're a problem. I'm a threat to their security because I'll know where they live and could burn them."

Felicia played with her nails, expressing some concern in her eyes. "Marcia is also convinced that Macy's hid some cameras in the Ladies' Intimates changing rooms, and is selling videotapes of us girls in Consumer Electronics. She may be given to paranoia." She leaned back in her chair. "But, something's goofy. The janitor left a note on the door that somebody was outside the office taking pictures though the windows last night after midnight. And the phone lines sound like tin cans on the ends of dental floss."

Brent stared at the old brick mill behind Felicia, and then mumbled, almost to himself, "The extension of the witness theory is that somebody is looking for the witnesses so they can ice them for testifying against their man, but that they probably won't kill me until after I've led them to the witnesses."

McNear's Mill

"Kind of makes me glad to be sitting right next to you here out in broad daylight." She regretted the jocular remark as soon as she made it.

"What's on the disc you got last night?" he asked.

"You probably don't want to know. Actually I don't know either."

Brent stared at her. "What means 'I don't know either'?"

"'I don't know either' means it's encrypted."

"What?"

"Code, Skipper. Two and a half pages of four-letter groups, double-spaced, not a recognizable word in the bunch. A few lines had numerals. By my rough count there's about twelve hundred groups, and the chances of making that many without spelling out a single four-letter word, like the one you're about to say, are nothing short of astronomical. But it gets better."

"How can it get any better than that?"

She shifted in her chair, apparently uncomfortable about adding any more load on a mind that was already reeling. "I looked at it for two hours, and finally found some recognizable words by running two or three groups together."

"What words?"

Felicia looked at her feet, then across the river. "I'm sorry to say this, Brent, but I could join some groups into VILLA VERDE, EXPLORER and all three of your phone numbers." She paused. "I'm really sorry it had to be that." He lived on Villa Verde Court. And he had wondered after last night if his unlisted cellular phone was secure. No such luck now.

Brent drew a deep breath. Neither of them spoke for a long minute.

"Patsy knows?"

"Your call, Boss."

They watched a little 14-foot Lido move up the river on its outboard. The tip of the mast barely cleared the D Street Bridge. They lingered a while longer...

The Lido disappeared down the river.

Brent finally broke the silence. "Who breaks codes?"

"The same people who make them, but now they use a computer with a thousand times more horsepower than mine has to make an algorithm that they scramble up with another computer just as big. The good guys make them, the bad guys break them with their computers, but the good guys have bought some time. There are no secrets in the '90s, just delays."

"Know anybody who could take a run at it? You're into that stuff."

"Not codes, I'm not. I do know one guy, a brother who was in rehab with me, who was a crypto in the Army before he got busted up and wound up in a chair. He played with codes on Loma Linda's mainframe when the hospital wasn't running it full bore. He could take a run at it."

"You know where he is?"

"Still at Loma Linda," she said. "Went to work for them in the data processing department. They've got a big mother down there – maybe it can unscramble this. You sure you want to know?"

"Got to. Can you send it down somehow? Tell him to keep it to himself – I'm worried about Patsy now – she'll probably be the next one with an echo on her phone."

"My advice would be not to talk in your sleep. This is going to work out OK, I promise you." She let go of his hand and turned toward the bridge. "Let's roll."

❖   ❖   ❖

Dave Nichols was sitting in the break room with Vladimir Belsky, with Lydia Wainscroft standing and talking to them. These three taken alone represented three of management's larger challenges to L&H, and seeing them talking together reminded Brent that the whole could be worse than the sum of the parts.

Vladimir claimed to be a direct descendant of Alexander Graham Belsky, the first telephone Pole. He was wilder than a March hare and made the local news a year ago when he tried to emulate a countryman, a pro football player who reportedly could eat light bulbs. The ball player couldn't, nor could Vladimir, and he spent three days in Fairfax General getting his esophagus put back together.

Lydia, the distaff version of Vladimir, was a French horn player in the valley's small symphony, not a bad group. She was married to a boring music professor at State U, but had recently moved out and was temporarily living with Katy. And Katy was getting tighter by the week with these two off-hours maniacs. Brent's fondest hope was that Lydia wouldn't start dating Vladimir.

Brent thought about how long it seemed since Monday, when Dave locked horns with Katy over who should have received the floor call from the pilgrimage of relocating executives from Compaq or whoever-it-was. And how he got his yucks setting up a snare that would run Dave all over the valley. And the tall knockout that came in to see about Dave's Pacer – who was she? And drinks with Dave later? Her? Brent passed that off as a Katy, just pulling his chain. The gal was probably looking for the escrow office next door and stumbled in here by mistake. The stunt with Dave was dead. Brent hadn't seen Patsy enough in two days to work it out, except for Monday night at the Green Mill Inn, and their minds were on anything but Dave Nichols that night.

Too bad Doeman hadn't run into Dave first – they were a pair made in heaven and could sit around and swap fashion notes and Slim-Fast recipes.

No, Doeman was all Brent's. Six houses to see this afternoon. Six Doeman load-and-unloads from the wagon. *Can't wait to see what she's wearing at one o'clock.*

Brent looked around for his cassette tape case. He began his day as the dreaded Scorpion, and then allowed it to erode him to the pencil-pusher, as Felicia had so delicately described him. This erosion might have been due in some measure to the revelation that his name, address, phone numbers and probably what he called Patsy in the post-midnight hours was being bounced off satellites into smoke-filled rooms for the convenience of strangers. And the leader of the pack would be in this very room in an hour and fifteen minutes. He needed a walk on the reservoir. To hell with lunch.

He found his tape case – the Scorpion was back. Brent knew that the Scorpion rented John Wayne movies and that anybody who rented John Wayne movies would surely walk to the beat of John Phillip Sousa. The March King it would be – Brent Douglas on the path, with the Marine Band in tow. Look out, reservoir people; the Scorpion was on the move.

CHAPTER EIGHT

Wednesday noon: J.P. Sousa on the reservoir...

At one time not terribly long ago, small towns like Rio Verde all across America had volunteer fire departments, with merchants and millers and teamsters awaiting their chance to race to a burning building with high-pressure hoses and fire axes and chainsaws to destroy whatever the fire missed. In Rio Verde, as they were in most small towns, the fire laddies were summoned by a horn, which by national tradition was tested each day at noon, amid the underlying hope that a building wouldn't catch fire at exactly high noon and burn to the ground while the erstwhile firemen-in-waiting sat in Fundas' Fountain having a burger. Progress inevitably came, and in its wake paid firemen stood at the ready in the engine barn. Rio Verde's horn, like those in most small towns, passed into history.

But not for long. The townsfolk instinctively relied on the horn as a daily bellwether of the municipal circadian clock, and the sense of time basically went all to hell when it quit blowing. Some even said their hens wouldn't lay, and local milk production sagged. This was characteristic in all small towns whose volunteer fire departments' horns were abandoned.

So the Rio Verde horn was restored. Or actually replaced by a new one, on the roof of the new firehouse just by the D Street Bridge, triggered by a signal on short-wave radio WWV from the Naval Observatory in Colorado at *exactly* noon each day. Brent heard the horn blow as he sat on a wooden bench in the dirt parking lot along the reservoir, pulling on his walking shoes. A dozen other cars were parked in the lot, and people were walking or jogging around the shoreline. It was hot, and still – a little Mercury was luffing its sail out near where the Sequoia River supplies the reservoir. The two occupants were having their lunch and didn't seem to care whether they moved or not, so long as they could keep enough way to use the slack sail for shade.

Brent shoved his wallet and wristwatch under the front seat of the Explorer, stuck Sousa in his Walkman then the Walkman and the car keys into a nylon fanny pack with the earphone cord hanging out. He threw the empty tape box back onto the dashboard, pushed the Walkman's *play* button and started along the one-mile asphalt circuit that had kept him from going batty since he had become manager of L&H. This all preceded Doeman's arrival into his life – today's walk would be the supreme test. But here, cooled by the pond lined with low-lying tamarisks, the stumpy little terrorist and the confusion she brought to his life seemed a world away.

He walked, trying not to march in cadence to the music, with the pond to his right and a hill shaded by eucalyptus and native oak trees rising to his left. *The eucalyptus,* he always marveled, *are so mature and numerous – can it be true that they didn't even grow any closer than Australia until a few hundred years ago…?* He scanned the hillside for the little coastal deer that frequented the area, the pond for beaver or trout in the shallow water, the sky for the cormorants that would occasionally dive and snare a fish from right under his nose. No cormorants today – a 747 was flying a little higher with the landing gear hanging on a slow approach to the airport a half-hour drive across the bay.

The reservoir's down a little.

Brent had a tree stump pegged that just broke the surface when the reservoir was full. It was two inches out of the water today. A couple of joggers in nylon shorts and brief halter tops approached him – neither waved nor smiled, but Brent held out his open palm and the closer one touched it as she went by – a gentle low-five. The path users had a code of tranquility – the majority who jogged or walked alone had come here to enjoy their own thoughts. Few on the path, even those who had used it for years, knew many others by name, nor spoke each day past a nod, if even that; yet all shared a collegiality. He was coming to the end of the sloping hills, toward the dam where the valley's manmade ditches were fed from the reservoir. A massive old concrete structure with ancient cranks and boards controlled the flow of the water. Today they were open – the irrigating season had begun.

❖   ❖   ❖

A bicycle slowly approached him from across the bridge over the outlet dam. Bikes were prohibited on the narrow pathway, and this one stood out like a sore thumb among the pedestrian traffic. The rider was tall and slim, and as the distance closed he could see her light blond hair pulled back tightly from her forehead and ears into a little bun on the top of her head. Long, powerful legs drove the pedals as she pulled the slight upgrade to meet Brent, and he saw not even a slight hint of a valley in the taut skin on her chest above her orange batik print croptop as she leaned toward him over the handlebars. A pager was clipped to her white cotton shorts.

She was tan and toned, and beautiful. And she looked familiar. The Rolex. The long neck and a figure so shapeless it redefined femininity and desire. The face was haunting. He tried to picture her without the Elton John shades, hooked behind ears that were accentuated by the austere hairstyle. He recalled another thin woman with huge blue-gray eyes – *ice on fire*.

The Falcon.

Two days before a woman with eyes like ice on fire came into the office for some BS reason that never really washed. He cast her in his mind then as "the Falcon" – an innocuous progression of his Scorpion fantasy that he often took a ribbing for. She'd used the phone, looked around, stared at Brent and left. Katy pulled his chain about her interest in Dave Nichols' Pacer. Baloney. This lady had something to do with Doeman and her band of thieves.

Dave Nichols' Pacer

She rode on, not looking at either side of the path. Brent watched her over his shoulder. She never looked back.

But he hadn't come here to worry about these damn relocated witnesses or those who would like to do them in. The relevance of a tall blonde on a bike who may or may not be the same blonde who came to his office paled in comparison to the sinister Doeman, who would plant her stout body in his office in another 42 minutes. For the moment his mind was on J. P. Sousa, the view of the town and the mill and the tall oak trees and his search for the great blue heron who had been lurking in the reeds 50 yards in front of him for the past few weeks. He couldn't see her yet, but she could hold so still that he'd lose her from one lap to the next. An older couple approached, as they did most days at noon, he in his usual deerstalker, and she in her floppy old straw hat with the gingham band. Brent nodded, and they smiled back.

The heron was at her post.

The path meandered between the reservoir and the river, and a few sailboats luffed in the river. Brent looked for a guy he usually saw on a one-man scull, a beautiful teak hull fitted with brass oarlocks and polished oars, pulling along the river. In the heat, he had probably gone to a morning or evening regimen. The old railroad tracks that were laid along the river to the bridge and the mill were all but removed, the crossties rotting in the gravel roadbed. Across the river were some of the last open meadows in the valley, and few Holsteins had gathered under a weathered loafing shed. The wind had come up just enough to keep the temperature comfortable, and the Mercury had unfurled its mainsail and was drifting toward the river under the elevated bridge, the old wooden structure just high enough for a small sailer and wide enough for walkers.

12:30 p.m. He turned from the railroad tracks toward the parking lot, the piccolos dominating the last 16 bars of *Stars and Stripes Forever*, a sure signal that his concert was coming to a close. On a normal day, which he hadn't known since Monday, he would easily walk three laps during a lunch hour. Today, even a second would make him late for Doeman. He thought about calling Katy on the cellphone with a message for Doeman: "Brent's been kidnapped by a station wagon loaded with lonely nuns from the hospital in Fairfax. He conveys his regrets to Jane for breaking their one o'clock appointment."

Good, Brent. Right now your clients would just as soon that their enemies would kill you to save them the inconvenience. Why not call an Irish Catholic and have her lie for you so the whole Maryknoll order can join in the chase? Maybe she could call what's left of the Branch Davidians and the Dan Rostenkowski Fan Club too, hack them off, and make your whole life look like a Peter Sellers movie.

The thought passed, and he walked by the Parcourse, occupied by a pair of particularly attractive and well-proportioned lasses doing some kind of new exercises on the parallel bars, obviously beneficial for their bust lines and the *glutei maxima*. Whatever they had been doing, it was working. He considered telling Patsy about their unique routine, then thought the better of it. Sousa had already clicked off in the fanny pack, and he unzipped it to store the earphones and get his car keys. He slid the key into the door lock.

The Explorer was already unlocked.

He pulled the key back.

It had been locked. He knew it.

He looked at all the glass. No damage. Somebody had opened the door with a key.

Now what?

He opened the hatchback and sat down, and changed into his street socks and shoes. Nothing had been apparently disturbed, and there was little in the wagon to steal – a few tape boxes and a couple of real estate files.

A white van started over the auto bridge toward the county highway. As it turned away from him, he had a split-second view of the passenger. Elton John sunglasses and a chignon.

The Falcon. Maybe here to distract me if I showed up while the driver of the van was still in the wagon. But doing what? Nothing was taken.

Brent thought about that. He thought only for a second about how they got a key. Hell, these people get unlisted telephone numbers like they're in the Yellow Pages and take shorthand in Cyrillic. They can probably pop car doors like pistachios. But why would anyone get into the car if they weren't going to take something?

They were leaving *something*.

This wagon's probably got a transmitter hidden somewhere.

He knew better than to try to find it – he'd read enough spy novels to know they could make one look like a bulb in the dome light and that he could tear the thing down to the frame and never find it. He slammed the hatchback and sat behind the wheel, feeling an uncharacteristic urge to remain quiet.

The office meeting and Rafé's presentation and the hour with Felicia in the sun and the walk with the March King had taken his mind off the whole witness thing for most of the day. But as the van disappeared toward Rio Verde, his fear for the unknown – the late-evening calls to an unlisted number, the encoded transmission with his townhouse address, the mysterious blonde, Jeff Terrell's foreboding recollections – returned to center stage in his skull. He headed for the office.

❖   ❖   ❖

12:55 p.m. He thought about bugs. Where do they put them? Who is *they*? How far do they transmit – does somebody have to follow me? Maybe it's just a tracking device they can home in on. From where? A satellite? A submarine? Is somebody with a moustache and a scimitar in an air-conditioned trailer at an airstrip in Cyprus watching me, right now? Can they tell if I'm on Post Street or a block away on Western Avenue?

Brent was prone to soliloquies. Not necessarily to their solutions.

Damn. I'm not even alone in my own wagon. His phone chirped under the front seat. He answered: "Yes?"

It was Katy. "Where are you? Your little girlfriend's here, been here for 10 minutes with ants in her pants ready to go look at houses. You on the way in, Skipper?"

"Thank you for calling, Mother. I have an appointment at the office at one o'clock and I'll just about make it." He wasn't about to say anything sensitive if the wagon was bugged.

"By the way, my car's running rough and it would be helpful if I could borrow yours this afternoon." He remembered that Katy's car was rumored to be registered with the Center for Disease Control in Atlanta. "On second thought, Mom, maybe Aunt Felicia's would be better – could you arrange for that while I drive over?"

The line was quiet for a moment. "You scare me sometimes, Brent. Somebody got a gun to your head? Just say 'everything's fine, dear' and I'll call the highway patrol."

"Don't do that, Mom. I'm coming over the bridge now. Ask Felicia about her car, and give Jane a nice cup of tea for her nerves."

Brent looked at the clock on the office cupola – one straight up. He walked into the lobby, and glanced into his own office on his way to the receptionists' counter.

Unbelievable. Doeman was sitting there, in baggy tan coveralls with extra cargo pockets on the pant legs in addition to the myriad of storage in locations normal to her. Her hair was covered by a scarf resembling a hospital scrub cap – he wasn't sure that it wasn't one. She had her stuff spread all over the table across from his desk – connected papers of some sort, like a print run. In a plastic basket like the supermarkets give shoppers who don't feel like trundling a cart around was some ungodly collection of her notion of house-hunting tools – he could see her measuring tapes, a small level, two cameras, a videocam and some cartridges, a Panasonic dictating machine. And, of course her briefcase and that damn Texas Instrument calculator. She didn't see him.

He motioned for Felicia to follow him around to the bull pen. Katy just watched, apparently still struck dumb by the car phone conversation. She finally said, "I'm sorry, Brent. Whatever it is, I'm sorry. I will wonder if I've been a good friend to you after you're gone. But I'll come visit you."

Brent turned to Felicia. "Somebody's bugged my Explorer, probably not somebody from Doeman's locker room. I need your Granada."

"Everybody in the valley knows my little coupe. What if somebody sees you and that crocodile together in it? What am I supposed to say? National security?"

"No. Brent security. If the bad guys can hear us they can hear addresses." Brent wondered who was "bad" and who was worse on this preferred-client list. "I'll bring it back with a full tank."

"I'll get the key. And the key to the gas tank. Leaded gas, if you can find it."

Brent walked into his office and clicked his computer. Opus and Bill the Cat had been at play – the screen went to *HouseNet*. "Hi, Jane. Nice to see you."

His heart was pounding. The squat woman in coveralls resurrected a 35-year-old fear of the broad-beamed school nurse at Fairfax Elementary who used to sneer at him while she dug out a sliver or slowly peeled a sticky Band-Aid from his skin, millimeter by millimeter.

"Ready to go see a few houses?"

"Seven. I'm fine, thank you. And thanks for the disc of the transmission. My mother's attorney had some revisions to the family trust that I needed to sign. I guess you have a notary in the office."

Family trust, my ass. And she knows I know better. "The receptionists are notaries. Seven houses? Great. Beautiful day for it, isn't it?" Her need for a notary could prove interesting. At the minimum, the receptionist would want to see a driver's license or photo IDs. Would her name be Jane Doeman? Sure. *On at least two of the dozen different IDs in that ugly little duffel bag she carries for a purse.*

"Here are the seven I want to see. And I brought some equipment so that I can send some information back to my clients. Perhaps Felicity can transmit it on her modem after I embed it into our company software language."

Felicity?

"She'd be glad to." Brent looked at the seven homes Doeman wanted to see. All were on lockboxes, and vacant. Interesting – the chances of that are slim, Brent told himself. Then he told himself that he had to quit turning minutiae into substance, before the soliloquies drove him into a deeper state of paranoia than these clients were already doing for him. He then told himself that telling himself things repeatedly was a sure sign of collapse. Next would come arguments with himself, soon followed by losing the arguments. The final signal of his exodus from sanity would come as Katy started looking normal and well-adjusted.

Brent sorted the seven printouts into the sequence they would visit them in. Two were starter homes, three were mid-range for the valley, the two remaining were expensive. Quite expensive. "We're going to start with the less-expensive ones. Ready?"

"No. Let me see the order we're going in." She opened a map that had been lined off in block square grids, with shorthand characters marking every other grid axis. Brent showed her where each listing was on the map, and she marked it with Roman numerals. Then she took seven sheets from her briefcase, each of which had a corresponding Roman numeral and printing in characters he didn't recognize – some looked like meteorological symbols, other like symbols from a physicist's elemental chart, and few that looked like the screen of his computer after he screwed up one day and hit some SHIFT+CONTROL option that he shouldn't have.

What captivated him was the barcodes – dozens of stickers on each page, aligned with the characters which were probably some category or descriptor of each listing. He'd never seen barcodes in a real estate context before. She put the sheets in order and stood up.

"Let's go."

CHAPTER NINE

Wednesday afternoon: Doeman's tour...

Then they walked from Brent's office, broker and client, Yogi and BooBoo. BooBoo carried her little bag of tricks, and the smaller accoutrements of home-shopping in the various pockets on her pant legs, upper sleeves, the breast, hip and side pockets and canvas fanny pack, pulled tight enough not to slide down and off her fanny. Yogi was hailed by Katy, today in braided pigtails and a 49er rugby shirt: "What time In would you like your little man slid to, Mr. Douglas?"

Brent looked at the magnetic In/Out board. God, how he wanted to see *Patricia* B as I*n*, even just for a minute. His time away from her was eating on him. He watched his present date, the object of his present affection, the apple of his eye, his client for three escrows, the elegant and multifaceted Jane, known in some quarters as BooBoo, walking to the parking lot in her designer coveralls from Oshkosh and clanking like a telephone lineman in full pole-climbing gear. The turquoise hospital scrub cap was the frosting on this cake. Benham was off pouting; Doeman was the reality.

"Why thank you, Miz O'Rourke. About two hours would be fine, which would be 3:30 for you math majors. I'll look forward to seeing you then." The few agents in the bull pen that could see Yogi were smiling.

Felicia piped up: "Remember, Skipper. Think unleaded. Tomorrow would be fine. And brake is left, gas is right, I think. And if you drive into my 'hood, please tell them you stole it."

Brent walked behind Jane, now some distance ahead of him in the lot, both heading for the Explorer. A thought flashed into his mind.

She's not that unattractive...

Short, yes. No ballerina. But the fanny pack had cinched in the waist of her coveralls and she didn't look *that* bad. The thought was gone as fast as it came. He started to get the cellphone out of the Explorer. Only then did it occur to him that the phone itself might be the bug or have one inside it, transmitting whether the phone was on or off the hook. Bad idea.

"We're taking the black Granada. Thought you might be more comfortable getting in and out."

Both stood by the passenger door of the Granada. "Thanks. I had a tough time in your wagon yesterday. I'm kind of short – don't know if you noticed that!" She stood close to him as if to emphasize her diminutive stature, and smiled up at him. He felt her ample breast press against his forearm, shift slightly, and then move away.

Brent sensed that talking to himself and answering, then arguing and losing, and finally finding Katy to be a sage and prescient advisor, was beginning to pale as a barometer of sanity. He found that his soliloquy was now plumbing new depths, first by taking note that Doeman indeed had a waist like most other girls do, followed by a feeling of newfound intimacy with the woman when he felt her warmth against his arm accompanied by a pretty smile.

Confusion raged within him – he hadn't forgotten her belch in that armpit restaurant and the eleven-thirty call to his unlisted number. Or neither the coded message nor the penetration of his wagon an hour ago.

She was still trouble. The brush against his arm was only an accident and the smile was gas – just like babies get, to fool the world into thinking they're happy. *Trouble* is the only way to view this terrorist…

❖　　❖　　❖

He cranked the Granada and drove toward the first listing. Listing #I of VII. "Tell me a little about the clients looking at this house. Do they have kids in school? Where will they work?"

"All of my clients are retired. There are three of them, and only two have children. I'd rather not talk a lot about them – their privacy is important to them, and it's for your own protection too."

Their privacy is important to them.

Jeff Terrell's words in the break room, verbatim.

"I *need* protection." *She admits it? Jesus…*

"It turns out we've got the run of all the listings you want to see today," he told her. "They're all vacant and I have a lockbox key to them." Brent eyed the battery of tools in the basket on the back seat, and stuck in various pockets in Doeman's coveralls. He noticed she had her own cellular phone.

"I probably won't have to go into too many, just number four. I mostly want to see the outside and get a look at the neighborhoods. With any luck, we can write three offers tomorrow morning after I confer with my clients. And if our relationship goes well, there will be seven more clients wanting homes we can start looking for next week. The company would like to set up a meeting with you first, since there will be quite a bit of money involved." She turned to look a Brent. He wondered if she saw him suck in a quick breath of air, or noticed the sweat breaking out over his mustache.

Seven more witnesses? And even more assassins looking for those seven? And Brent Douglas alone knows where they all are?

...and the company? That word again. Meeting – where the hell do I meet them, on some submarine moored outside the 12-mile limit, disguised as Shamu?

"When might this meeting be?"

"Soon. Isn't this the street? Slow down." She started looking at her hieroglyphics on the clipboard. He stopped in front of the house. It was a small frame house, with large windows in the living room and the bedroom to the left of the front door. There were few trees on the lot, or the lots on either side, and the homes were close together throughout the neighborhood. Brent liked the house.

Doeman didn't. "This is quite open from almost all the way around. More trees would be nice, especially with that picture window." She pulled out a compass from her left thigh pocket and let it stabilize. "Don't worry; the compass is compensated to work inside a car. The house has a north exposure, and we don't really like that." Brent could have showed her north without the compass.

She stepped out, and pulled a camera from her basket that Brent would die for – an Apple QuickTake that converted an optical image right onto a floppy disc. Like the Polaroid of the late 1940s, it was instant, but could put an image onto a laser printer in color, or a TV set, or be transmitted over a phone line. They were expensive, but the price was dropping rapidly and soon every real estate agent in the industry would have one. As would most of the rest of the world.

She took a few pictures while Brent admired the camera. It had the heft and shape of a pair of 7x50 binoculars with a lens on only one side. Indentations for the fingertips of both hands on the top of the grey case cried out to Brent to pick it up and play with it. It would do anything a film camera could do, then alter the picture's size or focus or zoom, right on a computer monitor or a TV screen. When the picture appeared the way you wanted it, a button "saved" it onto a disc.

Jane sat back into the car almost like a lady, a far cry from the Doeman half-twist that amazed the crew in Carl's Barbershop yesterday.

"Drive."

She had a facility for words.

Out from the shopping basket came a dark brown case about the size of a cigar box, with cords running out of it. One ended in a standard telephone jack, another in a cigarette lighter plug, and she pulled Felicia's unused cigarette lighter from the socket in the dash and plugged in that cord. Brent assumed she had low batteries in whatever the thing was, but she wasn't talking. He drove. She plugged a chrome marking pen-size device on the end of the third cord, and a bright red light at the end of the tool started to flash, rapidly.

She swept the tool over a few barcodes she had marked on listing I and the brown box chirped. In a second she was done and she put the contraption on Felicia's console. Listing II was only a few blocks from I, and they arrived. She liked it. It was surrounded by trees and had small windows. Brent figured out what she liked – an affordable fortress. She liked the peekhole in the hobbit door and the separation from the neighboring homes.

"Want to see the inside?" Brent fished for his lockbox key.

"No. Thanks. I'll just take a few pictures." Brent got out with her and watched her take pictures of the home, then away from the home to the street and adjoining homes. She measured the fences and made a few notes on her encoded sheet on the clipboard. She was animated. He saw the smile again, as she talked quietly into her dictating machine. He couldn't hear her.

Back in the car, she made more notes. The whole showing had taken 15 minutes, none of them inside the home. "It's a doll house. We'll make an offer on it."

It's a piece of junk inside, with the hell beat out of the kitchen and bathrooms. He'd seen it on an open house four months ago.

The barcode reader flew over some of the stickers – Brent tried to watch as he drove to III but nothing on the sheet made any sense to him anyway. She put the reading device away, reached for her cellular phone in the cuff pocket of her overalls, and turned it on. It "woke up" with a beep. She then plugged the phone jack from the brown barcode reader into the back of the cellphone and moved a dial on the reader.

She entered about a dozen numbers on the phone pad and "sent" them. It dawned on him that had they been in the Explorer and had it indeed been bugged, the bugger could regenerate the tones off the recording tape onto a computer and find out who the buggee was calling. Whatever was at the other end finally answered in a tone, not unlike a fax tone. Doeman hit a button on the readers, probably "send," Brent reasoned, as he drove with one eye and watched with the other.

The reader made a noise that sounded like Morse code. Fast Morse code. The transmission was over in about 10 seconds, and Doeman "ended" the cellphone and "paused" the reader. Then she tore sheets I and II from her clipboard, wadded them up, and tossed them into her briefcase.

❖   ❖   ❖

Listing III was into Doeman's mid-range price category, and the difference from I and II showed. Unfortunately, the home, while a good listing needing only minimal work, was perched atop a slight hill, very open, with huge picture windows in the living room, dining room and what Brent knew to be the master bedroom. Doeman looked at it through small binoculars, breast pocket right side, as they approached it from down the lane. "I can see right through it, from the center window out the back!"

Dining room window through to the kitchen window-wall. Some buyers, less concerned with getting their asses blown off as Doeman's all-stars are, actually like an open home. Seven more of these paranoids over the horizon? God help me...

The stop was brief. A few pictures with the digital Apple camera. Brent wanted to play with it, to sight through it and take a shot himself, but wouldn't give her the satisfaction of asking. Back in the car, she played out her usual routine with the barcode reader. Listing IV was almost across the street. Eucalyptus trees a hundred years old ringed the white Georgian replica with five Ionic columns across the dramatic front entrance. This was a beauty. Small windows. Private. Under-priced. He pulled through the open gates into the cobblestone driveway and under the *porte cochere.*

"We'll make an offer on it – maybe even for the general. This is a nice home. I'll take some pictures and put it on the list." She did her thing with the camera – side and front, a few from the front patio.

General?

"This one is beautiful. I could live here myself." She made notes furiously in her Cyrillic shorthand. He pulled out onto the county road, another sale under his belt. About 10 minutes.

General?

"Who's the general?"

She appeared flustered. "Ah, our general manager. He's looking for a top-end home but his wife loves anything that looks like Loire Valley."

Loire Valley? What the hell's she talking about? That place is as Loire Valley as Tara is a pagoda. Loire Valley homes, with their green mansard rooflines and stark white masonry walls were never big in this valley – the grape growers and wineries to the south didn't want anything to do with that French wine country in their midst.

Doeman's kidding me.

She bar-coded her speed-sheet on listing IV. She pulled a black marker from her cleavage, where she had already collected a six-inch scale ruler, a Bic pen and the temple of her sunglasses, and put a large + + + under the IV. She put listing V on top of the clipboard.

Her phone rang. And rang. As she turned and leaned against the seat to pull her laptop computer from the briefcase behind her, Brent caught a glimpse of a long fold of pale skin and a mound of soft flesh rising well above the zipper in her coveralls. She noticed his glimpse, now maturing into a stare, and accommodated him by holding still for a moment longer before retrieving her laptop. The phone still ringing, she opened the laptop until it "woke up," plugged it into the ringing cell-phone and let it answer. The screen on the laptop was hard to read in the sun, and Brent didn't see change on the screen as the message was received. She keyed the phone off in about 10 seconds – about the time it took Felicia to receive two and a half printed pages last night.

What was in this message? His jock strap size?

They already had about everything else there was to be known about him. Only by this time next week there'll be seven more people trying to find him...

Listing V would be a keeper, Brent reasoned, by the Doeman criteria. It was secluded. It didn't seem to matter if the interiors of the homes looked like the inside of a goat's stomach, so long as the homes were secluded. V was a dandy, an old stone Federal with verdant trees and shrubbery, the only open view toward the reservoir with a pleasant window up the river. She'd like it. And that would be three sales – they might not even have to go to VI and VII.

He was thirsty, and a Seven-11 market was on the way to V. He recalled that he was seated not with a woman but a temple, nutrition-wise, a fact established at lunch at the Heron yesterday. He wondered what temples liked to drink, or did they just sit on bodies of water and absorb it? Actually, he'd missed lunch and a burger would go good right now, but he was saving room for a steak at Patsy's. And two fingers of Jack Daniel's while he's cooking them. Maybe some white corn to go with the steak and a good bottle of local merlot.

And dessert. Patsy's specialty dessert, a delicacy reserved for Brent alone, was out of this world. And non-fattening.

"Would you like something to drink? There's a market up ahead, and cool patio at listing number five."

"I could go for a cold beer."

A *beer? The temple drinks beer?* He looked at her. Even she had a surprised look on her face.

Brent carried a pair of 16-ounce Buds out of the market and parked at listing V about two minutes later. Doeman loved it. It had been vacant for a month, and looked like the Temple of Doom. She brought her usual equipment, took the usual pictures and mumbled into the pocket dictator. Brent found a redwood swing hung from a huge Norwegian maple branch in the view corridor looking up the river. He went back to the car, got a blanket from Felicia's trunk, spread it out on the dusty swing and plopped himself down.

She can take her damn pictures 'til hell freezes over. I'm on a break. He cracked a beer.

Doeman showed up about three swigs later with her plastic market basket and started unloading the paraphernalia from her coverall pockets into it. She recovered a Bic pen from her cleavage, and a small scale ruler that Brent hadn't noticed in his earlier inventory. She pulled off her nylon hiking boots and opened her own beer.

"We're done, Brent. I've got three good candidates. Save the other two for next Monday for the rest of my people. Good brew – thanks."

Monday?

"Where do we go from here, Jane?"

"I want purchase offers in hard copy by tomorrow afternoon at one. Make it four – might as well grab that first place too. The price was right. Enter 95 per cent of asking price on all of them, cash at close of escrow. We've worked with Sunset Escrow before in LA – let's use them again. If the seller doesn't like that, we'll pay the title insurance, but they *are* going to Sunset in Rio Verde.

He recalled Jeff's comment: *the closing check came to another branch of the local escrow company. We never saw it here…*

She fiddled with the barcode reader and notes on her clipboard, and pulled her phone from the basket. While she plugged the reader into the phone and dialed a dozen numbers from memory, Brent stared at her. That raven hair could be attractive, with a little work. Pretty teeth – white and even. Big brown eyes – long, full lashes and dark eyebrows. A smallish waist, cinched under the fanny pack belt earlier. And sitting here with a barcode reader propped on it, a flat tummy. He remembered the legs, the whole view of them in the denim skirt falling into the wagon yesterday. Short, and heavy, but in a Rubenesque sort of way. Not a small derriere, but her small waist only accentuated it further.

In all, she was attractive. He remembered his brief view of the smooth skin on her full cleavage. Hell, she could be *plenty* attractive. She could be a beauty. So why did she go through both days looking so damn repulsive? And the personality: D*rive. My body is a temple. You have an appointment at one tomorrow.* She was a beautiful enigma with the personality of a SkilSaw. His mind went back to Mr. Broker as she spoke:

"We talked about this before. Instead of my Visa, I'll put $2,500 into each escrow as earnest money deposit upon signing the four offers. Escrows are to close in 30 days. I have power-of-attorney for the company to sign the offers and escrow instructions. I'll give you a certified copy of that power to sign as soon as I see the preliminary title reports." She wasn't turning any hole cards until she knew the houses had merchantable title. Smart lady. Smarter than I though she was. He'd love to see the power-of-attorney – at least he'd know what state, or nation, she hailed from.

"No problem on the earnest money, except for the PAs for the individual buyers. Do you have those too?"

The phone finally connected, and she pushed the *send* key. "We won't need them. The company is buying the houses and will quitclaim them to my clients after recordation. This is not your concern. Would you rub my feet?" She swung her legs up onto the swing next to his right hip.

Bingo! Brent thought, almost ignoring the fact that he was now rubbing her feet like he frequently rubbed Patsy's. Quitclaims. That's how they could conceal the identity of the true buyers. The "company" bought the properties, through an escrow. Then they deeded them out to the individual buyers, or maybe they never would – what's the difference? If the clients or employees or witnesses or whoever didn't record the quitclaim, or recorded without title insurance, they could record them to Mickey Mouse or Indiana Jones or whoever the hell they wanted to and live in peace behind their eucalyptuses and walnuts and oaks. A lot of work and planning, but one real estate broker could bring it down. To some degree he was protected too: Even if the *revenginistas* shoved swizzle sticks under his eyelids he could truthfully scream that he didn't know where Mickey or Indy lived. That thought alone gave him comfort for about seven seconds.

His strong hands had worked on her feet during this whole mental exercise in Conveyancing 101, and while he hadn't paid much attention to her feet, Doeman had. Her head was back on the end of the swing, eyes closed, and she was smiling. And moaning softly. Since their chance meeting, her personality and warmth had run the full gamut of emotion from A to C. Now, as the sun filtered through the leaves a hundred feet over their heads and the lazy river a quarter mile down the grassy slope lapped at the reeds and disappeared around the green hills, and the Holsteins mooed and the unique scent of eucalyptus filled the air, she appeared happy, possibly even human. He raised her foot over his knee and continued the massage.

"Brent, you mentioned a place for lunch that had a great menu and a view of the river. Do they serve dinner there too?"

He thought about The Shadows, a few miles down the county road toward Fairfax. "Yeah. A good one."

"Let's go, tonight. I don't think you liked that Heron place too well. Can I take you to the shadow place tonight?"

Brent's mind, now off title insurance and Saturday morning TV kiddie-show grantees, was in low idle, enjoying the view of the river and the weight of her calf on his thigh.

The barbecue…

"It sounds good, but I have plans. Thanks anyway – maybe I'll take a rain check?"

Doeman pulled her legs back abruptly and sat up straight. "Get out of if somehow. I need this night – I'd like to look like a lady for you at least once. Next week's no good. My supervisors will be here in town with me and it'd never go then. Think of it as a business meeting that your job requires. I'm spending a million bucks with your company and I'd like to take you to dinner. Tonight."

She plopped her arms across her chest.

Business. Inevitable. The piper would be paid. Be it good business, or suicidal business with her band of fruitcakes, he was looking at four escrows. She had the horsepower, apparently, to go over his head to the owners of his firm if he spurned her. He couldn't rock the boat.

They sat, staring at the river.

Patsy would have to wait.

"What time would you like to go? Six OK?"

She smiled. "Great. I'll look nice, I promise." She pulled off the scrub cap.

Brent thought about the bugged Explorer. Funny how the mere presumption of a listening device had ripened in his mind into an accepted fact in four hours – taking the Explorer tonight was out of the question.

"Do you have a rental car?" he asked. "My wagon's only hitting on five."

"I turned it in. Can you borrow another one?"

"Maybe." He thought. Felicia's was out – she needs her own car and couldn't trade for the Explorer. He'd deal with transportation somehow. "Let's travel. I've got some work to do yet, and I need some escrow numbers to have an account set to pay the deposit into tomorrow."

He had work to do, but it wasn't to do with the escrows. He had to tell Patricia Benham that the steaks and white corn would have to wait for another night. This would not please her. And the special dessert...

Damn!

Brent held the door for Doeman, and handed her the basket of tools. She pulled the sheets for the first four listings and ran out 95 per cent of each in her calculator. Brent's mind was on the call he had to make. He drove Doeman to the bed-and-breakfast downtown and she jumped out easily, in contrast to the side show she put on while evacuating the Explorer.

"See you here at six," he nodded. She was smiling.

Brent waved, drove the Granada two blocks to the office and parked it in Felicia's spot, pulling the seat back up to where she liked it. He took the four listings, an empty Bud can and the scrub cap out of the car.

He set out to make the toughest phone call he could remember ever making in his life.

He walked into the office. The whole bull pen seemed to be staring at him. Alice and Holly were behind the glass at the hot desk. He laid Felicia's keys on the counter.

"Thanks, gorgeous. Give them back to me in the morning and I'll gas it up."

He moved his little magnetic man to *Out for Day*. Katy noticed that, and said "Appointment that good, huh? Get a date for tonight, maybe a little din-din at the Heron? I hear the mantis and cedar-bark plate is excellent on Wednesday."

"Sold four listings and got a date for The Shadows. Six." He walked into his office. Both receptionists followed him in.

Katy: "May we remind you of a certain obligation with Miz Benham, tonight, her place, steak, with the probability of getting your clock wound, which might be in the best interest of everyone in this nuthouse? This Doeman broad is setting you out of your mind. And ours."

Felicia: "It's my Granada's effect on men. Makes them crazy. Even faithful men like Skipper. Don't keep the date – Patsy will drop you like a ton of bricks. She's already PO'ed about lunch yesterday. You're in deep doo-doo. Four sales aren't worth it – Patsy's too good a lady."

Brent lowered his head onto his desk. "Don't have much choice now. It's a client thing. She'll understand. She has to."

Pilot and co-pilot headed for the door, two pretty faces in shock. Or possibly in deep disgust.

Felicia spun around: "Would you mind gassing up my car *before* you call Patsy?"

3:55 p.m. Brent stared at his telephone for several minutes. It didn't move. He pondered the words he might select. "Hi, Patsy, this is Brent,"

came to mind. Beyond those, he encountered difficulty. Maybe she wouldn't be home and the whole coast cellular net would be down. Maybe he would be taken hostage by a carload of nuns. Maryknoll. Maybe he should face the music.

Butch's now-famous interrogatory to Sundance *who are these guys?* had formed the metaphor of Brent's past few days. Another scene from the same movie now seemed apropos: When surrounded by the Law, the outlaws joined hands and spent the entirety of their jump, from a high cliff to a river below, shouting in unison one four-letter expletive. Brent bit the bullet, pushed Patsy's home speed-dial button, threw back his head and formed the same expletive behind clenched teeth. Her phone rang…*ssshhhh*…and rang….*eeeee*…she answered…*yit!*

"This is Patsy…"

"Hi, it's Brent. Douglas. How are you?"

Douglas? How many Brents does she know? "Hungry. You sound goofy. Heard you were going to show some homes this afternoon. Do any good?"

"Looks like four houses – 900 thou, give or take a few. Strange happenings going on around here, though." It dawned on him how long it had been since he'd seen her, and how little she knows about Doeman and Company.

"I played volleyball with Katy last night and we had a beer afterward. She told me about it – some of it. You think all of that can be happening?"

"There's more now. This morning Felicia told me about a data transmission to this Doeman sweetie that arrived in code. They've got my unlisted number at home. They bugged my wagon during lunch. It all looks like an effort to move a bunch of government prosecution witnesses into town with no trail behind them. And I'm the loose end that could expose them. It gets worse – seven more are coming next week."

"It can't be that bad. Let's work it out during dinner. You're probably getting yourself nutsed up over nothing."

The D-word. He knew it would come up. Hang on, Brenty-boy:

"Actually, I'm calling about dinner. I have a conflict – their relocation specialist wants to have dinner with me tonight, and was pretty insistent. I tried to reschedule but it wouldn't work any other way. Can we move the barbecue to tomorrow?"

Relocation specialist. He liked that. Genderless, businesslike, professional. Put into my place, what could Patsy say?"

"You inconsiderate asshole!"

Oh.

The black phenolic resin telephone handset turned to something dead and cold and wrong in his left hand.

"You insensitive, selfish, inconsiderate asshole!" Patsy tended to repeat herself when she was upset. Having addressed that, she continued. "I'm sitting here with two porterhouse steaks, corn, and wine; a full moon four hours from my deck and a lacy little ensemble from Victoria's Secret that wouldn't cover up one of your relocation specialist's knees. You call her back, mister, and break the date and have your ass over here by six or you and me is history." He could hear her starting to cry.

"You're upset." He wished he hadn't said that – upset might have been an improvement. "This thing is ugly and I've got to humor her. It's gone beyond worrying about commissions. If I stand her up, I may be history. The only way I'm safe is by being of value to *them*. And don't ask me who *them* is. I think *them* is the ones *they* is looking for for ratting *them* out in court. And only I will know where *them* lives."

"Katy said you're either half nuts or in great danger. She's worried about you – the whole office is. And the danger option seems realistic right now. We'll try for tomorrow. I'm not too keen on you keeping company with that little beast but I'd rather have you in one piece in the long run. I love you, Skipper."

"Thanks. Your support means a lot right now."

Then he recalled his other dilemma.

"Oh, and Patsy?"

"What is it?"

"Could I borrow your Taurus tonight?"

The dead cold object in his right hand was quiet for a few seconds, until Patsy let him have it out of both barrels, likening him once again to an orifice that was brought up several times in prior conversation, together with a litany of other well-chosen Anglo-Saxon words and a vivid and unabridged description of his latest dinner date.

Then the line went as dead and cold as the phone handset.

And he sat, still, in his office.

4:15 p.m. God forbid that he take a short break from his problems with Patsy and the analysis of potential crossfire from two teams of assassins converging in his skull, but he did have a chore to do. He dialed Sunset Escrow, an office he knew well just across the bridge and a few doors up the street from the Blue Heron. He had used them a bunch – they had a good title "plant" where the duplicate of the county's land records were researched, and two of the valley's best escrow officers. Their aging office had the character all escrow offices ought to have, a companion to the old L&H real estate office he could see out his window. Doeman said Susie Santini was designated to receive the wire transfer of the earnest money funds. She always cracked him up and would make some tough escrows pleasant. Or at least tolerable.

"Hi, Toni. This is Brent Douglas. Is Susie around?"

"Not today, big guy. Or tomorrow or Friday. She got the chance to go to a tax-deferred exchange seminar, kind of rush-rush. A lady from our San Bernardino office flew in last night to fill in for a few days. You'll like her; her name's Laura Bigelow. I'll put you through – she should be off the phone in just a sec."

Brent hung the handset over his shoulder and looked out the window. Jeff's words in the break room came back to him, as Jeff's words had for the last 24 hours: *It closed at Bay City Title, but some officer who had come in from LA to take Gwen's desk while she was on vacation did the escrow instructions and the deed. Funds were wired in from another Bay City branch, so nobody in Rio Verde ever saw a check or a draft.*

Strange.

Strange indeed.

He hung on the line. Laura came on, and they introduced themselves. She was quite cordial, and quite loud. He held the phone away from his ear.

Does she know anything about this, or did she just go where Sunset sent her? Does anybody at Sunset know anything's out of the ordinary?

Laura gave him four sequential escrow numbers – all ending in SS – Susan Santini's code. Susie would probably close all four of them, without a clue, or a care, where the closing funds came from. Nor would Brent ask her to find out. No sense getting her mixed up in this...

Their talk was pleasant, and Brent promised to come by tomorrow and say hello. He would need their electronic funds transfer address for the four files he'd create in the morning.

Katy walked in and sat down. "I bear news."

"Speak, oh pretty messenger. But bear good news only. I got enough of the other." He could tell from Katy's expression that good it would be.

"You have wheels. A sky-blue Taurus, as a matter of fact. Loaned by a lady who loves you enough to give you a car to haul your new date around but hates you enough at this moment to blow your butt off with a shotgun if she lays eyes on you. Her words."

"Thanks. How do I get it, given the veiled hint of danger to me surrounding her home?"

"We're going to dinner at the Sandpiper at 5:30. You can go by after that, leave the wagon keys on the left front tire, take her keys from the same tire on the Taurus and beat it. And don't bring it back after your date, if you know what's good for you. She'll trade with you tomorrow."

"I have the feeling I owe you."

"Big-time. Actually she said she wants to pick up some 21-year old Dustin Hoffman studmuffin and play Mrs. *Robinson* with him in the back seat of the Explorer while whoever has the thing bugged thinks it's you and Doeman. Maybe there's a Mr. Doeman. Add him to your growing list of enemies."

"How does she expect to land a 21-year-old?"

"She said something about a secret – somebody's secret, was it *Victoria's*? – that she bought for some old fart who doesn't have time for her anymore."

"Thanks." He laughed out loud. It was music to her ears. The office hadn't heard his distinctive laugh for a couple of days.

Felicia poked her head in, on the way out and home. "Guess you know you're got two Fords to fuel up tomorrow. Give Jane my best, Tarzan. Are you going to her vine or yours after dinner?" The paper clip in Brent's hand flew just over her head and out into the lobby.

4:50 p.m. The Explorer turned off Villa Verde Road into the rock-lined townhouse driveway and nosed into Brent's carport. He got out, his tie hanging loose and shirttail half-untucked, and walked to the mailbox pedestal. BRENT DOUGLAS HAS WON A MILLION DOLLARS! Ed McMahon had personally written on the large brown envelope. He chucked it into a can placed there for that purpose. Aldo Martini walked out of the shadows. "Hi, Brent." Brent spun around, surprised.

"Hiya, Al." The Martini family had been in the valley almost as long as Rafé Morales' family. They grew 60 per cent of the grapes in the valley and sold them to the vintners. Aldo sold his own land to some golf course developers for a price that would choke a horse, and busied himself as the virtually-volunteer handyman and town crier at the 20-unit town-house, with the abundant flower beds to tend and the company of the congenial residents as his only reward.

"Ah, they're killing me with work, Brent." He had a full head of glorious white hair and a thin mustache to match, in striking contrast to his rugged tan face. He tugged with strong forearms at the red suspenders over his well-worn chambray shirt.

"You're breaking my heart," Brent laughed. "How's your golf game?"

"Ready whenever you are. Bring your wallet – I've been hot, mid-80s. That's fair warning. By the way, your carpet cleaners got here, left about an hour ago."

Carpet cleaners?

Brent mulled that over. They were ready for cleaning, and he'd thought about doing it, but couldn't remember calling anyone. He didn't want to involve Aldo in this.

"Who came, ServiceMaster? I think that's who I called."

"Wasn't them. Don't know who it was, just a plain ol' white van with two guys, one white, one black. Got here about one."

"Did you let them in?"

"Said they didn't need a key. You must have given them one."

A *white van.* Do locks mean anything to these people? "That's right. I remember now. Both of them, kind of short guys?"

"Not these two. Both real tall, wearing brown coveralls and blue knit watch caps. The white guy was the skinniest guy I've ever seen."

Yeah, and with the best fanny you've ever seen going the other way on a bicycle.

The van with the Falcon must have left the reservoir and come straight over here. "Thanks, Al. Good to see you."

He unlocked his townhouse, with the wry notion that it didn't seem to matter what the hell he locked up lately anyway, so why was he bothering? The carpet hadn't been cleaned, no surprise, and nothing was missing, no surprise there either. He looked at the clock – one hour to Doeman-time. He cracked a beer and walked to the stereo cabinet. He turned on the amplifier. The CD player was already on. Maybe he left it on last night. He started whatever disc was on. Nothing played. Did he unload the disc carousel last night? He couldn't remember either way. He shut the system off.

The sliding door onto the second-story deck was open, but he never locked it anyway. He yanked his tie off, threw it over the carved cigar-store Indian on the deck with some other ties, and plopped his tired tail on his chaise – part of a Brown Jordan set the founding fathers had given him as a bonus when he bought the townhouse. The view up the river between the oaks this time of year was breathtaking.

Laurence Harvey's belief in the Manchurian Candidate syndrome was beginning to manifest itself: The mind is merciful, and slips into idle when overload approaches.

CHAPTER TEN

Wednesday night: A table for two...

A man in a sport coat is a rare sight indeed in Rio Verde during warm summer evenings, but Brent had just ordered a dandy from L. L. Bean, and he pulled the new summer weight navy coat on over a light blue short-sleeved shirt. He was glad that his folks had given him Frederick as a middle name – years later, the BFD monogrammed on most of his oxford shirts offered a tacit insight into his attitude toward life: Big Friggin' Deal.

He was anxious to witness what Doeman would wear to join him. Maybe the coveralls or the denim, but more likely for an evening out, a silver lamé sheath, so that the townsfolk might know that he had brought a large baked potato of his own to dine with. Hiking boots of black leather, perhaps with silver toes, and a number of bracelets that clanked like cowbells as she moved. What surprises could an *haute couture* tomato like her perpetrate? And who would see them? Would she belch again, as she did at the Heron? Patsy had friends; hell, the whole valley knew her. And he had parents, fine folks in Fairfax who occasionally ventured out for a mid-week meal.

His final act upon leaving was to take one match from a matchbook and hold it just below the lower hinge as he pulled his front door closed. The match was pinched between the jamb and the door. If anyone entered the townhouse, the match would fall, unnoticed. He learned that in the *Crimestoppers* section of Dick Tracy in the Sunday funnies when he was a kid.

Al's morning glories in the bed by his door were beautiful. He cut just one with his penknife. A posy. Perhaps just two gazanias. And a day lily. The portulacas were flourishing; Al wouldn't miss four. Lavender is nice. The candy-stripe dianthus was gorgeous and plentiful but her stalks too short for his intended purpose. Ditto the begonias. A zinnia, and another. A duo of marigolds. And, one tall cosmos, perhaps the focal point.

Brent knew better than to screw with Al's roses…

He closed his penknife, and carefully laid his floral booty on the passenger-side floor of the wagon. Leaving the wooded complex, he pushed a Neil Young tape into the player. Did he lock his door? Who cares? Nobody in Rio Verde uses a key anymore anyway.

Patsy's house was only a few minutes away, on the other side of the gentle hill. He pulled into the driveway next to her Taurus, and put his car key on the front tire before he forgot it. He took the flowers from the floor and found a rubber band in the jockey box.

He dropped the rubber band over the antenna of the Explorer, and then carefully held the stalks of the purloined petals against the antenna, one by one, until he ringed it, with the cosmos as the tallest, then working down to the shorter stalks. He mixed the colors and the heights, and when all were in place, he raised the rubber band over the stalks to hold them in place. The bouquet was perfection. How long could any woman remain torqued with a man of his sentimentality?

Time would tell…

He locked the Explorer, took the key from her tire, and started the Taurus. It was clean and new, and an ancient 101 *Strings Play the Great Love Themes* was playing in the tape deck. He let it play.

Five more minutes' drive would put him in front of Doeman's bed-and-breakfast, dead-nuts-on six straight up. He was conscious of his heart rate rising, and felt his palms, moist on the bulky steering wheel. He thought about what he'd say. What they'd talk about. No business. What they'd do after dinner – no clue about that one. Today she wanted her feet rubbed, asked him so naturally that he forgot every rotten thought he'd had about her and massaged them without a second thought. What would she like him to massage later?

❖   ❖   ❖

He turned into the parking lot next to the bed-and-breakfast. It was an authentic Queen Anne, built during the turn of the century. Wedgwood blue with extensive white bric-a-brac,

Queen Anne Bed & Breakfast

a turret with the original curved glass, and matching lace curtains tied back behind every leaded window. A Tiffany lamp glowed in the parlor window. Native stone planters surrounding the home hosted the most-imitated flower beds and shrubbery in the valley. Many thought the serpentine lights along the roofline of the mill and those in the downtown park were arranged 90 years ago just to frame this old "painted lady" in their soft glow. A figure was sitting on a park bench in the forming shadows of the gloaming, under the honeysuckle-covered treillage of a wrought-iron arbor near the ornate entry into the home. She was wearing a broad-brimmed hat with a bowed sash that complemented the period theme of the bed-and-breakfast, and in the flickering light from the replica Victorian gas street lamps she completed a scene that would have made the front page of a Sunday rotogravure of three generations past.

He stepped out of the Taurus as the figure in the hat turned toward him. She rose to walk from the park bench across the deep lawn in the yard, still some distance from him. She wore a floral print dress, quite tight through her slim waist and deeply-cut between the lace-trimmed shoulder straps. White satin tights ended in a lace band at her ankle, cased in dainty brown suede granny boots. From her shoulder a large wooden-handled purse of fabric matching her dress hung from a long strap. Brent mused that Edith Head herself might have matched the costume to this scene.

As they converged in the brick walkway encircling the dim street lamp, he could see the feminine curve of her full hips and thighs. They stopped under the lamp, facing each other. He was captivated with the smoothness of her athletic arms and deep valley of porcelain skin in the revealing bodice of her peach dress.

Doeman.

"Hi, Brent. Ready for dinner?"

He said nothing. Thirty-six hours of recollections raced through his mind. Her mysterious and devious behavior of the past few days. The contrast between the amorphous nearly-bare fanny sprawled across the front seats of his wagon in front of the office, and this shapely rear end in a graceful dress. She looked up at him, a wistful half-smile brightening her face. Her short black hair swept across her forehead, then back beneath the straw hat. She wore tasteful silver earrings and a simple bracelet – no black Casio diver watch tonight. And the smell of gardenia, her fragrance forming the perfect dot under the question mark that this whole evening had turned into.

She didn't move. She had him on the ropes, and she knew it.

He lifted her left hand toward him. Fingernails, so rough and uneven this afternoon, now polished to an iridescent peach pearl glow, very close to the color of her dress.

"Wow."

"I beg your pardon?"

"Wow, you look great."

Great, nothing – she looked beautiful.

"Thanks."

"I've got to ask: What came over you? You look beautiful!"

There. He said the b-word.

"The past few days I've been busy night and day, before and after I see you, and just haven't had time to primp. Tonight I wanted to look like a lady for a change. But don't get used to it – tomorrow and the days next week will be ball-busters and I'll probably go back to my coveralls. They're utilitarian."

Brent replayed her words in his mind, trying to remember if *thank you* were two of them. Ah, the enigmatic Doeman.

You're welcome...

❖   ❖   ❖

Jane allowed Brent to open her car door, gathered in her long skirt with her right hand and sat down gracefully, then lifted her knees lightly, arched her toes and swung forward into the seat.

Amazing. Brent contrasted it to the skin-show she put on for the boys in the barbershop gallery yesterday.

The unmistakable, and lingering, aroma of her gardenia fragrance immediately permeated the Taurus. Brent loved gardenia; he hoped Patsy would also, in her Taurus, for the next few weeks.

Doeman turned up the 101 *Strings* on the tape, slumped back in the seat and closed her eyes. She looked peaceful.

The ride to The Shadows took only 20 minutes, and they reached the restaurant on the grassy bluff where the river slowly ceases to flow until it becomes a lake. Light from the campfires and Coleman lanterns of a dozen campgrounds sparkled like fireflies on the island beneath the bluff in the delta. The delta's small islands thinned in the distance, until the water filled a broad open lake. As the twilight yielded to darkness the lights of vacation homes defined the lake's shoreline.

Doeman, her eyes still closed, didn't move. Brent touched her shoulder, gently.

She spoke. "I love that music."

"Yeah. It's old, but it's nice." He walked around and opened her door. The night was warm, and she left her light sweater in the car. He took her hand and helped her from the low seat.

"I made reservations for two, under *Smith*," she said as they walked.

"OK. Who's Smith?"

"That's the name the company uses on its Visa cards, and I want to be consistent."

"Is Smith the company's name?" He instinctively put his hand on her waist, guiding her through the trees on the way up the walk. Only then did he notice that the back hem of her dress was open to well above the knee.

"No."

Oh.

She walked silently for a hundred feet. "I'd rather not talk shop tonight." She took his hand as they walked into the restaurant's foyer.

"Smith, party of two, please, with reservations." He glanced around, wondering who from the town was seated nearby; noticing that this Smith fellow resembled Douglas, and where was the willowy Patsy? The pretty hostess looked at the reservation list, and then looked up with a questioning glance.

"Ah, yes. Walk this way." Brent smirked at the classic line from *Young Frankenstein* and knew that few indeed could walk the way the hard-bodied college coed-turned-summer hostess was gyrating. Following behind her, he hoped it was a long walk to their table. Doeman was even smiling – could it be she was reading his mind?

Brent, ever the gentleman, held Jane's chair as she sat at the table. The view from their table was spectacular – over the hurricane lanterns on the tables of the restaurant's outside deck a floor below, to the fireflies on the delta, then along the shoreline of the lake. Over her shoulder in his line of sight glowed the skyline of the big city across the bay.

The talk was small and separated by long, but not uncomfortable pauses over a carafe of the local chardonnay. After a few more minutes, they ordered. The candlelight flattered Doeman's pale skin and danced in her dark eyes, and the shadow between her high, full breasts deepened whenever she leaned toward the table. He sat with both hands on the stem of his wine glass, and she reached across to take them both in her hands and hold them as she broke the silence:

"Tell me about Brent Douglas…"

Brent Douglas was shocked, was the first biographical fact that he might have revealed, but he didn't. He thought about that. Was the interrogator only a rather lovely lady, far from home, enraptured by the view and the touch of his hands, now curled around hers? Or was she still the evil woman she had seemed to be for the last 36 hours, the stumpy tip of a clandestine iceberg that he didn't want to melt all over him? How much did he want her to know about him that could possibly help her clients' future attempts to compromise him?

"Not much to tell, for having walked the rock for 45 years." He repositioned his hands over hers. "I grew up in the cluster of lights over your left shoulder and started at State University. Went for three years, then had a chance to get into the Navy flight program and finish up my degree while I was in the service. After 13 months of flight training, they discovered I was half-blind and transferred me to flight engineer school. I did three hitches, about 80 per cent of the time right over that hill behind you as an engineer on a P-3." Which would mean nothing to her. "A big four-prop job that wakes up the North Bay when it takes off and flies back and forth over the ocean all day and night looking for submarines."

Maybe your submarines.

"I dated a lot, but never married. Came close a few times. Wished I had now – I spend a lot of time with the guys in the office and their kids in Little League. It would have been a good life."

"Do you think you'll ever marry?"

"Yup. Got a great lady all picked out. I'll probably ask her to tie the knot by the end of the year."

This to the casual observer would juxtapose why he was holding Doeman's hands ever-more tightly, captivated by her low neckline and the candlelight dancing in her eyes.

The salad arrived, and they withdrew their hands. They ate in silence. A string quartet was playing Bach on the deck below and the sonata filtered into the dining room through several screened windows. The salad dishes were whisked away, and the waiter refilled their wine glasses. She took his hand again. She remarked that had it not been for

Mendelssohn, the works of Bach would have been lost to the world. Not bad for a woman who didn't know a Tudor from a Loire Valley home earlier in the day. Or who burped like a stevedore in the Blue Heron café. He recalled a book he read years ago about multiple personalities – this chickadee could inspire a sequel. But whichever persona she was emulating tonight, her warm hands felt good in his.

Quite a few people were enjoying the evening on the lower deck. Most were captivated by either the string quartet or the moonlit view up

The Shadows Restaurant

the river, but one woman had repeatedly looked up toward the dining room where Brent and Jane were seated, glancing back and forth along the picture window as if she were looking for someone in particular. She spoke occasionally to a person in the chair across a small cocktail table, but Brent's view of that chair and its occupant was obscured by the banister of the stairwell leading to the lower deck. Brent looked back at Jane, who was now almost gazing at him. Their entrées arrived. The Shadows had the best food in the valley, in the nicest setting, with superior service. He was glad to be here tonight. He thought of Patsy, but at this moment he was glad to be with Jane. He was taking a certain comfort in the knowledge that this was a temporal relationship, and tonight would close the book on the social aspect of it.

They made some more small talk during the main course; even while Jane pointed out that their business relationship demanded that they remain objective in their off-hours, or some such supercilious crap. While she was remaining objective, Brent felt her calf moving, slowly against his. She began talking in great detail of her childhood, her large family and her college education at an American university in the Far East.

She was one of the five children of a language professor mother and a munitions broker father. He had a group of nine or 10 partners who visited the hot spots of the world, ensuring that one side or the other of whatever altercation was in vogue was supplied with sufficient ordnance to get the job done. Evaluating the merits of the beef or their job was not a part of his.

The little cartel, which moved her family around the globe with some frequency, came into existence shortly after the fall of Diên Biên Phu in the mid-1950s and managed to stay one jump ahead of the conflicts in the Middle East, Central America, Northern Ireland, Afghanistan, the African Third World, and to some degree, within the United States. Wherever the milk of human kindness had ceased to flow, Jane's father and company would be there, bargaining to supply guns and bullets, new or salvage aircraft, missiles or bombs, electronics and whatever else the traffic would bear; buying from one faction and selling to another who would put them to whatever use suited them. Jane's father was a conduit, not a conscience.

A busboy cleared their table. Brent turned his coffee cup over and held Jane's with his free hand, questioning her. She nodded and he inverted hers too. Coffee was served. A sterling tray of sugar and cream was brought to the table but neither used it. She intertwined the fingers of her right hand with the fingers of his left, and continued:

The cartel also supplied men to work the equipment – a pilot with combat time in a MIG, a crew who could fire a French Exocet missile, a Brit who could service a Harrier's jet engine, ground soldiers or technicians or *saboteurs* with experience in deserts or jungles. Or office buildings or industrial plants or regional telephone switching facilities.

Christ, these mercenaries were running an international catalog store and temp agency for global mayhem.

She continued, as if anxious for Brent to know, in order to validate her day-and-a-half of spooky behavior. Brent waved off the waiter with a dessert tray for the moment, then looked into her pained eyes and silently invited her to continue by raising his eyebrows.

The men in the cartel got greedy, or careless, or both, a few years ago. In the classic tale of the right hand not knowing what the left hand was doing, one group of the cartel based somewhere, she wasn't sure where, sold a number of fighter aircraft to one side of a confrontation.

Her father, unfortunately, didn't know what his branch office was selling or to whom, and sold the opposing forces in the same rift a large number of the same model aircraft, throwing in a few hardy men to fly them and fix them.

Battle was inevitably joined, and Jane said her father later related that the ensuing carnage looked like an airborne OK Corral. The common electronics on the planes couldn't distinguish the good guys from the bad, relatively speaking, and the heat-seeking missiles they sold them consequently weren't too selective after they were launched. While the *generalissimos* running the supersonic fray were not terribly aggrieved by the loss of four dozen tall young men with white scarves, most of whom were provided by Jane's father, both sides were madder than holy hell that a couple hundred million U.S. dollars' worth of fighters, all bought from the cartel, had been turned into a stack of junk aluminum without furthering their respective noble causes.

The cartel was in hot water, and the illicit-arms grapevine went into overdrive. The other customers around the world analyzed their enemies more closely and found that they too had common ordnance with the aggressors from across the river or over the hill. Brent reasoned that the first rule of success and survival in running an international arms mail-order house was to sell to one side or the other, but never to both. Jane went on.

People were looking for my father.

And he didn't do anything illegal. Honest, he didn't...

Brent tacitly agreed. If the Navy ever decided to upgrade from his old turboprop Lockheed P-3 *Orion* subchaser, assuming there were still submarines to chase after the *détente*, they would probably strip the sonar gear off them and remove the racks that held the depth charges that blow submarines to smithereens. Then they'd sell the Orions to some outfit that dropped borate on forest fires then donate the radar and sonar gear to universities who could modify them to find earthquakes or track the migration of Alaskan double-breasted mattress-thrashers or for some other arcane purpose. Jane's father and his friends could legally buy a surplus Orion and ferret out where the electronics wound up. Finding depth-charges on the black market didn't seem to be a big challenge in today's world, and in six weeks the cartel could retrofit a Navy war machine that did Yeoman service without international peer for four decades, to sell to the highest bidder. Legally.

Mostly...

Brent listened in rapt attention. Recalling the chain of events pained her, and sharing it with him had brought her close to tears. But she brightened in concluding with the recent news that the cartel families who had gone into hiding were soon to be reunited. Only after she fell quiet did he realize that she was again gripping his hands tightly with hers, and that her leg was pressing hard against his calf. He sensed that she had not yet been able to bring herself to tell the story to any other person, and the 15 minutes she spent telling him had been a great cathartic.

They sat quietly. And Brent thought that *he* had trouble. He had only a few states'-evidence witnesses and the handful of those seeking retribution against them to deal with. Docman's father and his lusty privateers had stepped in it big-time – men, organized men, who lived by the sword in a world trying to avoid one, men most apt to fight and die for a cause they weren't sure of themselves, and now spread out around the four corners of the earth awaiting only a phone call to congregate and rekindle their conflict. These were the ilk that Jane's father had crossed. Her story told, she stared out at the fireflies of the campfires on the delta.

Brent noticed the woman on the lower deck again look up at the dining area, again slowly back and forth across the windows. She was probably attractive, but a shadow fell across her face and he couldn't really tell for sure. Her blonde hair fell below her shoulders. She was quite tall, judging by her long slim legs crooked below her chair and crossed at the ankle. Her form-fitting black dress with a Nehru collar and short sleeves rose easily to mid-thigh. A jade pendant hung at her narrow chest.

Brent stared at her for a heartbeat too long and he felt their eyes meet, although hers were still in the shadow and he couldn't pick up any expression. She captured his glance for a moment longer than a stranger seeing another across a room normally might, and then she looked back at her friend across the table and continued their conversation. Only her companion's light khaki trousers and cordovan moccasins were visible to Brent, his identity concealed by the stairwell. Brent continued to watch her, but she didn't look back.

An old girlfriend? Hardly – he'd been with Patsy for five years…

The waiter reappeared with the dessert tray and a carafe of coffee. Doeman eyed the cart like a chicken eyeing a June bug.

Brent decided to seize control: "A mud pie, and two forks, if you please!" Jane put up the requisite and expected argument that all women learn at their mothers' knee, about dessert and calories and everything going to their hips and such. And, as all women never do, the words *absolutely not!* never came up in Jane's protestations. They would split a mud pie.

Jane pushed her chair from the table and rose. "I'm going to powder my nose real quick before dessert." She took her purse and weaved between the tables, getting not a few second glances from several male diners. Whatever mud pies she had split during her lifetime, maybe just one or two too many, had gone to all the right places and avoided her waistline entirely. She looked damn good.

He looked at the lights of the city beyond the hill, and campgrounds below. He glanced down and the mysterious lady in the shadows who had kept looking upward at him, or someone.

She was gone, the khakis and mocs with her. Their table had been bussed, and reset.

Nuts. He wanted to see what she looked like, uncoiled and standing. Oh, well…

More coffee arrived, with a complimentary cordial of *crème de cacao* and the mud pie, divided into two plates. Jane returned, and Brent rose to hold her chair. She saw the mud pie.

"I really need this dessert now," she said, squeezing some skin on her brawny left bicep with her right hand. "I just saw the world's skinniest woman in the ladies' lounge. She admired my dress and I admired hers. I offered to trade her mine for her little black dress, and she agreed if I'd throw in my…" Jane had pulled the straps of her dress an inch or two apart and tugged them up slightly, then stopped herself just short of saying "…*knockers to go with it.*" Embarrassed and blushing, she continued. "She wanted a picture of my dress so she could find one like it, and had her date take a picture of both of us when we came out into the foyer."

"Was she from around here?" Brent prided himself on knowing every lady in the valley worth looking at, and this one was.

"I don't know. If you ever saw her, you'd know her though. Rail-thin, pretty and the lightest gray eyes I've ever seen, with just a hint of blue."

Brent realized she was the girl in the black dress in the shadows on the deck below, who caught his glance and held it. A small tremor traversed his body, and he dropped his fork. The people seated around him looked his way.

Falcon.

He retrieved the fork, and tried to act normally, or as normal as he could when his three-hour King's-X from Doeman-by-daylight is shattered by a visit from the Falcon. Why the pretense of the dress to get a photo of Jane? Who would want the picture that couldn't have taken one with a lot less theatrics? Had the Taurus been bugged too, while they dined? Nothing fell into place, and he mentally decided to hell with all of it. He was going to enjoy the evening and let tomorrow be damned. But he did know that he had to keep Doeman quiet on the trip back to the bed-and-breakfast in case the damn Taurus was now bugged also.

He looked at his gorgeous date across the table and knew the only salvation to the snapshot in the foyer was that no one could possibly see Jane photographed by candlelight and recognize her by daylight in her working garb.

The check arrived in a rich leather folder; she slid her company credit card into it and pushed it toward the edge of the table. She folded her napkin neatly in front of her, and suggested that they take a walk when they got back to Rio Verde. The waiter returned the check and she removed the card and figured the tip, then slid the voucher into the folder and the customer slip into her purse. Brent thanked her for one of the nicest dinners that he had ever enjoyed, surprising himself that the words weren't hollow in the least. She patted his hand and took it in hers as they walked from The Shadows into the warm night air.

❖   ❖   ❖

Neither was in any hurry to get to the car, really only a hundred feet from The Shadows. As they walked he questioned his own intentions. In three short hours he had become attached to Jane – her beauty and her civility, and her facility for conversation. Had he been smitten by the half-sad look in her eyes when he first saw her under the Victorian streetlight? A duckling, ugly before that meeting that had transformed itself into a fair vision to behold. Was this a longing for male acceptance and approval? Was the revelation of her father's present plight a plaintive cry for help?

And what about Patsy? She had been his steady for five years, and his best friend. They had traveled together, laughed and loved into a hundred sunrises, seldom had a difference of opinion that survived into the next day, and recently had started making vague plans for their future. She was squared away, a woman bringing no baggage into their relationship, at ease with their friends.

His ambivalence tonight bothered him.

He opened the passenger door, examining the interior when the light came on, half-expecting some evidence of the continuing intrusions that seem to accompany any occasion when he had turned a key in a lock. None was apparent; her hat and sweater the only objects in the car. He settled down in the driver's side and turned toward Rio Verde. The 101 *Strings* tape continued, Jane nestled up against the corner formed by the seat and the door and took his hand from the gearshift knob, rested it on her knee and held it. During some of the tighter turns on the river road, he borrowed it, replacing it when the road again straightened.

After four segments of music, they approached town, and Brent gave her a gentle squeeze that brought her back from wherever she had been. Where it was, it was pleasant, if her smile was any indication. He parked in the bed-and-breakfast lot, walked around the car and helped her out. He reached over the seat and retrieved her hat and sweater, and draped the sweater over her shoulders. He held her hat in one hand, and her hand in his other. They walked slowly along the cobblestone river promenade between the bed-and-breakfast and Walnut Park. He had seen her first along this promenade at dusk. Now the gas streetlamps contrasted against a dark sky, brightened only by the full moon low over the horizon across the river, enhancing the paleness of her dress and the green of the lawns and the foliage bordering the path. The reflection of the lights on the peak of McNear's Mill's roof danced on the water, and a pianist in the mill's garden courtyard was playing a Scott Joplin slow drag, accompanied by a cornet and a baritone – Brent thought he could hear a French horn also – Lydia Wainscroft? The musicians, volunteers all, had been playing for tea dances during the past several summers on Wednesday evenings. On the weekends the college kids took over the courtyard with their own brand of music. The turn-of-the-century slow drag blended easily tonight with his lady's costume and the idyllic setting.

Several minutes' leisurely walk brought them near the D Street Bridge, and Brent could see his office, the crisp white walls illuminated by the Victorian lamps surrounding it. They came to an unoccupied park bench under an arbor draped with wisteria, and she pulled him toward it and sat down. He sat to her left and she scooted over to close the distance between them, her thigh against his. Neither was particularly talkative. A good-sized cabin cruiser moved up the river, the unmistakable smoke of Kingsford charcoal briquets masking the exhaust of its well-muffled diesel. The white stern light and red nav light on the craft's port side were echoed a dozen times as the low wake rippled the water behind. Brent laid his hand on Doeman's shoulder, and caressed her neck between his thumb and forefinger. She rolled her head back into his grip.

He broke the silence. "Our relationship changed tonight. I'm glad you talked me into dinner."

"I knew you had me pegged as a genderless pain in the ass. I wanted you to remember me as a woman."

He glanced down the front of her dress, and inhaled the gardenia fragrance. Remember that, he would. "What lies ahead for you?"

"A lot of work, I'm afraid. We promised we wouldn't talk shop, but tomorrow we'll write four contracts so you can submit them to the owners. They should be accepted. Next week my superiors will be in town to inspect the four homes and help me find more – up to seven more. It may be necessary for you to attend a meeting with the executive board, possibly late next week. We'll pay your expenses."

"Will you be there?" he asked, surprised.

"Maybe."

Nuts. Brent had relied on their temporal relationship to keep his mind off her fingertips on his thighs and the large warm globe of flesh against his upper arm. The prospect of a meeting out of town was inconsistent with that comfort zone he had built up tonight. They may meet on another warm night, under other gas streetlamps and wisteria, and hear another Joplin rag and laughing voices drifting across another river.

They sat in silence for a long time. Another boat passed – a small Omega, more drifting than sailing. The music ended and soon cars could be heard starting in the parking lot by the mill. She took his left wrist and turned it, looking at his watch.

"Walk me home, Brent. Tomorrow's a busy day. But don't be in any hurry."

They returned to the bed-and-breakfast at a snail's pace. They started to turn from the river path toward the grand staircase to the front door, but she pulled his hand and they continued into the shadows between the painted lady and the river. He stopped and half-sat against a planter box facing the river. She stepped in front of him and leaned back into him, wiggling a little to ensure that she was in total contact with him, from the backs of her calves to her shoulder blades. He put his hands on her waist, and she pulled them around her, flat across her tummy.

"Just hold me for a minute."

Brent recalled some reference to objectivity during dinner, and her perception of objectivity jibed with his just fine. He massaged her shoulders and both sides of her neck, then crossed his arms across her chest. His forearms brushed against her warmth, and she pulled them in closer. They stared in silence at the river. He rested his chin on the top of her head. Her hair smelled fresh and clean.

She broke the silence: "Tonight has been the greatest night of my life. I'll never forget you. My desire is beginning to scare me – I never thought I was capable of feelings like these." She stepped away and turned, then fell into him on her tiptoes, their bodies touching from knees to lips. Her fingers curled behind his neck. "Be still for a moment. We'll never touch like this again and I want to remember it."

We'll never touch like this again.

A weight suddenly came off his chest, but not her warmth against it. The torment was over, not a heavy breath too soon, because a split-second before he had been on the verge of tracing his fingertips beneath the V in the front of her gown and holding her in his hand. He had never seriously considered that until she led him into the shadows, but once there he had calculated the probability that if he did, he would be led inside and upstairs to an antique four-poster bed for a night of objectivity, after which he would never see Patsy again. That was not good – too dear a price to pay for an evening of indiscretion.

The contrasting probability, as he thought with that part of his anatomy which all women suspect all men of thinking with when the moon is full, the wisteria sweet, lacy lights reflect on smooth rivers and warm feminine bodies press against them, was that he could cup his strong hand under her full warm breast and then take a quick knee to the groin, blow four escrows, lose his job, then be tracked down like a dog by Jane's deranged father for feeling up his daughter. And finally losing Patsy anyway, not that his life-expectancy would then permit a lengthy engagement.

We'll never touch like this again.

Make it count, Brenty-boy. He caressed her back then slid one hand down onto the curve of her bottom and pulled her closer.

"I'll never forget it, either," he said, truthfully. "I'll walk you home." They held hands, and he lifted her hat off the fence post and plopped it onto her head. "You look cute in a hat!"

And she did.

The kiss at the door was soft and short; a kiss a groom could give his bride with her father and the parson looking on. She stood at the heavy mahogany door framing an oval window of leaded glass, as he walked toward the Taurus. He looked back – she waved, slowly, with just the fingers of one hand.

CHAPTER ELEVEN

Later Wednesday evening: All in the family...

The Taurus smelled of gardenia, one of the grandest fragrances ever to spark the embers of romance. Unfortunately, Patsy wasn't around to enjoy the spark as he was, and even less fortunately, he was in her car when he was afforded the pleasure. Sensing that the scent of gardenias in her car would only rekindle her meltdown of earlier today, he ran all four windows down with the buttons at his left hand, and shut off the air conditioner so a remnant of the fragrance in the coil wouldn't inspire another ugly discussion six months from now. Assuming that six months wasn't an overly optimistic expectation of his longevity.

He ran the Taurus in where the bugged Explorer usually berthed and left the windows down for the night. Locking things in Rio Verde was rapidly losing its logic to him. He slipped the key in the doorknob of his townhouse, but just before he pushed the door, he remembered his sure-fire *Crimestoppers' Textbook* tactic. He looked at the door jamb on the hinge side – the red match head was where he left it five hours before. The door had not been opened.

Or the assassins had read Dick Tracy *as kids, too.*

Brent had a ritual path he followed upon returning home from an evening out: The new canvas sport coat, a dandy, hung in the guest closet, shoes kicked off on the way to the bedroom, keys and pager on the dresser, check the answering machine on the unlisted phone by the bed, no blink; lamp on by the bedside, trousers wherever they land replaced by running shorts, shirt being unbuttoned on the walk to the kitchen, lamp over the dining room table flicked *on* enroute, shirt tossed in the direction of the hole in the clothes washer off the kitchen, missed, check the business line answering machine, no blink, cold beer from the refrigerator and bottle cap toward the spittoon (cuspidor as his mother preferred to call it), missed, through the unlocked patio slider, necktie, if any, joins the others on Super Chief, Brent into Brown Jordan chair looking up the Sequoia River. Or, in inclement weather, Brent into Lazy-E-Boy in the den.

Brent followed his path.

The moon was high now, and a lone anchor light glowed up the river, probably on the cabin cruiser they had seen earlier. He reflected on his day.

Landau started the day by screwing up his office meeting, his first office meeting in the new building, with his mindless rambling about the joys and burdens of real estate, a paean all had already heard and knew would only be updated with the inauguration of each new occupant in the White House. Rafé did a great job with his multiethnic presentation, the high point of the day.

He recalled Doeman's deep porcelain cleavage by candlelight.

Well, Rafé was right up there, anyway.

Felicia gave him her analysis of the disc purloined from Doeman's home office. It confirmed a sophisticated level of skulking that he wasn't prepared for. And his address was in the disc. Whoever these folks were, they were serious. The disc bothered him.

Brent missed his lunch, but fortunately an unknown party took his mind off food by getting inside his Explorer without a key and probably putting a transmitter into it. Probably on the same frequency as the one on his telephones and the one in the townhouse. He did a quick tonic chord progression on his little Martin tenor uke, close to the ficus on his deck, the better they could hear him if that's where they hid a bug.

Doeman, as usual, was her typical flat-wave personality with her screwy shorthand and the barcode reader, blasting data off to God-knows-where over her cellphone. But the camera. How he loved that digital camera. Her criteria for house-hunting defied logic – the bromide of the industry was location, location, location – hers was obscured, obscured, obscured. Tomorrow he'd write four offers, the halcyon act of a real estate agent, writing an offer – akin to running a four-minute-mile, pitching a perfect game in the Series, hitting a clean G over high C in the choir, or preparing the perfect soft-boiled egg. But it was all wrong. The buyer hadn't seen the houses, the challenge of the negotiation was bypassed, and who the hell knew where the money was coming from? One of his favorite escrow officers had been uprooted, and she probably didn't even know why.

And his girlfriend was not pleased.

Not pleased? "Not pleased" would be an improvement. She's madder than hell. She knows basically nothing about Doeman save for watching her caboose falling into the Explorer in the parking lot Tuesday, and she has heard from Katy that you wouldn't take her to a dogfight if she promised to lose. Yet you break a barbecue date with Patsy to take Doeman to dinner, then have the cajones to borrow Patsy's car to take her out in. And it ain't over yet. In fact, if Patsy hates gardenias, it's just starting.

OK. "Not pleased" might fall a little short. Brent enjoyed these little chats he had with himself.

Finally, before his mind departed the day's business arena, he thought of Aldo, and the news that his carpet had been cleaned, which it hadn't, by a black man and a white man, one of which wasn't. How they let themselves in to his townhouse pales in comparison to the question of what they did when they got in here, what they looked at, what phone numbers they have, personal address of his parents and his friends, a few business records and tax returns, his service record and why did they take his new Grisham paperback?

And no, winning a million from Ed McMahon didn't do much to assuage his anxiety.

❖   ❖   ❖

He fetched another beer. The hour was late, but the night was warm, and sleep was not looming large as an activity that interested him. He plunked on the uke.

The events of the day were frightening, which he wouldn't deny, were he to detail the whole chronology at its present stage of evolution. Felicia came the closest to knowing that big picture. And best-pal Patsy, his ever-stalwart confidante, had labeled him with an epithet that she usually reserved for others, the lowest of pond-scum, and then maybe only once in each year. She had used a three-year supply on him in one phone call, just before she laid a death threat on him should he darken her door. No, right now she might not be the person to help seek any rationale in his evening with Doeman.

The cabin lights in the cruiser had been shut off, as had most of the lights in the farmhouses along the river channel. Only an occasional set of headlights passed down the county road. The valley was going to sleep. He thought about dinner.

People were looking for my father.

And, he didn't do anything illegal. Honest, he didn't.

All of a sudden Brent smiled, then threw his head back and broke into a loud laugh, the laugh of a man who hears a joke at work but doesn't get it, forgets about it and then goes home and the punch line finally connects at nine o'clock that night. The laugh of a man who thinks he's got it together, but when he's handed the solution to a puzzle in a candlelit room, with soft music playing and moonlight falling on the river, seated across a table from a voluptuous woman with dancing eyes and the aura of gardenias and her calf against his, he finds that he couldn't have figured out 2 + 2 without a calculator.

He'd been looking for relocated witnesses. Not a bad theory at all. They were known to exist, certainly; and most needed a roof over their heads. They were hot commodities, and Lord knows a few people wouldn't mind finding them for whatever illicit reason.

But Doeman had brought the last piece of the puzzle to dinner. Her clients were her family, and their friends and former business acquaintances.

Nice euphemism, Brenty-boy. Business acquaintances. Try gun-runners, mercenaries, soldiers-of-fortune, turncoats, traitors, thieves who would embezzle from their own government and all the others for a profit.

The clarity of that escaped him in the restaurant. In the candlelight he was ready to nominate Jane's father for a Nobel Prize.

Those were the people he was finding a home for, the ones who didn't want to be known or trailed. Quite a client list.

And seeking them, and Brent after he knew where they had relocated, were gun-runners, mercenaries, soldiers-of-fortune, turncoats, traitors, thieves who would embezzle from their own government and all the others for a profit.

Brent looked his empty beer bottle and debated whether to have another. Why not?

He hearkened back to the good old days in real estate, about 4:30 this afternoon, when dealing with spooky clients was an honorable endeavor, when the people you sought homes for were all amassed in one country or one jail, and the people looking for them were all of the same stripe. An aggressor that narrowly-defined is easy to deal with. For the Scorpion.

But now, we find Doeman's father, from his own country, probably not Mr. Popularity in that country anyway, in league with a half-dozen other sinister sorts, émigrés from the other countries where greed is practiced, which is all of them.

They practiced their craft with men of like persuasion, who bought Mr. Doeman's wares for the singular purpose of taking what they didn't have coming by creating widows and orphans and terror and intimidation until they had what they wanted.

All were happy, or at least stable, until the day or night that a few dozen F-4Es or A-37s or 101s or whatever the two warring customers were sold, annihilated each other in unison and canned up into the sea, or the jungle, or the desert. Brent never heard. All he knew was that the Merchants of Menace were out of business with some dissatisfied customers in chase. The Falcon had to fit in with them. Why to Rio Verde? Hell, our cops didn't even own a radar gun yet.

Maybe that's the answer right there.

His problems didn't change dramatically as a result of this nocturnal analysis. He was still the hub of the wheel rolling through deep doo-doo, and as the saying goes, once your feet are off the ground it doesn't matter how high they hang you.

OK – why the romance? Why the foot-massage at listing V, the mystically beautiful Victorian lady sitting under the arbor in the gaslight by the bed-and-breakfast tonight? The closeness, the touching, the warmth, the manner and laughter?

Was it a cry for help? Were she to remain as cold and impersonal as she had been for their first two days in her search for a normal life for her family, a barrier between them would eventually grow, and her effectiveness would be hindered. Yet, had she allowed the evening to ripen only a short step beyond where it stopped, and had she invited him up to her chamber for the love-making that was inevitable from the moment that they left the arbor to walk back to the bed-and-breakfast, his capacity for clarity of thought would have been diminished by the affection that would follow, and her purpose would be compromised.

Objectivity.

God, how he hated that word that she used during dinner, its relevance having now become crystal-clear.

If that was her conscious plan this evening, it had worked. But he doubted it was orchestrated by forethought or malice – the feelings were too genuine. No actress could have played the part. He cared for her; he understood her plight and would do his level best to solve it.

1:13 a.m. He turned out the lights and went to bed. He was restless, thinking most about Patsy and how nice a freckled face and a headful of auburn hair and her warm breath would feel on his shoulder, a slim leg across his thighs.

He drifted. Jane drifted into his mind, left, returned. He imagined what it would be like to snuggle up to her.

We'll never touch like this again.

Her words, in the shadows behind the bed-and-breakfast.

Probably a good way to leave it...

The Manchurian Candidate syndrome that carried him off to the arms of Morpheus a night ago when his thoughts went to overload, didn't work at 1:15 Thursday morning.

Or 2:15 a.m., or at 3:15. Sleep never came.

CHAPTER TWELVE

Early Thursday: The cold shoulder...

It was the kind of morning in Rio Verde that a movie director would await for months on end, to capture a scenic panorama of a small American town replete with a river of just the right width and hue, and mature dark green trees of sufficient size to shade a two-lane country road with aged barn-wood fencing meandering along either side. Inside those fences, some black and white Holstein cattle return from the milking barns to spend their lazy summer day along the fences whisking an occasional fly with their tails, moving tentatively closer to the fences when the urban families in the rental cars stopped to visit with them.

If the script took the filming into a town, then Rio Verde could host that endeavor too, on narrow cobblestone-curbed streets, still wet from

Downtown Rio Verde

the street sweeper that went through before dawn. Ornate bronze hitching posts and granite stepping blocks placed two world wars ago were still ready at many curbs, so that the ladies in the cast might not be inconvenienced by the height of the hansom cab that would spirit them off to the I.O.O.F. hall for a morning of whist. A few doors down from the Alhambra, the firemen had driven their retired old engine, still kept in commission for the Fourth of July parade, to the curb by Walnut Park. The open-seat 1928 Seagraves' tall black tires, the grain of the wooden ladders and spoke wheels, and the brass headlights and bell above the bright red water tank formed a pleasant complement-in-time to the black and brass-trimmed locomotive of similar vintage displayed in the park.

The oak trees on the hillside that lifted gently from the river parted occasionally, revealing the second stories and peaked roofs and turrets of the Queen Anne painted ladies that marched up the hills. A few bore the bulging onion domes evoking the Russian influences of some of the early fur traders from the Polar climes seeking winter respite in the temperate valley. America saw many a heroine bride on the silver screen, marching down the aisle of one of the town's four archetypal white clapboard chapels, their four-sided belfries rising above the oaks and the turrets.

Only the reddish-orange hull of the *Steamer Gold* was missing from the scene at McNear's Mill across the river, sparkling maize flowing down a rusted galvanized chute from the mill's elevators into the hold behind her white superstructure, as it flowed every morning when the fire engine and the locomotive across the river were still in their youth. The bridge was raised this morning for a good-sized Hans Christian. With their milk-white hulls, light teak decking and transoms, and bright brass hardware aplenty, many said they were the most picturesque of all small sailboats. Her sails were stowed as she moved slowly down the river on her diesel,

The Steamer Gold

the cocktail pennant still flying from her mast as a forgotten vestige some manner of sybaritic gaiety that took place on board the night before.

In all, it was a morning that would not find the townsfolk the least bit surprised should the popular Brent Douglas, clad in an old plaid cotton shirt, Levis and his shit-kickin' boots, see his fair and freckled Patsy, driving her surrey with the fringe on top and a dashboard of genuine leather down Western Avenue. Her auburn hair would be falling in long thick pigtails into bows to match her yellow sundress and hat, and he'd feel moved to hop aboard and scoot her sexy little Sooner rear over, take the reins from her soft white hands, push his straw Stetson back from his blonde forelocks and lift his voice in a chorus of *Oh, What a Beautiful Mornin'*... for the whole town to enjoy.

❖   ❖   ❖

But on this morning, a song was not to be. Notwithstanding the fact that Patsy and her surrey were nowhere in sight, one glance by the casual observer into the Taurus with all the windows still rolled down would be enough to tell that the normally affable Brent Douglas was not himself.

In the short line of cars held up by the drawbridge, now lowering behind the Hans Christian, was a man who had laid awake the entire night, fending off demons and gargoyles, phantom carpet cleaners in brown coveralls and hairy-chested cryptographers swinging scimitars and faceless blondes staring at him in darkened restaurants in Marrakech and Kuala Lumpur. Two visions recurred all night long with each toss and turn – first the moonlit rear view of a beautiful vixen with jet black hair packed like a seed in a grape into a peach-colored Victorian gown, her manicured fingertips caressing his thigh. Then the vixen turned toward him, revealing in the bright office lights a butt-ugly harpy with all the warmth of a snake, bent on a purpose that would not survive dissection by honest men in the cold harsh light of day and using her abundant feminine wiles to subvert his judgment to further the welfare of those who did not deserve his talents.

All night he had watched the red numbers change on the clock at his bedside. 2:41. 3:28. 4:16. The shades were growing light. 5:28. The sun was up. 6:00. The radio came on – the Giants lost in the tenth, and Clinton was going to Oslo this fall.

6:05 a.m. Up, shower, coffee on the deck. The cruiser in the shallows was still anchored. A graceful sloop was anchored upriver, maybe the Hans Christian he'd heard about. Sleepy.

Two pieces of toast, no juice left. Clothes unimportant – who cares? White short-sleeved shirt, navy trousers, beige Mephistos. Patsy hates white short-sleeved shirts with dark ties, says they look like something a customs agent would wear. Change tie to light paisley, blue flowers, hate that tie. Hate ties period.

Call Patsy. No, too early, a bearded man with a saber is monitoring the call in a trailer at the airstrip in Cyprus anyway. Have a banana. Back to the deck. Ten more minutes won't hurt.

He sat for fifteen, maybe twenty minutes. Late. Left the townhouse.

❖ ❖ ❖

Great. The drawbridge is up. Leave late once a month and that's the morning when the damn drawbridge raises.

Jane. She was pretty. Soft. Night was perfect, gaslights, music across the river.

We'll never touch like this again.

Good. Came too close. Have too much to lose.

People were looking for my father.

And he didn't do anything illegal. Honest, he didn't.

Bullcrap. She's in denial. I'm not. The sun's up, the gardenias are gone, I'm running an office. She's a client. If she wants to buy a house, she can damn well step to the line and act like a buyer. And screw this fictitious grantee baloney. Patsy and I live in the town, and I don't want to share it with a bunch of mercenaries. To hell with all these people, especially Jane. He was increasingly annoyed about her exploitation of the perfume, the cleavage, the fingertips, the shadows, the sad story of dad and his band of thieves. If dad got his ass in a sling, he could get it out himself.

OK, Brent. You've convinced the assassins. Now convince yourself...

The Scorpion had spoken. The lady behind him tapped her horn – perhaps the Scorpion would care to come back to earth from his drowsy soliloquy and follow the rest of the parade across the river.

As the office drew up on his right over the east side of the bridge, he hoped that he could maintain his Scorpion persona throughout the day. He knew all he had to do was keep his mind off the break-ins, the phone taps, the coded messages, the carpet cleaners and that weird blonde that kept showing up. Scorpion too soon faded into the background. Brent the pencil-pusher kept facing reality, growing more squir-relly each morning that he drove into work. Jane's revelation of the nature of her clients made them seem more auspicious. He was tired, cranky, and scared.

He was late – 8:15 – 'way late for Brent. Thank God, the Granada was in the parking lot.

Felicia had the doors open, the lights on, the coffee brewed, the Xerox on, and the phones unforwarded.

"Morning, Skipper. Do you remember Pam Stone, Betty's daughter?"

Pam was a receptionist-in-training that Brent brought in last week to help with the switchboard during the summer. Felicia had entered two wheelchair tennis tournaments and swore that this was the summer that she was going to make her mark. In both the past two years she had worked her way up in points at regional meets, picked up a few bucks for endorsements, and had been seeded in the semifinal meet that would have made her eligible for the national tournament in Winter Park. And both years she had had her doors blown out by the same player. Or, more succinctly, that "damn honkey southpaw," as she described her honorable opposition.

Tomorrow, Felicia would journey to Irvine to again wage battle against the southpaw, whom she admitted had become quite a good pal. They were going to room together before the fray began on the courts and planned to get into a little trouble in Newport Beach, win or lose.

Katy had joined the sidelines of the 'Niners. She'd be gone a bunch, too. And Felicia was getting some invitations to join Rafé with their multiethnic program. She'd need time away from L&H. Hiring Pam was a good move.

"Of course I remember Pam. Nice to see you, we're all glad you're here." They shook hands.

Of course, I remember Pam. Every guy in the office remembers Pam, Pam of the L&H company picnic renown, Pam in the sleek and shiny-when-wet one-piece jet black swim suit with the high French-cut legs and the brass zipper 'way down the low-cut front, the tan coed that stood the men of the office on their ears every time she leaned over, and finally caused Betty to leave the picnic early in disgust with her male coworkers. What Pam lacked in intelligence, which was considerable, she made up in verve and gusto. But today she looked businesslike in a white blouse and plaid culottes.

Let's see what tomorrow brings.

Brent got his coffee and went into his office, starting to close the door until he saw Felicia heading his way.

"You don't look so good. Sleep come a little tough last night?"

"No. It didn't come at all."

"How was your dinner with Doeman?"

"About the best I can say is that she is one beautiful schizophrenic. Two women rolled into one – absolutely poles apart, sharing one body."

"And I heard quite a body, at that."

Whoops.

"Who told you that?"

"It's the word on the street. Actually, I stopped for doughnuts and ran into Margaret Cooke. She and Jack were at The Shadows last night, and if I didn't know better I'd swear you were with someone else, anybody but Doeman. A *dress*? What's with that woman — Margaret said she was a looker."

"She was last night. But the look was incidental – she told me a story that will curl your hair."

"That I can do without, thank you. But I would like to hear the story. She called already; she'll be here at 10:30. She wants to wrap up four escrows and get a disc by noon because she's got a satellite feed at two. Maybe you can fill me in after that."

Brent thought back to Tuesday about Doeman's reference to GMT. "I thought the satellite feed was at noon."

"It got moved back. Did you say 'feed', like you're getting the lingo? What's next, 'Baud'?" She giggled.

"Try this lingo: 'bye.' " He thought better. "Wait. Did you hear from your friend at Loma Linda about the code?"

"I talked to him last night. He couldn't logon their mainframe until midnight. He's going to call me this morning sometime." She left to join Pam who had moved a chair behind her desk and was taking calls.

8:50 a.m. The time was at hand to call Patsy. Margaret and Jack Cooke were friends of Patsy's, and it would stretch comprehension to hope that Margaret, known in some quarters as the Mouth of the South, had not seen or talked to Patsy by now. Nor that Jack, a racquetball buddy of Brent's but consummately pussy-whipped by Margaret, would exert any influence as a man among men over his wife to zip it while this little tryst got sorted out and put into perspective, which should take the women of Rio Verde until about two o'clock today.

He closed his door and speed-dialed her house. Ten 'til nine – she might be gone. He thought again of Butch and Sundance. *Ssshhh*…it rang…*eeee*… "Hello?"

"Hi, it's me. How ya doin'?"

"Skip it. You have more balls than a bowling alley – borrowing my car so you can take some three-bagger client to dinner, at her insistence, and showing up at the hottest spot in the valley for the locals with some-body with the face of an angel and built like a brick shipyard."

Uh-oh.

"She looked OK. Better than she looked around the office. I didn't dress her."

He could have gone all morning without saying that, and heard Patsy's comeback before she said it: *No, but I suppose you un-dressed her.*

"I heard she looked a damn sight better than OK."

No comeback? She's slipping.

"According to Phyllis Waters you and every other guy in the restaurant never took your eyes off her big milky-white hooters sticking out of her low-cut peach dress, and she wore out her cute little lace tights rubbing them up against your white ducks."

White ducks? What did she think I was – the parking valet?

"They were my canvas slacks."

Phyllis Waters was incredible. She couldn't tell a cop what color Rolls-Royce flipped and burned on her front lawn if it happened twenty minutes ago in broad daylight, but put her in a dark restaurant with a friend's steady and she rivaled a videocam for gathering detail.

"And I suppose you held her hands all night just to keep her from getting into her purse for the switchblade she was carrying? What happened after dinner, a little dancing cheek-to-cheek?"

"Actually, we faced each other."

Brent hoped a little levity might take the edge off the conversation, a presumption that would prove incorrect. He recalled once telling her that it took 41 facial muscles to frown but only seven to smile. That approach didn't work either.

The Footbridge

"And no, she didn't have a switchblade. She was telling me a story about her father and it was kind of difficult for her so I did hold her hand, yes. Most caring men would do the same for any poor woman in a similar situation."

"I'm touched. Did the story continue after dinner along the promenade? Jan Titus and a few of her friends had been at the Alhambra and saw you all lovey-dovey over there too."

Christ – did anybody stay home last night?

"We weren't lovey-dovey. We were just talking about the offers she's putting in today."

"Give me a break, Douglas. What's next, *she followed me home; can I keep her*? And offers – cut that crap too. I think I can figure out the only offer anybody made last night, and I'll skip the obvious reference about putting it in."

Brent could hear her choking up, tears not far behind.

"She wasn't the least bit attractive when I saw her at the office. What did you bring out in her to make so many people say she looked so damn good? You say you didn't dress her – did you *undress* her?"

Aha. She isn't slipping after all.

"N…"

"Put yourself in my place – how would you feel if I went out and made ga-ga-eyes at some stud in The Shadows, all your buddies told you the next morning about what a hunk he was, and I told you I was just doing my job, and life goes on. Would you like that?"

In the first place, guys wouldn't light up the Rio Verde switchboard about you like some people have obviously been doing about me.

Say that, Douglas, and all this will become only the warm-up show for the main event that will follow.

"N…"

"No, you wouldn't a damn bit, and you'd be hot too. And that's the boat I'm in this morning – the laughingstock of Rio Verde. The whole town knows it. Brent got his fiddle tuned by some stacked dark-eyed stranger while little Patsy sat home. And he used Patsy's car to get her to the motel. That's what the whole town's saying. And isn't that pretty close to what happened?"

Brent waited to see if she would answer this question too. She didn't. He was anxious to hear how the whole town knew about his soirée already this morning.

He assessed his predicament. Had Patsy known how really circumspect he was last night when Doeman was warm against him in the shadows, and how he wanted to be true to Patsy even under the spell of the gardenias and the gaslights and the moon shimmering on the river, she would have lightened up about three notches. Conversely, had *he* known while in the shadows with Doeman that Patsy would reward his deep fidelity and love with this screaming, shouting conniption fit, he might as well have parted the V in Doeman's bodice with his fingertips and then taken her up to her chambers. And still be there. What the hell, he was a marked man anyway thanks to Doeman's clients. Except for Patsy, he had nothing to lose.

Motel?

What *motel?* For Christ's sake, she was staying at the bed and breakfast on Western Avenue! "How'd all this lead to a motel?"

"In my car, probably. Look, I've had it with you and your nutball Scorpion fantasies and this little sexpot client of yours. My sister and two of her friends rented a condo this week in Balboa and have to give it up Sunday, and they've invited me down. I'm going. Liz is giving me a ride to the airport. Personally, it's none of your damn business. But as my all-powerful and omnipotent Mister Manager, you're entitled to know. Katy has my number, if any business comes up. It shouldn't. Put the Taurus back in my garage when you can and then go figure out how to get your newfound lady friend's low-slung ass into your own wagon."

She was crying.

"I hope we can work this out, but you've really hurt me. 'Bye."

Click.

Two men from Shepherd's Antiques in Fairfax were delivering the rehabilitated fan taken from Fundas' as Brent walked out of his office, still reeling from Patsy's diatribe and a little befuddled as to how she could leap to so many conclusions and get so much help from her friends, so fast, to assist her into the leap. He had hoped that his empathy for Doeman's grievous plight might have merited a little more support. But he had wounded her, and that bothered him. He had taken a walk along the river from a wisteria-covered arbor to the shadows of the painted lady, risking all he loved along the way. He had wounded his best friend.

The antique restorer's work was beautiful. The big round motor housing, eight weeks ago tarnished black and coated with the dust and grime of eighty years and a million revolutions, had been machine-polished beyond a depth and luster he'd ever seen on any brass hardware. The embossed turn-of-the century *General Electric Motor Company* script around the waist of the motor housing, imperceptible under the tarnish, had been meticulously re-lettered. The mahogany blades had been stripped of the old varnish, re-stained, and shot with Varathane to protect them for another eighty years. About the time it would take Patsy to cool off.

Brent decided that on Saturday morning he would hang this tribute to the founding fathers from the rod in the bullpen, to be swinging in all its former grandeur as the troops arrived on Monday morning.

Unless, of course, Patsy called and told him she'd pick him up at John Wayne airport for the short trip to the condo for the rest of the weekend.

Realistically speaking, the tribute would welcome the troops in grandeur Monday morning next.

He looked at the receptionists, a third crewmember now aboard, all plugged into their earpiece microphones. The phones were busy for a Thursday morning, and Pam was taking most of the calls.

"I'm going down to Sunset Escrow and pick up some wire transfer slips for Doeman's files. Anybody want to take a walk?"

No takers. Strange. Pam, no, she was in training, not really invited. Felicia begged off, explaining that she was awaiting a call from her crypto buddy in Loma Linda with the results of his nocturnal number crunching on the big mainframe computer in an effort to break Doeman's coded transmission. But the look in her soft brown eyes told him otherwise. She plainly didn't want to go with him just now. Not at all like her...

And Katy, always a sort to enjoy a yogurt on the way back from downtown, with a shortcut through Walnut Park and five minutes in the gazebo with Brent, was diffident. "I think I'll just work through my break."

Strange.

And the crew in the hot desk counter in the lobby – Lydia looked away as he glanced at her. She was talking on her earpiece microphone, but the lamps on her phone were dark. She was not a woman prone to talking to herself. Alice just looked at him. No smile, no stare, no frown. Just a look. Tom Yarbrough walked in the front door with a client. "Hiyo, Tomás. How ya' doin'?"

"*Fine, Brent. How are you?* Tom never called Brent *Brent.* Skipper, big guy, Scorpion, numb-nuts, probably not around a client, but never *Brent. And how are you?* Tom's never been that stiff and stilted.

Brent walked back into the break room to get a cup of coffee to walk with. Holly, Edith, and Paul were sitting in one chrome booth. All looked up, none gave more than an obligatory smile or nod, and they turned back to their conversation. He filled his driving cup with the slotted lid across the top and went out the stainless steel door of the break room into the bright outdoors.

OK. *I get the message. Patsy's hot, so they're all hot, and I'm taboo in my own office.*

❖   ❖   ❖

The Sunset Escrow office had the atmosphere that he had wanted to convey in the décor of the new L&H building. L&H didn't do badly, considering the realty company had ten times the floor space of the escrow company with five times the people working inside it, and a few concessions had to be made to bring it in on any kind of budget.

Sunset was in a small office on Western Avenue. Like many offices and retail stores in downtown Rio Verde, and indeed many other downtowns in rural America, it had a high ceiling, almost two stories, and a loft. An intricate pewter gas lamp with crystal chimneys, converted years ago to incandescent bulbs, was suspended by a stout chain from the center of the high ceiling.

A counter separated the entry lobby from the four heavy wooden desks beyond, an escrow officer on either side with her secretary, or technician as most companies called them in the '90s, at a desk in front of each officer. A receptionist, here the lovely Toni, sat in front of the storefront window, probably a leftover from when the office was a retail store years before. The canvas awning was extended against the morning sun over the sidewalk.

Inside, it looked like an escrow office where disinterested third parties have conducted the business of conveying real estate since the dawn of public property ownership in England in 1215 A.D., their instructions issued by the buyer and the seller of the property, and their job not complete until their instructions were fully carried out.

When you hold the sum of $........, you are to record a deed conveying ...... *to ......*

Deep dark paneling that an architect would get shot for specifying today, but authentic for the period, reached to the hammered tin ceiling with a repeating crosshatching of concentric circles – probably the building's original ceiling. The glow of the brass banker's lamps' green glass lenses fell on each desk. Photographs of the valley and its landmark buildings were hung from the walls – the showcase photo was one of this block's buildings with 1920-vintage cars parked diagonally at the street's grassy median, Escrow Office plainly visible on the awning.

A refrigerator-sized forest-green safe with four-inch gold leaf lettering Valley Escrow and Trust Deed Service sat on huge casters on the wall behind Toni, bright nickel steel rods holding it closed since the early 1940s. Smaller gold lettering dated the company to 1911. Displayed across from Toni was an old Burroughs 12-column adding machine on a spidery black stand, a full 120-button keyboard with a motor as big as a coffee can that made the streetlights go dim as it ground and ground until an answer appeared in the windows over the buttons. On the counter was a heavy black cast-iron notary public seal, used for a hundred years to squeeze an embossed legal seal onto a document until the advent of photocopy machines that could not "see" the white-on-white impressions nor print them onto a copy.

Brent stood with coffee cup in hand, looking at Toni and the history surrounding her. She didn't really fit here, as pretty as she was. In these surroundings *she* should be a *he*, with a balding head and a thin mustache, a long-sleeve white shirt with armbands at the elbow, a vest over his suspenders, and a green eyeshade over a little gold *pince-nez*. And he should be frowning, overwhelmed by the gravity of the awesome responsibility of conveying clear title to the parcels of Rio Verde.

Toni was frowning. Brent doubted that the awesome responsibility of escrow was overwhelming her. "What's bothering Toni? You look like the pretty girl in the hemorrhoid commercial."

"So who do you want, Brent? Laura? I'll get her – she's in the back room."

So was everybody else in the office. And what's eating Toni? She always had a smile for him. She was Sunset's version of L&H's Katy – never a bad day, at least to the visiting public. She walked back around the counter. "She'll be right here. Have a good time on the waterfront last night, Casanova?"

Ergo the hemorrhoid-sufferer's smile. She was a friend of Patsy's, albeit quite a bit younger, but Patsy brought 30 escrows a year to Sunset and had grown close to Toni in a big-sisterly sort of way. He ignored the question. Laura Bigelow walked out of the back room and toward the opening in the counter.

Brent looked, and then looked again. Laura looked like a cross between Clara Peller and Whistler's Mother, possibly the squeeze of the guy in the green eyeshade who should have been sitting at Toni's desk. She appeared to be well into her 70s, a tiny grey-haired woman in a dated dress. She transferred her cane and extended her small right hand to Brent. He could see that she wore a hearing aid on a strap around her neck, a device he had not seen the likes of since he was a child when his Uncle Vic kept a hearing aid the size of a Walkman in the chest pocket of his bib overalls with a fat cord leading to a speaker in his ear.

And curiously, *pince-nez* eyeglasses.

Laura was a self-propelled artifact in an office already nearing museum status.

❖   ❖   ❖

"Hi, I'm Brent Douglas, from L&H Realty." Brent extended his hand also and she shook it vigorously. "I hear we're going to close some escrows together."

"EHH?"

These escrows could seem longer than he'd planned on. He raised his voice and spoke in the direction of her hearing aid: "We're going to be closing some escrows together, for a buyer named Doeman." He wondered to himself why he was making eye contact with her chest and not her eyes.

"OH, THE DOEMAN FILES. COME WITH ME." Amazed that such a small person could generate such a decibel count and pondering whether her hearing had been damaged by listening to her own voice, he followed her around the counter to Susie Santini's desk. Toni looked downward at her desk as they walked.

Susie should have been here. She was his favorite escrow officer, back in the days when he opened an escrow once a week. He thought of her and would liked to have been a mouse in the corner of whatever higher-level machinations that resulted in Susie being parked in a 1031 exchange class while Laura opened her four SS escrows.

"HERE IS THE ELECTRONIC-FUNDS-TRANSFER RECEIPT. THE MAIN SUNSET OFFICE SENT TWELVE THOUSAND DOLLARS TO BE USED FOR THE FOUR ESCROWS. IT'S MORE THAN WE EXPECTED BUT IF THERE'S AN OVERAGE, I'LL JUST JOURNAL IT AS A CREDIT TO THE BUYER'S ACCOUNT AT CLOSE. DO YOU NEED ANYTHING ELSE NOW?"

Brent thought. No – the dulcet tone of an acid rock concert over the loudspeakers in Candlestick Park might be nice, but "NO, THIS SHOULD BE ALL I NEED FOR NOW. I'LL LOOK FORWARD TO TALKING TO YOU WHEN I GET THE SIGNED OFFERS BACK." He realized he was still looking at her chest as he spoke. He would have to work on that. "SEE YOU TOMORROW MORNING!"

He headed for the sidewalk door with the EFT slip. Toni was still staring at her desk.

"EHH?"

He let the screen door close behind him.

He walked back toward the bridge. The fire truck had been backed into the barn, and the grass was still wet in Walnut Park. He missed Patsy or Katy or Felicia – one of them would usually join him when he took a mid-morning walk to escrow or the post office or the bank. But this morning he felt terribly alone, like the hero of an Edmund Dante classic sentenced to life without human contact or warmth. And the sentencing didn't take long. Ten hours after an ill-advised walk along the river his love, those in his own office, and now even an escrow receptionist were giving him the cold shoulder.

He sat, alone, on a park bench for a few moments. 9:15. Doeman would be along all too soon, and he had to keystroke four offers-to-purchase and earnest-money deposit receipts. Not a gargantuan chore at all with the *HouseNet* software, but time-consuming.

He thought about Doeman as he looked across the park at the bower where they sat last night after dinner. What would she be like this morning? He debated whether she was really a schizoid or not, and whether he really understood the term. He recalled that everyone who ever read *The Five Faces of Eve* became an overnight shrink. And if she *did* have multiple personalities, would their existence put to rest the questions that raced in his mind, or only pop up a few more to dodge tonight as the red numbers on his alarm clock cycled through until dawn?

He walked back to the office, entered through the break room's door, traded his plastic walking cup for his Garfield cup, filled it, and went back up the tile path to his office. This trip through it was Pete Stephens and Ann Hathaway who first looked through him like he wasn't there, then nodded a thin *Good morning, Brent.*

His message box was empty, but he did remember that he hadn't checked his VoiceMail earlier this morning. He speed-dialed the system and then his 72677456 *Scorpion* code, a throwback to a life when international intrigue was still great fun.

Thank you for calling. You have one new message. Press one to play.
He pressed 1.

"Today, two—thirty—two—A—M. This is Officer Driscoll calling at 2:30. Just for your information, I encountered two subjects driving a white

1992 GMC van going through your dumpster. They said they were looking for aluminum cans and departed promptly at my request. No further action will be taken unless you request it. I have the license number of the van on file, but I won't run it for ownership unless you file a police report. Call if you want to, Brent."

Now they're in my trash.
He pressed 2 to store the message, and hung up.
What could they get out of my trash?
The space bar on his computer brought *HouseNet* to life. He pulled the first address that Doeman wanted to make an offer on to the screen, and then pulled down the PURCHASE AGREEMENT & DEPOSIT RECEIPT FORM window with his mouse. The standard state form, minus the information he would add in the next few minutes, appeared on his screen.

They could get the listings that he'd assembled for Jane yesterday.
Brent's fingers ground to a halt, and he sucked in his breath.

In preparation for her first visit, he had pulled up 12 listings and printed them. She trashed most of the file, replacing it with the screwy bar-coded hieroglyphics that she'd brought along herself, much of it generated after her 11:30 call to him Tuesday night. They left the office with only her own sheets with the barcodes and the map that he had made.

The rest had gone in his wastebasket with the plastic presentation folders. It was all in the dumpster by midnight when the janitors left. Twelve listings, only seven Doeman decided to look at, five she actually visited, and four she would make offers on. But if someone is looking for the four homes she selected, twelve is a lot better number to start with than the thousand listings in the valley.

He'd played right into their hands. For people of their ilk who bug cars and houses with the same abandon as most agents put up *For Sale* signs, and who transmit their mail in four-letter groups and barcodes, sorting through a dumpster is child's play. He put them on the right course and gave them some sensitive information on a silver platter. And he compromised Doeman.

Arguably, he could file a police report, forcing the system to cough up the identity of the owner of the van, but this, too, was problematical:

Under oath, I state that while nothing of any great value was taken from my dumpster except for some beer cans, the two perpetrators in the white van were known to be annoyed because four of their new A-4D fighters were splashed by my clients' A-4Ds over the Indian Ocean, and the perpetrators were seeking out my clients' new home addresses, which might have been in the dumpster, so they can kill them...

Rio Verde did not operate an asylum, but in the wake of filing that police report it might be inclined to float a bond to construct one for Brent Douglas.

The van was probably stolen anyway.

He stared at his screen. He finally came to the conclusion that he wasn't derelict. Where was it written that a broker has to shred listing information that a client doesn't want, or ingest it if he's seized by the bad guys from Century 21 or ReMax? Doeman should have foreseen the problem and taken what he offered her to do with it as she saw fit, given her slightly bizarre expectations of the real estate process. But she didn't, and now she had to presume that her adversaries knew not the specific four she was making offers on, but at the least those within a 12-listing menu. Their job, whatever it was, would be easier.

Should I tell her?

His fond recollection of the soft deep valley between the shoulder straps of her dress by candlelight was obviously hampering his judgment. Or objectivity, as she might say, in her sweet, low voice.

No, you idiot, you don't tell her.

The only thing less predictable than a wild animal is a wild animal sensing danger. No. You're a real estate broker, not the *Scorpion*.

10:10 a.m. Twenty minutes to Doeman time, the rest of four contracts to be keystroked. The trash, if any, may be stolen; to hell with it. Get some coffee and print the contracts.

CHAPTER THIRTEEN

Later Thursday: Doeman's turn to sweat...

Felicia brought Brent his morning maple bar, and that's about all. Her smile and usual warmth were not in evidence.

"Thanks, gorgeous. I thought you were mad at me."

"Let's just say you've done brighter things. Why The Shadows, for God's sake? Of all the restaurants in the valley, why there? And why in Patsy's car? I feel bad about that because I engineered it. If I'd known Doeman was going to look anything like all that I've heard about her this morning, and if I'd known you were going to The Shadows, I'd have stayed clear of it. Now I'd even like to take back the Tarzan and Jane wisecrack."

So much water had gone under the bridge since 4:30 yesterday that he'd forgotten about that. Brent decided that at the least it was better to be chewed on than ignored. "You're right, and I'm sorry, not only for Patsy's sake but everybody else I've hurt."

Felicia smiled, the first in his direction from anyone this morning. "Don't worry about it. It's done. What I mostly want is for everybody to get this stunt of yours behind them and get on with life. I'm leaving tomorrow for the meet, and I don't want this fight between you two hanging over my head."

"Neither do I, but we may not know for a while what the little lady plans on doing about me. She's leaving for Balboa today for the weekend. Won't be that far from your meet, actually. By the way, did you hear anything about the code from our crypto?"

She looked at her hands, folded in her lap. "Yeah. He didn't break it, but he got a line on its origin. And it's weirder than we thought. It's an old code system that worked pretty well for quite a while until they uncorked those ungodly Cray supercomputers. Apparently it's still in daily use for some lower sensitivity-level transmissions."

"But pretty sophisticated?" Brent was hoping to learn that it was used by some backwater government, not a real superpower threat. "Who uses it?"

Felicia looked back at her hands, then out the window of the office. She reached over his desk and took a bite out of his maple bar, an act of familiarity right up there with Horton Landau putting his gunboats on Brent's desk. Then she looked at him.

"We do. "

Then they both stared out the window.

"Who's *we*?" he said after some time.

"*We* is the CIA, Naval Intelligence, Army Security Agency, the State Department, Treasury or ATF – folks just like us." She turned and started for the door.

Brent thought about that. "OK, then who's the bad guy chasing Doeman?"

She stopped. "Maybe another one of the above. Or she's an agent that's turned, and they're trying to plug the hole. Using our lines to transmit her data fits either of those theories. Her phones are tapped, and she knows it. One agency is relocating foreigners for some coalition they're trying to curry favor with, and the other agency wants to know who they are. You might be smack in the middle of a federal turf war."

"Why don't they just get a subpoena? Or shut this thing off at the pass before they buy anything?"

"Subpoenas take judges, and judges are political. And maybe whoever's tracking her wants to find out who's going to move into the houses before they make a move. If the money's coming from foreign governments like you said, then the buyers are probably pretty hot fish. And it's easier to shoot up Rio Verde and grab them than it is to extradite them from some burg with no treaty."

"Then I'm safe when it's over. My own government will ensure that I'm out of the crossfire."

"No, you're probably in *worse* trouble. If the Ayatollah were after you, you could call the feds for help and get it. But if you're in the middle of a turf war and if the CIA decides that you could screw up a million dollars and five years' work, you'll have a tough time getting help from the State Department or the FBI. They call people like you radicals, and one side or the other blows your butts off in the name of the common good before you can say Ted Koppel."

"How come this is so clear to you?"

"Probably because I sleep all night, and you don't. And my buddy at Loma Linda worked for these maniacs. I spilled your story, sorry, and he filled in the gaps. It isn't the first time they've brought somebody in out of the cold, but the fact that there are so many moving to one town, and all locating through one real estate broker, blew him away. But the scenario holds water."

Brent looked out the window a while longer. Felicia just sat, wishing there were something she could say or do. He finally turned toward her.

"Thanks. And for the maple bar, too."

She closed his door behind her. The look in his eyes told her that he needed some time alone. From what she'd heard yesterday, and now with these few tidbit updates, she knew his whole hunter-hunted scenario might have gone by the boards.

❖   ❖   ❖

10:20 a.m. Brent decided the only thing he could do now was play Doeman's home-search out to a conclusion. Felicia's friend may be right. If so, his life was idyllic ten minutes ago by comparison to his lot now. Then he only seemed caught between one dark force attempting subterfuge and skirting the law of the land, and another trying to unravel the first one's efforts. He had harbored the notion that if the party got too rough, he could take refuge within the federal legal system. Now, the forces still seemed dark, yet both sides wore white hats. The guys were all good guys, there were no bad guys, not guys he could bring out into the open and hope for a shred of understanding within that legal system.

He'd read of the term *out in the cold.* The Scorpion of Rio Verde was out in the cold.

He pulled *HouseNet* back up on the screen, and furiously key stroked **Jane Doeman** wherever *the buyer* appeared on the form, the *sale price* she computed for each offer where appropriate, followed by *terms:* **Cash at close of escrow.** He didn't even know her address. He entered the addresses of each home in the *address* field, and **$2,500** in the *earnest money deposit* field, *to be held by* **Sunset Escrow Company,** followed by the Susie Santini SS escrow number that Laura Bigelow had assigned each purchase agreement.

Only then did he notice one thing they all had in common:

They were all REOs.

REO in the patois of the real estate industry is *real-estate owned*, a book-keeping category where banks keep properties which they have fore-closed upon until somebody else comes along to buy them, usually at a depressed price. Banks and other lenders don't look for top dollar as much as they look for a quick turn to get the non-producing asset, their eu-phemism for a loan that somebody probably screwed up by authorizing, off their books. REO has a slight mystery to it, and were a bank's share-holder to ask for a translation, the "owned" part has a positive connotation.

By thunder, we must be doing great. Look at all the real estate we own!

Brent tried to factor that commonality into the growing Doeman equation. He gave up. No answer made any sense, a recurring conclu-sion that he was fast growing accustomed to. But the commonality was interesting.

He sent the purchase agreements to the printer on the credenza behind him, and they started spilling out in hard copy, ready for her signature.

Without a moment to spare. A cab drove into the lot, a short figure seated on the passenger side. She now had a Pavlovian effect on him. His heart started to beat faster, and visions flashed through his mind like strobe lights flashing in a 70s disco parlor.

A *slim waist*. Bogus carpet cleaners. *Gardenias*. The bug in the Explorer. A *steak and Jack Daniel's*. The blonde in the restaurant, photographing Doeman. A *great blue heron, in the cool, peaceful reeds*. His new Grisham novel, gone. A *Joplin slow drag quadrille, under the moonlight*. A pleasant flashback, followed by a jarring one. Jeff's unintentional words of warning. H*is duckie slippers under Patsy's nightstand*. Susie Santini gone, replaced by Laura Bigelow.

Doeman had matured into an instantaneous five-foot-one cause for a head-on collision in the synapses of his mind, and in she walked.

She looked normal, not heavy, and not slim, not pretty, yet not par-ticularly unattractive either. Her gardenia fragrance lingered, yet not reinforced by another dose. He watched for a remnant of the warmth she telegraphed last night, but saw none as she nodded to receptionists and walked into his office. He looked at the swell of her blouse under her blue blazer and remembered her warmth against his chest last night in the shadows. Her hair was attractive, but without the sizzle it had the night before. She looked nice, businesslike, but probably wouldn't have garnered a second glance in a crowd.

A far cry from her undulating trip to the ladies lounge of The Shadows that fascinated every man there and apparently every woman too, if one could believe the departing Patsy.

❖   ❖   ❖

"Hi, Jane, how are you this morning?"

"Fine, Brent. Kind of late though. I'd like to stay with this and get it onto a disc and transmitted to the home office as soon as I can, and get out of town for the weekend. Can Felicia slave a disc into UNIX for me again? I'm still having trouble with my laptop's power supply."

All business. "No problem. I have the hardcopies ready, if you want to review them. Why don't you sit at the table and take your time, and I'll make sure Felicia doesn't leave for lunch before your disc is ready."

He stepped out the door to vacant stares from the hot desk crew and not much more from the receptionists. One more button on Pam's blouse had fallen loose and her myriad attributes were beginning to grace the lobby. Katy didn't look up.

"Felicia, Doeman wants the offers reduced to Unity before she leaves. Can you hang around long enough to do it so we can get her the hell out of here?"

"Gladly. And it's UNIX. Going for coffee? I could use some lemonade."

"Done." He picked up her glass and navigated through a sea of icebergs in the bull pen. Even the guys were glaring at him.

How did I get into this much trouble so fast?

The break room was empty, and he sat down alone in a booth, and pursued a new thought: So much of the work of so-called professionals this week had been amateurish. Why were Doeman's aberrations from normal social behavior so erratic? If the Falcon's agency is indeed opposing Doeman's family, why did they send an agent a Hollywood producer would cast for a James Bond flick? With those big grey-blue eyes and long graceful legs she was about as subtle as a sand wedge. And why the break-in at the townhouse? *Carpet cleaners?* Why did they take three hours? If professionals unlocked the Explorer, wouldn't they relock it? Why did the Falcon want a picture of Doeman? And can a pencil-pushing real estate office manager attract so damn much bugging and trash-collecting? Do the real secret agents of the world get down to this level?

He thought of some of the bungled police capers in the news, some bungled up by the top-level gendarmes of many nations. All the world's Barney Fife's weren't in Mayberry. Nobody's perfect. And most national security cases aren't the stuff of spy novels. Recent events in Rio Verde were making the international espionage community look like a Chinese fire drill.

Boy, if my tax dollars are subsidizing this carnival, I'm disappointed.

All that's all true if Felicia's friend is right and it's an inter-agency beef. The good news would be that her friend's all wet, and it's only just a bunch of lawless international terrorists, outcasts in their own countries and sought in all the rest, loose on each other.

That's great news – for a day or so I was worried.

His mind went back to the night on his deck that he told himself that these little soliloquies to himself are non-productive and ultimately will contribute to his insanity. He picked up Garfield and Felicia's lemonade and strolled through the adoring crowd in the bull pen to this office.

Doeman had done her usual number on his contracts with her Hi-Liters and motioned for him to sit down, eyeing his coffee. "Would you like a cup?" he offered...

The temple, who enjoyed three cups last evening, wasn't drinking this morning.

"These are very close to what we want, but I need to make a few changes."

Brent pulled up one at random on his screen. "Tell me the changes, and I'll enter them. Will they be the same for them all? The computer can change them all at once."

"Yes. On the buyer lines add *or nominee*."

The change would read *Jane Doeman or nominee*, preventing the seller from pulling out of the contract if a person other than Jane Doeman elected to go into title. That change could bother a seller who was carrying back a promissory note, in effect loaning a part of the down payment to a credit-worthy buyer, if that buyer tried to run in a flake at the last minute. In this case it wouldn't make much difference to the banks who owned the homes because they would sell to a capuchin monkey at this point if the beast didn't have an IRS lien against it at the time of recordation. But it bugged Brent because it put one more impediment between him and learning what was going on.

"It's for your own good," she commented. "It isolates you from the buyers' identities."

She was right.

How could a woman change so in twelve hours? Last night, her calf on his ankle, and all four of their hands around the stem of a wine glass. This morning they were like strangers.

Next, insert the phrase: *Seller shall be obligated to accept legal currency of any economic council member country at par value as of close of escrow. Discount fees, if any, charged seller to convert closing funds to U.S. currency or other currency of seller's choice shall be paid by buyer following close of escrow."*

"What?" Brent knew what she said but he couldn't believe it.

"You heard me. I want that in the contracts, all of them."

In other words, a buyer could use chicken lips if such were the coin of the realm in some country Brent never heard of that had done business with Jane's father. This would bug the banks that owned the houses, but anything is better than a REO on their books.

"That could be a problem."

"It won't be. Trust me. Write it."

.   *Her gentle way with words was returning.*

"I thought you were transferring funds in from Sunset Escrow's home office."

"There's been a change in our plans. Our comptroller might want to use currency, and I want to leave that door open. Type."

He entered the phrase, ignoring the reference to a comptroller. "Next?"

"A new clause: *Buyer shall be deemed to have constructive title to effect placement of liability and hazard insurance on the property, and sellers herein shall, in consideration of buyer maintaining insurance, grant sellers the right to enter and inspect the property and conduct reasonable repairs."*

She's good, he thought. She wants the run of the places and has sense enough to insure them all to keep the sellers happy and out of a lawsuit. And she doesn't want the sellers back on the property.

No problem. Bankers seldom become sentimentally attached to their REOs...

Brent hunt-and-pecked the keyboard for a few minutes. "Done."

She handed him the disc from the digital camera that she had been using yesterday. He downloaded it into his computer, and a photo of the Federal-style home they looked at yesterday appeared on his screen, in verdant color, better color than he could capture with slow Ektachrome film in his Canon EOS. He sorted back and forth on the video disc, embedding several photos to correlate with each listing.

My God, how he'd love to have one of these cameras for the office. Or for Patsy's big grin on Sunset Beach in Oregon.

"That's it. Print them."

Yes, ma'am. Brent moused the printer icon, and the LaserJet behind him started to hum.

Doeman looked at her watch, a very feminine Seiko in place of the big black Casio she had worn earlier in the week. "I'm going back to my room for a while. It's been a long morning and I'm a little tired."

You're tired? I haven't slept for 30 hours.

"I'll just walk and be back here about four o'clock to sign the papers and work out the escrows." He walked her out the front door amid the glares of the hot desk crew and the receptionists, save for Pam who wasn't in on the L&H feeding frenzy that had been nourishing on Brent's carcass all morning.

Brent thought about Mike Driscoll's call about the dumpster incident early this morning. He'd already decided not to tell her about it. She was an assassin who could cover her own tail. Then he thought about the dark eyes dancing in the candlelight.

"Can I talk to you for just a minute?" He stopped her by the iron loveseat under the canopy.

She was taken aback and looked at his hand holding her forearm as it had last evening. But she was no more surprised than he was as he looked at the same hand. He released her.

"If this is about last night, I don't want to talk about it. For reasons you don't understand, it is hard on me to think about it. I don't regret a minute of it, and I'll never forget it, but I don't want to talk about it. Period."

"This is nothing to do with last night. Sit down." He pointed at the loveseat, and they sat with as much daylight between them as they could manage.

"Last night someone went through the dumpster behind the building."

Why did he bring this up? No turning back now...

"They told the cops they were looking for aluminum cans, and they probably were. But you threw a bunch of information into my wastebasket yesterday, you're going through a lot of trouble to preserve your clients' privacy, this is the first time in this building or that one over there that our dumpster's ever interested anybody, and I think you've got to assume that what was on my desk might be in the hands of someone beside you and me."

There.

She paled, hard for a girl with no tan to do. She stared at her shoes and the sidewalk, and he felt for the first time since he met her Monday that she had finally lost her ungodly sangfroid. And she didn't like it.

She thought, quietly for a long time. Lydia and Tom walked out of the office for lunch, an escrow runner parked and brought some documents in, and Dave Nichols walked in behind him. They all looked at Jane, trying not to stare.

She didn't move.

He awaited a tongue-lashing, deserved or otherwise, for not protecting the security of the transaction. It didn't come. The runner from Bay City escrow left.

She finally looked up, then at him.

"Did a white van have anything to do with this?"

Now *he* was surprised but hoped it didn't show.

"Not that I know of," he lied.

She sat quietly for a few more moments.

"This may change everything. I need… I need time to think. I'm trying to remember what was on those papers. I need time."

She rose and walked toward the D Street Bridge. He didn't.

"I'll be back at four. I may have to call the home office for instructions. I'll see you then."

He watched her on her path over the bridge, walking slowly, her usual starch and assurance drained by his words.

Scenarios pro and con about the white van raced through his mind for only a second or two until he remembered his self-imposed ban on one-man soliloquies. He did it, it's over, let the chips fall where they may. And for the first time this week an unexplained occurrence didn't seem to paint him further into a corner. How could Doeman's suspicion of a white van hurt him?

Well, for openers her suspicion could make her less predictable than she already is, he thought to himself before he launched into yet another self-soliloquy where he asked himself hypothetical questions until he went into brain-fade and ascending stages of paranoia. He left it at that.

Except for wondering whether she too felt someone breathing down her neck, other than himself last night in the moonlight, or if she'd noticed the van tailing her somewhere during the week. He left the thought at that. Thirty hours without sleep, with an intervening peak on the river last night in the moonlight with an angel, and a valley this morning with a devil-incarnate — same person — was taking its toll. He was dragging, physically and mentally. He missed Patsy and knew that that void in his life would last for many more days.

The crew ignored him, nothing unusual. He saw Pam with the headset on, and noticed that Felicia was readying herself for her grand exit to Irvine. He walked around the corner into his office and was grabbed from behind by two strong arms.

This it is. This is how it ends.

He looked down at the freckled arms across his chest, and emerald ring on the right hand.

"Go home, Brent. You don't deserve this punishment. I can't stand to watch this happen to you. Sleep. Everything will be all right. You and Patsy will be all right. This will pass. Go home and sleep. Don't even talk to me, just get out of here!"

Katy was a friend. She kept her grip, bordering on a bear hug, from behind him. She was in tears.

"I don't need a second invitation." He turned her around and looked at her. "Will you be OK? You look worse than I do."

"I'm fine," she said.

He led her to his chair, sat her down and squeezed her hand. "Thanks, pal." He closed his door behind him.

He stopped by Felicia's side of the counter. "What time are you leaving?"

"I thought I'd get away about three."

Brent looked at his watch. 12:25.

"Well, look at that; three o'clock, Brenty-time. Time to roll now." Standing behind her he put his arm around her shoulder and whispered in her ear, "Get outa here and go kick some butt in love sets. Good luck!"

Brent told Pam to man the phones and leave Katy alone for a few minutes. He moved his little magnetic man to 4:00, the hour of Doeman's return, and Felicia's to *Vacation*. That column on the board was starting to look pretty good to him.

The Taurus was awaiting him in the **MANAGER** space. He'd switch cars later. He got into the Taurus. Windows open all night and half the day, and it still smelled like gardenia. If Patsy thought she was wild this morning, she'd have plumbed the depths of a new meaning of the word if she had to drive it to work with *this little sexpot client of yours'* perfume wafting up her cute little upturned snoot.

He waved at Felicia as she was starting her Granada, and she gave him a thumbs-up.

Over the bridge and through the woods, he was home in five minutes, set the alarm for 3:30, stripped to his shorts in two more minutes, and was asleep on top of the sheets almost immediately.

The phone beside his bed rang at 3:10. He never heard it.

CHAPTER FOURTEEN

Thursday afternoon: A change in plans...

3:30 p.m. An annoying and recurring beep filled the redwood planked bedroom as though the room were getting a busy signal. At first it meant nothing to the sole occupant of the bed, lying supine in exactly the same position it landed in two and a half hours before.

The beep was relentless. Brent's preëminent distaste for alarm clocks rested in the fact that he seldom relied on them, as he was usually up with the sun on all but the darkest days of winter. And during that fortnight of time he was usually in no hurry to roll out of the sack anyway.

Thus the beeping fell on ears relaying to a mind for which the tone had little meaning, and worse, a mind that hovered between a real deep sleep and a mild afternoon coma. One does not spend thirty hours romping the riverfronts of Rio Verde with Doeman-by-the-moonlight on the one hand, and on the other dealing with the likes of Patsy and the daytime-edition Doeman, and the associated joy and serenity that both brought him, then go home and take a casual nap. Brent crashed.

But an alarm clock is unforgiving of trysts and terrorists – it wants one to *awaken*. Rather, one wants oneself to awaken, and sets the clock.

Don't shoot the messenger.

Brent finally realized that the beep wasn't a busy signal or a seat belt that wasn't hooked or the microwave telling him that last night's cold pizza was ready or his Orion subchaser was on final approach with no landing gear separating it from the runway. He opened his large brown peepers and looked at the ceiling.

That's my alarm clock.

Very good, Skipper.

He thumped with his fist in the direction of the clock. And again. And again. He silenced the lamp, the telephone, his pager, a pocket book (not his Grisham) and his picture of Patsy. And the beep continued. He rose to one elbow and looked at what was left on the side table. The alarm clock was doing its job. Pulse, respiration and temperature were returning. He looked at the clock, found *Alarm Off* and poked it. The beeping stopped. He flopped back on the bed, looking at the ceiling.

And he thought about his snooze. *Wait until I tell Patsy the dream I had!* Spies, sexy women, space-age computer stuff. You were even in it, you were madder than hell at me. And there was an ugly duckling that turned into a babe, like Agnes Gooch did in *Auntie Mame.* And another spy with legs even longer than yours. And the whole office was mad at me for taking this chick out, see, but we didn't really…

Nuts.

Number one, her head's not on the pillow next to yours, pretending she's still asleep and hoping you'll quit jabbering. Number two, it's unlikely to be there in the near future, and even that may be an optimistic time frame. Number three, the dream wasn't. It's halftime in the game of real life and you'd better come out of the locker room with Knute Rockne's words and the Notre Dame fight song swelling to a crescendo in your helmet, or you're going to get your ass kicked by somebody , and right now you don't know who, so assume it's all of them.

And, four, forget the 'spy with longer legs than yours' bit. All wise men know that all women hold all men accountable for all their dreams. "You must think a lot about long legs or you wouldn't be dreaming about them. Aren't mine long enough?"

Often, it doesn't take much effort to initiate a spirited discussion between two in love…

The afternoon was warm, and Brent chose for his ensemble for this late matinee meeting with the businesslike and objective Doeman-by-Day, a stylish pair of fine cotton shorts in royal blue and a coordinated surgical scrub shirt of teal green, a trendy white XL hospital laundry tag exposed on the back of the neck. He owned a dozen of these in varying hues and was given to wearing the scrubs on leisurely occasions, which this wouldn't be, because they were comfortable, looked just as bad tucked in as when left loose, and had a pocket for his sunglasses whether worn right- or inside-out. Birkenstocks completed the outfit. He was both cool and comfortable. The sartorial charades were over, the sides had come to know each other well, and the time spent would be brief.

The air conditioner would have felt pleasant in the Taurus, but the gardenia scent was tough, still hanging in there. He drove downtown with the windows still down. He noticed the clock on the panel: 4:02. Two minutes late, five more minutes to the office.

Doeman was like an emotional time bomb looking for a place to go off. Five minutes of cooling their jets in his office waiting for him might be a welcome time for normal clients to glance through one of the *People* magazines in the L&H lobby, but sufficient time for Doeman to go into one of her ugly moods, take it out on the receptionists, and in seven minutes, on him. He reached under the seat for Patsy's cell phone and turned it on. It "woke up" with a beep, but then chirped – low battery. Talk fast, if it dials up at all. On this phone, the office was *Memory* 2, Brent's townhouse was 3. He touched *Memory* 2, then *Send*.

Speed-dial-three might have a vacancy by Monday...

It answered: "Good afternoon, Landau and Holmes Realty." Pam had a nice phone voice.

"This is Brent. The phone's about gone so I'll make it fast. Tell Doe, er, Miss Doeman that I'll be there in five minutes."

"She just called, said she'll be a few minutes late."

"Good. I'll beat her. 'Bye." He touched *End* and the thing chirped out of life. He pulled the cord from under the seat and plugged it into the cigarette lighter to recharge it.

How would we run our phones and radar detectors if everybody in the world quit smoking? Brent liked the challenge of these quotidian little questions in life. *Why did kamikaze pilots wear helmets? What do you say to God when he sneezes? If an M&M melts in your mouth but not in your hand, what does it do in your armpit?*

Questions like that. Questions were healthy; soliloquies were sure preludes to insanity. He came to Old Sonoma Road and locked up the brakes and cranked the wheel. Patsy's house was two blocks down the winding road.

A red Miata approached him fast, hugging one of the curves. A pretty little car, an honest-to-God convertible, not just a coupe with the top hacked off. But it was the driver who interested him, blonde, with her hair pulled back into a ponytail. An angular fact, beautiful, tanned, a pair of Ray-Bans perched on her nose. She belonged in the car – a scene right out of a Mazda TV commercial. He didn't get a good look at her, but he wouldn't mind seeing her buzzing around the streets of Rio Verde more often.

He drove into Patsy's cobblestone driveway. The immaculate post-war era home had been upgraded about ten times, extensively land-scaped, and looked like a million bucks. And her neighbors' homes in the woody subdivision were all just as well-kept. The garage door operator was under her visor, and he stopped next to the Explorer, still in the driveway, Al's flowers still around the antenna. A sad sight indeed. He pulled the Taurus into the garage with the windows still down and put one of his cards on the horn ring. *Thanks for the use of the car.* Love, B. The flowers on his antenna, love's labor truly lost, were dispatched into the garbage can, sorry, Aldo. He glanced around the garage, knowing that when he hit the button he was out for keeps, saw nothing, hit it, and dove under the lowering garage door. One less detail to worry about later. He liked driving his own wheels.

A taxi was pulling into the L&H lot as he turned in and parked in Felicia's space, close to the entrance. The clock over the canopy indicated 4:07. Doeman paid the cabbie and walked into the building alongside Brent, but not with him, then straight into his office and sat down at the table. She said not a word, and didn't look real good, like a woman who could have used a little sleep herself. And a little sun. She was wearing the same slacks and blazer that she had worn four hours earlier, and he wondered what she had done to amuse herself during those four hours.

Brent stopped by the receptionists' counter and moved his little magnetic man In. "Do we have a *but-not-for-long* category, Kate?"

"I wish. How was your nap?"

He stepped behind her and returned the bear hug she had given him earlier. "I can't thank you enough. I feel like a new man. Or a new woman." He caught the disapproving look over her shoulder.

Katy nodded her head toward Brent's office and said, "Get in there and get finished and get her out of here."

As he stood behind her, they both looked out the front door at the same time. It was the red Miata, not an easy little buggy to miss in a parking lot full of real estate agents' four-door sedans. The blonde with the ponytail was still at the helm. Brent released his bear hug and watched her weave it out the back side of the lot, then turn toward the bridge.

Katy looked at Brent. "Not bad if you like blondes. She's been through here three or four times already. Must be looking for somebody."

He thought about that. Tall in the saddle, tan, skinny face, blonde ponytail. Mysterious.

Katy looked at him, staring vacantly at the bridge, the Miata now long gone across the river.

The Falcon's Miata

"Katy?"

Katy looked at Doeman in Brent's office, showing signs of growing impatience.

"What?"

"That's the Falcon, in the Miata. I saw her leaving Patsy's place fifteen minutes ago. That's her."

"The fox that came in here Monday and used the phone, and rode the bike on your path, and took Doeman's picture last night?"

"That's her. I'd bet on it. And now she knows where Patsy lives too. That's where I saw her coming from."

Katy took control. "I'll wait for you until you're through with Doeman. I have to wait anyway because I'm Felicia until all this data crap gets launched into outer space or whatever she does with it. We'll talk after that – it's no big deal, there's a million skinny blondes in the world, and you've seen one. Or two, or three, but it doesn't mean anything. A blonde never killed anybody yet. Go. Go."

She pushed him into his office.

"Hi, Jane, how ya' doin'?" He needn't have asked. She looked as low as he'd ever seen her, no longer the take-charge, businesslike, objective pain in the ass she started the week as, nor the new-and-improved tolerable, almost pleasant persona that she occasionally displayed as the relationship matured, and definitely not the demure, beautiful belle of the ball whose presence in Rio Verde was chronicled in every beauty shop and over every back fence in the little town this morning

…as the relationship matured?

He thought about that. He'd only known her for 48 hours. He had had clients in the past that in that same span of time he had barely only begun to feel comfortable enough to call by their first names. While he was never sure what this client's first name *was*, the relationship was mature enough that he had already debated between drowning her in the Sequoia River or hanging her low-cut peach peasant dress over a post on her Victorian bedstead. Or both. She wasn't an old friend, it just seemed so, and he felt that if he knew her long enough, she could become at least two friends, maybe more, depending on which one of her persona was in the office or the sack at any one time. A textbook love-hate relationship. But far from a *mature* one.

"I've had better days. The trash creates a problem, but we're going with the offers. Are they ready?"

❖   ❖   ❖

Doeman signed the copies of the contracts for delivery to the escrow company and the sellers. Brent didn't expect a long delay in getting the bankers to sign the contracts, save for the currency clause. Had they the street smarts to understand that, they probably wouldn't have the houses as REOs in the first place. The offers would "fly," as those in the industry might say.

Katy faxed the signed copies of the contracts to L&H's own computer, embedding it onto the disc just as Brent had printed them, but now with Jane's signature appearing on the disc. Through some process that Felicia had taught her, Katy slaved a copy of Brent's disc onto another one and handed it do Doeman. Brent put the hard copies of the offers, with the funds-transfer slips attached, in an escrow sleeve to take to the sellers, who would change one chickenshit detail just to show him who's boss, and then accept the offers as quickly as they could before somebody changed their mind.

Then came the telling words "You are not authorized to deliver these offers to the sellers at this time. I will notify you in writing via telefax when you may deliver them. Probably Monday."

Aha. Doeman was not steering the ship. Somebody higher had the final approval. He could tell that having to make this admission bothered her. She continued, "But I do want the offers to go to Sunset Escrow at this time so that they may prepare instructions and the preliminary title reports. I have talked to Laura, and she will do that tomorrow morning and put it all onto one disc."

Doeman's family must have some kind of horsepower, Brent thought. An escrow holder usually wouldn't do the instructions until the offer was in contractual form with all the parties' names in blood. Maybe little ol' Laura is the terrorists' housemother.

"Can they do it in UNIX?" Katy asked.

"They can do it in whatever DOS language they use. I cancelled the satellite feed reservation today so this will be sent on voice-grade telephone in the cl..." She caught herself.

In the *clear*. *Voice-grade*. She had unconsciously used a cryptographer's terminology. *Comptroller*, my ass.

Katy faxed the five four-page offers to Laura. Toni called back in a few minutes explaining that Laura was unable to come to the phone, but that the 20 pages had been received and would be processed by ten o'clock tomorrow.

Doeman looked at Katy. "Katy, Laura will bring you their disc tomorrow with the instructions and the prelim embedded. Convert it to UNIX like Felicia showed you, and transmit it to the number Felicia has for *Jane* in her Rolodex. Then run a magnet over it to destroy it."

It rankled Brent that Doeman was giving Katy orders. The deed was done. Four offers had been written, executed and transmitted to escrows and to the buyers. All that remained was to gain her approval to present them to the sellers who would, no doubt, accept them. Brent had sold four homes, nine-hundred eighty-seven thousand bucks worth of real estate, between a Tuesday and a Thursday.

He had turned handsprings for joy after his first sale in the real estate business, told that part of the world that would hold still to listen all about his triumph, then spent the next thirty days planning and replanning how he would spend his first commission. It was four times his monthly pay in the flight engineer's seat of an Orion.

Today the mood was different. Katy went back to her console without a word and Doeman sat at the table in his office, packing up her paperwork. He couldn't see anything in it that was worth protecting from the prying eyes of others. They, whoever *they* were, had potentially already learned the location of the homes their adversaries had bought. They didn't really give a damn what Doeman had paid for them.

❖   ❖   ❖

4:35 p.m. Doeman walked over to Brent's door and pushed it closed. He had already sensed that finishing the four contracts was not the end of her task this afternoon.

"Brent, the company has decided that it is necessary to meet with you, face to face, about the breach in the security that occurred with the dumpster, and solidify the ground rules for what may be up to seven more executives' homes in the Rio Verde area. I told them that I enjoyed working with you, and you should stay on board for the next few weeks' efforts. The meeting is set for tomorrow afternoon."

He pondered that one for a moment.

Up to seven people. The next few weeks. The company.

Was it time to bring the curtain down on this shenanigan? At what point could he bow out? The first contracts weren't even fully ratified by the buyers, nor accepted. Did he have 'a few more weeks' left in him with this schizo?

Yes. He did. He didn't really, but he had to follow through. Maybe he could put these four to bed, *then* bail out.

"OK. Where?"

"Hawaii is the central point for you and them. They're overseas right now, and will meet you there. The company owns property on the windward side of Oahu where you can meet in privacy. The meeting is set for four o'clock, Hawaiian time. Here is your ticket." She handed him an envelope.

Brent opened it. It was a garden-variety airline ticket, coach class, on a Delta flight leaving International across the bay at 8:10 tomorrow morning. A four-hour flight, arriving at 10:20 local time.

"I guess I'll go. What should I bring?" The paperwork was all on disc and would have already been sent to them by then, somewhere.

"Yourself. You shouldn't need luggage. We'll get you back to Honolulu after the meeting."

He looked at the ticket for the return time. It was a one-way ticket.

"How come it's a one-way ticket?"

"Our plans may change."

But my clothes won't. Or their change may be to go ahead and kill me after they see the cut of my jib.

"How do I get from the Honolulu airport to the meeting?"

"You will be met by a limousine at the airport. A driver will be holding a sign that says *Hawk*. You are Mr. Hawk as far as he knows."

Dammit. Another raptor to go with the Falcon.

He was almost amused – not enough letters in H*awk* for a VoiceMail code – they need five digits. But this was not an occasion for levity. He was being taken from his own turf to theirs. Not that his own had yet provided any degree of security.

He looked again at the ticket. He was traveling as B *Hawk*. They didn't miss much. He looked at it again – the space for *Issuing Agency* and *Method of Payment* had been blanked out with a piece of adhesive foil. He'd hoped to see what travel agency booked the ticket, or how they had paid for it.

"I'll be there. Are you going to fly over also?" His mind conjured visions of the pain – Doeman's tush parked next to him in an airliner annoying the hell out of him for four interminable hours, followed later in the evening by the lovely Doeman's abundant pale breasts spilling out of a dental-floss bikini top, the full moon above lighting the saltwater droplets clinging to each of them, as they gamboled together and made love on some deserted beach on the windward side of Oahu.

He wasn't ready for either possibility. He held out a slim hope that Patsy may take him back, after she plays with him for a while like a cat toying with a moth. A pleasant third option was hanging the rebuilt fan in the bull pen while listening to the Giants shutting out Atlanta on Saturday morning. That third option didn't loom as being real promising.

"No. I'm not really needed. I'll be back here in Rio Verde by midweek."

"You think I'll be home by sometime Saturday?"

"I don't see why not. There's a second segment to my instructions to you."

"Which is?"

"We have decided to close the escrows with currency, and you will transport it back to the Mainland for us."

Just dandy.

If these guys of Doeman's *are* agents of the federal government, it might be embarrassing for them to be caught, by whatever their screw-up, with almost a million bucks in folding green. Or in drachmas or rupees. Or chicken lips.

And another federal agency, say the Falcon's for example, would love to help them into just such a faux pas.

On the brighter side, acting as the courier would at least ensure that he'd get back here in one piece. Earlier in the week *Who are these guys?* kept rattling through his mind. It remained a fair question, but now he thought of Butch and Sundance in the movie, relaxing on the way *to* the bank in Colombia, feeling the sweat only on the way *back* to the tin mine with the payroll.

In his convoluted thinking he reasoned that if their money had to get back to the Mainland, they'd leave him alone until he got back here, a damn sight safer place to be than on some lonely Hawaiian back road. Of course, others may want the money, if they know what he's got in his satchel, and take him out on the airplane or the cab on the way back to Rio Verde.

He held his finger to his lips as in *be quiet*. Given the skullduggery that had gone on all week, he wasn't sure that the sweaty guy with the scimitar in the trailer at the airstrip in Cyprus wasn't listening right now. He looked at the brass fan motor from Fundas' Fountain lying on the floor of his office.

It could be a big transmitter.

You're losing it, big guy.

"Enough said," Brent cautioned her. "I get the picture. Let's keep it to ourselves."

"I understand," she said, glancing around his office. She rose to leave, and without thinking he put his hand on her waist and told her to have a nice trip. She moved closer to him until her hip touched his thigh, and stood for a moment, still.

Then she walked out of his office and toward the open French doors.

He thought about his hand on her waist, the warmth of last evening in redux. She turned and looked at him.

"I'll just walk. I want to stop at the Heron café one more time." She stopped again. "And Brent?"

He shuddered. A sweet smile, like the smile he last saw framed by the oval window of the bed-and-breakfast, came over her face.

Whatever she's selling, I'm not buying. Last time I saw that smile she was detouring me into the shadows behind the Victorian, and I damn near wound up spending the night. No. Go away. Then she spoke.

"Never mind. See you next week." Then she waved, slowly, with just the fingers of one hand.

❖   ❖   ❖

5:05 p.m. An all-expense-paid trip to the islands. What could be nicer? Meet some new people, see parts of the island he hadn't seen before, and solidify four contracts that would bring him about twenty-seven thousand bucks in commission, before Uncle. Is this business great, or what?

Katy poked her head in his door.

"While you were tied up six of your better friends dropped by. They're in the break room waiting for you. They asked me to come along with you. Let's go."

I *didn't think* I *had six friends left. Now what?*

Pam had left a few minutes before. She had done a good job and could probably keep the place afloat if nothing too out of the ordinary came along. Katy dialed the 7-2-# code to put the phones to the night number. He followed her back through the bull pen toward the break room. Tom Yarbrough was in his office cubicle, his back against the wall.

"Tom, can I see you? Katy, this is for you too." Tom motioned them back.

"I'm going to Honolulu tomorrow morning, flying out of International a little after eight. Can you run the office for the day? Should be fairly quiet from all I can tell. Felicia's gone too, so I really have to depend on you and Kate."

Tom looked at his friend and nodded. *Should be fairly quiet from all he can tell? He hasn't had his head in this game all week. The place is going nuts, and we're down to one experienced receptionist.*

"Glad to, Brent. I'll get in a little early, and I don't have anything going on in the field all day."

Katy appeared to be shocked. "Why do you have to go to Honolulu?"

"Doeman's deal. Her big brass want to meet me. We had a little screw-up, and I think they think I'm the culprit."

Tom raised his eyebrows. "That whole deal's been screwed up from day one. What happened?"

This was the first that Tom had indicated he knew anything about the real estate side of Doeman. He obviously had heard of Doeman-by-Night, and was one of the agents that ignored him in disgust earlier in the day.

"She trashed some papers that I made up for her with some addresses on them. Then we got a call from Mike Driscoll at two-something in the morning that somebody was browsing through the dumpster. I was dumb enough to tell Doeman, and now she thinks she's been compromised."

Brent finished the brief account and wondered if Tom had a clue about what was happening with L&H and Doeman. Tom looked blank.

"I didn't realize that our files were such hot stuff. Where the hell did you do anything wrong?"

"Guess it's a long story. I'll tell you about it when it's over. No secret anyway – buy Katy a yogurt tomorrow morning, and she'll fill you in. Her yogurt snack is part of the manager's responsibility anyway."

Brent's weak attempt at humor was answered by a weak laugh from Tom. Brent and Katy walked into the break room. It was empty.

"So where are these friends?" Their number was too many for his golf foursome and too few for his half-court hoops team, now in summer recess anyway.

Katy sat down in a booth. "Look in the refrigerator, then bring two over and introduce us."

Brent opened the door to find a six-pack of Henry Weinhard's beer with a Kelly-green bow around them. He cracked two bottles and handed one to Katy.

"You're a good buddy. I can think of nothing that could be nicer right now. Almost."

"Don't look at me like that. You have enough women in your life, maybe two too many. Did you know Henry Weinhard was an Irishman?"

"Yes, I've heard the song about him many times on my old Kingston Trio albums. A friend of Tom Dooley's, I believe. Cut the crap. What do you mean *two* too many women?"

"The first one is obvious. Doeman's turned you into an irrational animal. But the one that's bugging you subconsciously is probably this Falcon string bean because she doesn't hang around long enough to give you any read on her. Why does she get to you so much?"

"You said it. I can't figure out how she fits into the picture."

"She's probably the best friend you have right now, outside of me of course. If this fantasy about secret relocations and silencing agents forever that you've ginned up is true, and most of us think it *is*, the string bean's probably the only one on your side, but she can't tell you. She's just watching and waiting, letting Doeman lead her to whomever she wants."

"Why doesn't she just *tell* me? Why the white van bugging my house and my car and God knows what else? She could bring me in on it, and I'd be more effective."

"You're not sure what the white van's doing. And no, you'd be *less* effective because your responses to Doeman wouldn't be straight, and Doeman would pick up on it in a heartbeat. Then you wouldn't be of any use to anybody. She's OK. Doeman is the one to worry about. Take it from a woman. She's a schizoid nightmare. We all can tell. Doeman will hurt you, almost certainly, and she can do it. But Stretch might haul your tail out of it before you get hurt. Don't fight her."

They both sat quietly and enjoyed Henry's company.

He broke the silence.

"You in the spy business now?"

"No, I'm in the female intuition business. That's what this is all about. And you're outgunned." She went for two more beers. The lights went out in the main office.

He opened the bottles and slid one across the Formica.

"How's Patsy?"

"She's alright. I talked to her this afternoon. He sister picked her up, and she called from the condo in Balboa. Guess it's a pretty fancy place – right on the water. She could see Catalina, so it must be sunny and clear."

"I can't believe I got myself into so much hot water so fast on one date. I really didn't think it would turn out that way at all. Then I saw that little beast waiting under an arbor across from the locomotive in Walnut Park, and knew I could be hurtin' for certain."

"She must have looked pretty good," Katy admitted. "Problem is that Patsy knew more about it by nine by accident that she could have found out all day if she were trying, and it all came up wrong. Did you take Doeman upstairs?"

"No."

Katy smiled. "I didn't think so."

"And believe it or not, I was trying to shut it down most of the evening, but right at the end the male spirit kicked in, and I almost went for it. But I didn't."

"When are you and Patsy getting married?"

"I had hoped by the end of the year. But things are on hold right now, obviously."

"You guys will be OK. Just don't get between Doeman and that skinny blonde. If us girls are reading it right, they've got their own score to settle, and the government and witness things have long since been left in the dust. This is a female catfight now. Just get the money home and let the system work."

She looked at the clock. "I've got to get to the hairdresser's. I know you think this mop just happens, but it doesn't. Will you get dinner somehow?"

"Yeah, Take-'n-Bake pizza, an XL – don't know when I'll see food again. Maybe Canadian bacon and pineapple to get in the Island mood. Not much else is helping. I'm going to the *Islands* tomorrow! Wahines wearing nothing but tiny shells, short palm fronds, and a big smile just for Brent. I should be ecstatic! What the hell's wrong with me?"

"I'll forget I heard the *fronds* and *shells*. Your libido has already landed you into enough soup for one day. Remember I want to do a jig at Patsy's wedding, not your funeral."

"You'd dance at my funeral?" He'd seen her dance, and she was good.

"Depends who the band is. Don't think about shells this trip. They might be in a revolver, and thinking about that'll make you goofier than you already are."

It was his turn to look at the clock. He started at flight time, 8:20 tomorrow morning, turned back an hour for gate check-in, back another hour and a half to be on the safe side for driving to International and parking. A half-hour to get up, shower, and dress. He'd pack tonight.

"I've got to hit the deck by 5:30 Ayem. Are there two 5:30s in the day?"

"Why don't you call Hap and hitch a ride on the flight-crew shuttle? You can shave off a half-hour and save the parking hassle."

"Then I wind up getting home at midnight on Friday or noon on Saturday or whenever with no wheels."

"Call me. I'll get you. I'll be home all weekend."

"You'd do that?"

"I'd love to, Brent. Please let me do something for you. You've been through enough this week."

She pulled long red handfuls of her hair straight out sideways from her head, a signal that the hairdresser was calling. Brent threw the bottles into the glass-only bin. She gave him all of one of her infamous O'Rourke bear hugs, and he responded.

"Have a good flight, Skipper. Call me when you get home."

CHAPTER FIFTEEN

Thursday evening: Hawaii calls...

An ancient Chinese proverb warns that "If you want to enjoy an American restaurant, never visit the kitchen." Brent could never remember exactly how it translated from the Chinese, but that was close. The same might be said for a Take-'n-Bake pizza. They're delicious, as good as a parlor pizza without all the Pop Warner football players running amok and the video games beeping. But should one buy one at the Take-'n-Bake outlet across the river from the L&H office, it is best to take it home, preheat the oven to six or eight hundred degrees, turn out all the lights in the kitchen so the pizza can't be seen, then open the box in the dark and stuff the pizza into the oven for a couple of hours. The result will indeed be one of nature's most nearly perfect foods.

Brent was attending to his pizza and had started the oven on *preheat* at 250°. He opened a beer and went out on the deck. He had thought until he was blue in the face about the deeds that he had done this week. He had tried for three nights to put things into perspective, like the blonde in the Miata driving from Patsy's house. And as usual, the more he thought, the more confused he became. He recalled a class he took in college, a logic class taught by a mathematician, demonstrating how permutations increased geometrically with only a linear increase in the givens.

Any one event during this week, taken alone, could be easily explained. Doeman has some strange clients. Not the first time that's happened in the real estate industry. But, let a blonde fox ride by on a bicycle or a Grisham book disappear, and one event starts tying to another and the mind instinctively seeks a mesh. And, applying the prof's geometric rule of progression, nine explanations are now viable for those three occurrences.

Then Jeff Terrell brings up the relocated witness possibility, possibility becomes likelihood, likelihood becomes probability and then events to follow are naturally drawn toward that probability, now a *high* probability and fast being etched into granite as the sole logical solution. All the other explanations are discarded. A few more minor events, all easily explainable in and of themselves, like the carpet cleaners here yesterday and a disc full of four-letter codes with this address and phone numbers, are certainly no reason to become totally illogical. Such things could happen to anybody.

Hot on the deck, west sun is pounding on it. Check the oven; light is on, meaning oven is either preheated or preheating. Forget which. Patsy says spray Pam on something to keep the pizza from sticking to the cookie sheet. Does the Pam go on the sheet or the pizza? Probably doesn't matter...

A man just has to think things through and see all sides of a situation. Susie Santini at Sunset Escrow is probably really at the tax deferred exchange class. What's the big deal? Just because you're opening a few complicated escrows, with nominee buyers and deposits that come in by wire from the other end of the state, doesn't automatically give you the right to assume that Susie's been spirited off somewhere to keep her in the dark.

And the guys in the dumpster. That stuff probably goes on every night. Mike Driscoll probably just happened to drive in when the two were there. And white vans are a dime a dozen. And the one by the reservoir with the blonde in it could have been a different one entirely.

The whole Falcon thing is ridiculous too. There could have easily been four different people – one in the office for an unexplained reason Monday, another riding a bike by the reservoir. You don't know that the tall guys in the brown coveralls that didn't clean your carpet weren't two guys in coveralls, but you heard the word *thin* from Al and you naturally thought of the Falcon. And the one last night in The Shadows, thin, could have been anybody. And the one in the red Miata. Thin blondes with light-grey eyes with a halo of blue around the cornea are like white vans. They're on every street corner.

Not *like this blonde.*

You really have worked yourself into a snit over nothing. All these things are explainable. Once you get into that juvenile Scorpion mode you do it to yourself. You're too old for this, you're a businessman with people looking up to you, and you're acting like a Kentucky Fried Idiot.

Right.

That's why I'm leaving tomorrow morning as B Hawk with a ticket with tinfoil over the travel agent's name to go meet with people who will give me a gunny sack full of something to bring back and dump on Sunset's counter and walk out with four deeds showing Desi, Lucy, Fred and Ethel as the grantees. Real estate office managers all over the land are getting ready tonight for a trip like you are, just to bring home a million bucks in cash. You'll probably run into a few of them on the plane.

And your commission will probably come in chicken lips.

What time did the pizza go in? Probably ten minutes ago. I'll call it five just to be safe. Twenty-five to go.

Have to call Hap to get a lift to International. Damn nice of Katy to pick me up tomorrow night. Tomorrow? Maybe…

"Durst here."

"Douglas calling Dead Stick, come in Dead Stick. Go ahead?"

"That's *Captain* Dead Stick to you, sailor. And I've been listening to that bullshit ever since we left Hong Kong fifteen hours ago. You left out the *over.*"

"I forget where you say it. Do you civvy flyboys really say that when we're not listening?"

"What the hell do you want? I'm sleepy."

"I need a ride to International tomorrow morning. Does that Tijuana Taxi you guys run go every day?"

"Rain or shine, Skipper. Be at McNear School's east lot at five ayem. That's in the morning. Should be room. New guy drives. That's you. Don't keep the passengers awake. Nice talking to you. I'm going to bed."

"Thanks, Ca…" click.

Captain.

Five ayem?

The pizza was fit for a king, and the king left only one piece. The king wrapped it in foil with the others, this newest one on the bottom of the other foil piles in the fridge. This pizza filing system was oft-discussed between him and Patsy, the usual result being disposal of the entire collection, to start another on a new day.

Sun down now, beautiful up the river, as it had been the past few nights. The cabin cruiser was still moored where it was this morning.

What's this? The light was flashing on his answering machine. He hit the *play* button. An androgynous synthesized voice announced *three ten peeyem*. "Brent, this is your mother." Mothers always say that on answering machines, as if 45 years of hearing their voices weren't enough to recognize them. Dads just start talking.

"I'm a little concerned about you and Patricia. I heard an ugly story in Tyler's about you and some lady with long black hair in a low-cut

sequined evening gown, necking in a Corvette by Walnut Park last evening, and dancing close with her later in the bandbox to the music that was coming from the mill. The Corvette was still there this morning, and the rumor is that you spent the night with her. I can't find Patricia, but I certainly wish you'd call me when you get home. Your dad and I are worried about you both."

The Bandbox in Walnut Park

Dad's worried? I doubt it. Mothers always say that too.

Dancing in the bandbox. Not a bad idea, actually, the music was certainly loud enough, and it might have been quite pleasant. The bandbox in Walnut Park was a hexagonal turret, the floor toward the back worn thin by the pegs of three generations of double bass players all resting their fiddles in the same hole. For the one or two people in Rio Verde who missed the *Douglas and Doeman* show last night, the little Queen Anne bandbox would have made their spectacle even harder to miss.

He called Mom.

"This is the Douglas residence. We're not at home, please leave a message."

We're so embarrassed by our little boy Brent that we've left the valley forever in shame. Please leave a message.

"Hi, Mom. This is Brent, your son. I don't know anything about a 'Vette. Her hair is short, and the dress didn't have any sequins. We weren't necking in a Corvette or any other car." *No fib there.* "She's a client; I sold her some property today. Patsy is in Orange County with her sister. Everything's OK. And stay out of Tyler's market – Safeway's version of my evening out was much more accurate this morning."

He paused. Should he tell her he was going to Hawaii? Given the ripples already created by last evening, he decided against that. She'll only assume he had gone with the raven-black hair in a sequined muumuu. An interesting thought.

"Thanks for calling, mom. Everything's fine." Then a wry smile. "By the way, did they tell you that we were waltzing in the bandbox last night, both naked as jaybirds? See ya."

Dad would bear the brunt of that. But he could handle it.

He cleaned the kitchen, made some coffee, and set the timer for four-thirty. Another beer, and out onto his deck. The sun had set behind the low hill west of the river, and the view of the valley was too pleasant not to enjoy.

A couple of beers at the office and three more at home had taken the edge off his nerves. His outlook, however tangled up by Doeman, was stable tonight, and the suds had enabled him to deal with the dilemma, if not totally rationally, in an environment devoid of the terror he had felt off and on for the past couple of days. He didn't drink much, a six-pack would usually last him a week. Usually. But not this week. Next week, if this carnival continues, he'd bring home a case.

He sat in the chaise and pondered carrying that much cash. In the movies they'd give him a briefcase, sealed, and he'd carry it. Does airport security check it? What does he do when he goes to the john in the plane, take it with him? What's it look like – a canvas bag, a solid briefcase, a leather satchel? What's he do with it when he gets back home? How many people know that he has it? How does he know who to give it to? Maybe he can walk into Sunset Escrow, dump it on the counter, and get Laura to count it. ONE THOUSAND ONE, ONE THOUSAND TWO, yikes.

And is he an accomplice to something? Is the money stolen? Would he wind up handcuffed to the Falcon for three or four hours on the plane? Would she frisk him? Meticulously?

He was back to his soliloquies, despite his self-imposed ban on them. He wondered if he would ever be able to carry on an intelligent conversation again. The time spent with Katy and Felicia were the only times this week that weren't strained. He wished Katy were going with him.

Right. Just what they both needed.

He did need a beer. And an Alka-Seltzer.

What should he take? According to Doeman he'd be home tomorrow night, which might translate into Saturday morning with a late departure and the time difference. Wear light trousers, a shirt, open collar, a blazer, and white loafers. Look right at home in the Honolulu airport.

A briefcase? That would be two bags to carry aboard, but he planned on reading and wanted to take some toiletries. Maybe throw in a pair of shorts and a scrub shirt. For what? This wasn't a scrub crowd. I'll take the small Bean carry-on bag; maybe the briefcase will fit inside it.

What do people carrying nine hundred grand usually wear? Hard to say. Might have seen three or four today, all dressed differently. Probably doesn't matter.

He reached for the cordless phone by the chaise.

"Hi, Katy. I need Patsy's number in Balboa. I want to tell her what I'm doing tomorrow."

"No can do. How many have you had? You out on your deck brooding again?"

"Two Henry's at the office, a couple more here. I'm just tired. Yes, I'm on the deck, planning. No brooding tonight. *Que sera, sera.* Why no phone number?"

"Patsy's orders. She knows you're going; I talked to her earlier about her MacGinley escrow. They're out anyway. Some friend of her sister's has a place on, is it, *Lito*? Island and they were going there for the evening. Did you remember to call Hap?"

"Yep. Wheels in the well at five o'clock at McNear School."

"Have a good trip. Get some sleep. Love ya." Click.

Lido Island? That's where all the rich guys live. She's probably going to meet a commodities broker with a ponytail and a Ferrari. I may never see her again.

A new soliloquy is born...

He found his small canvas suitcase, more like a bag with two zippered compartments and fabric handles. It would hold everything but the kitchen sink and still qualify as a carry-on. Inside it from his last venture out of the valley was his black nylon toiletry case. He'd fill it tomorrow morning after he used everything he'd put in it. He looked at his bottle of Grey Flannel cologne. Patsy gave it to him for Christmas a year ago, and he loved the stuff but never felt right wearing it when she wasn't around. It had about a teaspoon of the liquid left in it, and he was rationing it. He threw it in the bag. It would be a good pick-me-up later in the day, he reasoned.

Most of what he would take would go on his frame, a frame that was reaching the age that it needed constant maintenance, like a daily walk and a few chin-ups and dips at the Parcourse at the reservoir, and crunchies in the morning before his shower. He was, in a word, pudgy at the belt, no thanks to a big dinner last night and deprivation of his daily walk while attending to Doeman's needs.

Housing needs.

The beer and the pizza, of course, were only a minor detriment to his physique. Man can not survive on maple bars alone.

A pair of shorts and a scrub shirt would be good, just in case he got loose for a while. A scrub shirt was easy; there was one hanging on every projection and fixture in his bedroom and most of the rest of the house. But his favorite Madras shorts and his swimsuit were not to be found. He took his Birkenstocks off and pitched them into the bag.

The missing shorts bugged him, the swim trunks he could account for. They were at Patsy's, kept near the hot tub for the inopportune and minimized occasions when the more modest came by to hop in the tub for a splash and a thimble of peppermint schnapps, a beverage invented centuries ago just for hot tubs.

Wonderful. I'll run around the island in Birkenstocks, a scrub shirt and a smile, no shorts. No sense calling attention to oneself when one is hauling nine-hundred grand in one's carry-on.

He packed a book, wished it was his new Grisham. He took his cameras. He never went anywhere without his palm-sized Olympus XA2 clamshell, and he packed the bigger Canon too. Hawaii is known for Kodak moments.

Two cameras, a book, a scrub shirt, spare skippers and socks and a pair of sandals. It's axiomatic that no one needs a lot of clothes in Hawaii, and most travelers take too many. He didn't feel he had overpacked.

He cracked one last beer and walked to the deck. He spotted his ukulele and thought for a moment. He picked it up and hammered out a few chords, finally a verse of *Salty Dog* toward the bugged ficus for the guy with the scimitar at the Cyprus airstrip. Much as he'd like to take it along, the uke would not return this trip to the land of its beginnings.

He thought a bit, vowing to himself that he wouldn't get into one of his convoluted soliloquies with himself. In Katy's words, something is haywire, something he couldn't fathom. Felicia's friend's analysis, based upon his experience with these people, was that the situation was volatile. And Jeff Terrell's wife, often known to sense that there was a paranoid chasing her, had added enough supposition to fact to keep it interesting.

Even Doeman had noticed a white van. He didn't hang around long enough to find out where or when she noticed it, but it must have been significant. And the blonde in the Miata.

He was thought out. The permutations had become exponential – too vast to deal with.

And, he was out of beer.

He was packed to travel, in a sense. He set the alarm clock for 4:30. The cabin cruiser had turned out all but its anchor light, and full darkness had fallen along the banks of the Sequoia River.

Brent went to bed. He heard his father's voice, and the phrase he always spoke on the eve of the more auspicious crossroads of Brent's youth.

Big day tomorrow, Tiger.

CHAPTER SIXTEEN

Friday morning: High Flight

Oh, I have slipped the surly bonds of earth,
And danced the skies on laughter-silvered wings...

As often as Brent flew in the Orions, he never quite overcame that fleeting instant when the subchaser, a rather large and ungainly piece of machinery on the ground, would lift its front tires completely and most of the weight off the rest of them, point its nose high enough to deprive those in charge of any clue as to what might be out in front of them, and then fly, just like Lockheed said it would. As the plane broke free of the ground it always make one stomach-churning dip back toward Mother Earth as her supporting air cushion gave way to the undisturbed atmosphere, briefly robbing the wings of their lift.

An instant later one gloved hand would lift the landing gear lever in the Orion, and another would shove the four throttles a few notches forward to a power setting that would have torn the engines off before the drag from the landing gear was smoothed into the wells beneath the wings.

The paraphrased words of aviator-turned-poet John Gillespie Magee, Jr. from his classic poem High Flight would often resound over the crew intercom, occasionally in Brent's voice:

Gentlemen, we have slipped the surly bonds of earth...

The brand-new Boeing 767 slipped from the surly bonds of earth at 8:22 a.m. a hell of a lot easier than the old Orion ever did.

My God, for a twin-engined plane this baby's really got some suds. The plane had turned onto the active runway at International and started its take-off roll, and the noise level barely increased as Brent was pressed harder and harder against the crisp new upholstery. The nose pulled high as it climbed out of International like a homesick angel, making an occasional course correction as Departure Control vectored it around other traffic. Brent could see a military something-or-other, a KC-10 aerial tanker maybe, through his window on the left side of the aircraft. It was a little lower and behind them, climbing and maintaining a course parallel with the 767's as they were both guided out to an imaginary radar intersection over the ocean. From there both would engage their autopilots and rely on satellites to guide them along their trips. If they were both going to Honolulu or Hickham Field, they would fly within fifty miles of each other for the next four hours.

Brent settled back in his seat, and although the plane was nearly full, the seat to his right was vacant. He had tucked his half-empty carry-on under his seat before takeoff, after first slipping a Dell crossword puzzle book and a pair of dark glasses into the pocket on the seat in front of him. He watched the flaps retract into the silver wing, and felt a slight power reduction as the crew eased the rate of climb, although they were far below cruise altitude. He had hoped that someone in the van that left the school so early this morning would be working this flight, but a tour of the cockpit was not to be. Only one flight crew left Rio Verde in the van, a Delta crew heading for JFK. The three attendants in the van were on an American trip to Dallas. Few talked to Brent, most were half-asleep on the 50-minute trip in the big 15-passenger van. For them the thrill of slipping the surly bonds of earth had long since ebbed into a weekly occurrence.

The sun was bright along the south left side of the westbound plane, at this early hour still behind the aircraft and reflecting off the wing and, no doubt, annoying the bourgeoisie in the first-class section. To Brent it was welcome light on his crossword puzzle book. He had come close to bringing a new Clancy novel but decided that anything Clancy had written lately would pale in comparison to the real-life side-show that had gone on in Rio Verde these past few days. And that was now being moved to the Islands.

He lifted the arm between his seat and the vacant one, turned sideways and pulled his right leg up onto the seat in a half-reclining position. The seats in the center row were empty; two people occupied the right-aisle seats far across the cabin. He felt very nearly alone, on his own airliner.

Coffee was offered, and he accepted, cream and sugar please and a few macadamia nuts to join the pineapple pizza he nuked at 4:40 to get himself into the mood. Lunch would follow in a few hours. He turned back to his puzzle. His eyelids were heavy. He'd been up for four hours already, with the most challenging afternoon of his life coming another 535 miles closer to him each hour. His head rolled back into the headrest. The cabin darkened slightly as the plane's climb took in into a layer of fluffy clouds, cleaving them until they inundated the thick wings and power plants. He slept, or did whatever that state of somnolence is called six miles above an ocean while people move about and talk, chimes summon the attendants' attention to the flight deck, and a week's recollections, from dumpsters to gardenias, carom off the hemispheres of a brain.

Whatever it was called, it overcame the Scorpion. The attendant took his half-empty coffee cup and closed his seat-back tray.

❖ ❖ ❖

> Up, up, the long, delirious burning blue
> I've topped the windswept heights with easy grace
> Where never lark, nor even eagle flew...

The left side of his face grew warm. Hot, actually uncomfortable where his head had slumped next to the Plexiglas window. The combination of the sun arcing higher above the horizon and a new vector that took the plane on a more southerly course had oriented the sun almost directly over his glistening forehead. He sat up in his seat and put his feet back on the floor. He glanced at his watch.

10:10.

He reset his watch to 8:10 local time while wondering if the trip's short duration merited the effort. Lunch would follow in about a half an hour. He lowered the sliding screen slightly to kill the worst of the sun's radiant heat.

He thought about the meeting at four and the route and the transportation to get there. A driver, holding a Hawk placard, would meet him, presumably at the luggage claim area of the terminal. Do I talk to him? Or her? Where are the others coming from? Jane had said that Hawaii is the *central point*. How does the driver know it's me? Maybe I should have sent Dave Nichols. Told him there'd be four escrows in it for him if he made the meeting at four.

The way the Douglas luck has been running Demi Moore would be holding the Hawk sign, Dave's meeting would be under a lanai on a beach, and the Bud Girls would serve snacks. Doeman's bosses would laugh and joke for a while then ratify the contracts, and they'd all take Dave to a luau later. And the buyers would all be celebrities and authors and scientists, banned in their own country but feted after they arrived in Rio Verde, welcomed to Disney World by Willard Scott and Mickey, and invited on the Letterman show with their brilliant real estate agent, Dave Nichols, who engineered their emigration.

And the sonofabitch would get my commissions, and then probably ask Patsy out.

Brent analyzed this latest soliloquy and wondered if the cabin pressurization was fully operational. The people across the way didn't look disoriented – it must only be out on his side of the cabin.

He thought about the transmission from Rio Verde to Hawaii. Did Laura get the instructions and the prelims done and onto a disc? And did Katy transmit it OK? Katy had worked with Felicia long enough to have a good handle on the data processing, but Felicia afforded a certain comfort zone. Without the documents he was stuck if Doeman wasn't to be there. And she wasn't, he hoped. The sweet smile, her parting shot yesterday afternoon, would be tough to resist on a warm Polynesian night.

8:30 a.m. Lunch should be rolling down the aisle soon. 10:30 in Rio Verde, six hours since his reheated pizza, 14 hours since the original version, 23 hours since his last maple bar, and 36 hours since his New York steak at The Shadows restaurant with Jane. As a hungry traveling man he was beginning to feel a kinship with the Donner Party on their journey.

8:32 a.m. *Where the hell is the lunch cart?*

He pulled out his crossword puzzle book. The sound of two pieces of stainless steel striking together resounded down the aisle, and he reasoned that it was either caused by the lids put over airline meals being nested, one atop another, or by the inlet guide vanes of the huge turbofan engine disintegrating twenty feet to his left and 36,000 feet over the Pacific Ocean. Either eventuality would terminate the discomfort he was starting to feel from certain starvation.

Happily the noise turned out to be the food covers clanking. The engine held, the altitude and course remained true, and a lunch cart taxied to a stop at his three o'clock, as they used to say on the Orion. Meat loaf was on the bill of fare, an excellent entrée with plenty of fruit and bread and a small salad. Brent later tried to sweet-talk the attendant out of another mini-loaf of the good stone bread, and she offered him a second lunch. He gladly took it, with another container of island punch, parking the standby meat loaf at the ready on the tray table of the vacant seat next to him.

Brent enjoyed the second serving, leaving naught but a piece of broccoli on each plate. He was not fond of broccoli. But all the rest was excellent.

Nourished, he rested again. The sun was now reflecting off the silver wing into the coach-class cabin. The blue of the sky seemed to meet the blue of the water below, and no defined horizon was visible. A few scattered clouds, benign and white like cotton balls, floated high over the airplane offering no respite from the sun's rays on the wing. Viewing out the window became difficult, with little to be seen. He lowered the shade and returned to his crossword book.

He drifted and thought of what might be happening at L&H, which seemed exponentially further away with each mile they covered, almost nine miles each minute. He smiled about Katy and her screwy 'Niner practice later that afternoon, actually not so much later. It was almost noon in Rio Verde. Could Pam handle the phones by herself? He longed for a walk around the reservoir and imagined how good a mile or so would feel right now after being cooped up for three hours. He wondered if Tom Yarbrough and the troops from the End of the Beginning would get the brass fan up while he was gone.

His drift continued, and he returned the pocket book to the seatback compartment. The plane's cabin was quiet now, few people moving around and the voices, laughing and talking earlier in the trip, were barely audible above the quiet whine of the engines and air conditioning fans. The sun was bright in the cabin, the passengers were going on vacation, most of them, it was early in the day at their destination and only noon where they had come from, but the mood in the cabin was somber, a quiet usually associated with red-eye flights out of the East coast.

Many were sleeping and had their seat backs reclined. He looked over the headrests up the long aisle to the restrooms amidships in the aircraft separating the aft seats of the first-class section from coach class.

He shuddered as if an electrical shock had snapped from one earpiece of his music headset right through his cranium to the other earpiece. He fell back into his seatback and took a few deep breaths. Then he sat up in his seat again and looked forward.

Six rows up, in the right seat of the center aisle, was a fist-sized blonde postiche just visible above the seat backs. He couldn't see her head, save for the upper curve of her right ear protruding from golden hair tightly-drawn upwards toward her barrette.

❖   ❖   ❖

She's probably the best friend you have right now. The string bean's probably the only one on your side, but she can't tell you that. She's just watching and waiting, letting Doeman lead her to whomever she wants."

Katy's words in the diner.

Brent sat tall and looked over the seats. The topknot didn't move, didn't turn from side to side, or lower. It just sat, immobile.

He continued to watch her. What would he see when she turned? He weighed the benefit of getting up, crossing from the left to the right aisle through the aft service area and returning forward up the right aisle, which would necessitate looking backwards and down as he passed her. Subtle. And what would he do when he saw her?

Howdy, Ma'am, you the new schoolmarm in town?

There wasn't a hell of a lot he could do. He just watched, and the postiche moved only occasionally as if she were reading a book.

His vigil continued. And the target held fast. He considered that it might be a postiche that somebody had crafted to set atop the seat cushion to slip him the rest of the way loose from his mental moorings, but he could see just enough motion to reveal an ear, or a sunglass frame as she occasionally looked up from whatever she was reading. But the tan, the angular sculpted face, and those big light-grey headlamps never came into view.

It's no big deal; there's a million skinny blondes in the world and you've seen one. Or two, or three, but it doesn't mean anything. A blonde never killed anybody yet.

He hated it when Katy was right.

Following a half-hour of sitting bolt upright in his seat to maintain his view over the headrests, he grew weary of watching the bun. Brent smiled. She could climb back over the seats with those long legs, plop down into the seat next to him, fold her sunglasses into her pocket so he could see her big grey-blue orbs, and he *still* wouldn't know a damn thing more about her than he did now.

But he remained captivated and continued to stare.

A flight attendant, the one who yielded the extra lunch, walked aft in the left aisle with no particular purpose, then stopped after she passed

Brent's row and turned to ask him why he didn't eat his broccoli. She was cute as a bug, and quite friendly.

He turned to look up, and he joked with her for a moment, then she left to answer an attendant call-light. The engines' pitch lowered, almost imperceptibly, and Brent felt the plane start into a gentle descent. Most passengers in the cabin probably didn't notice the change in attitude and the power reduction. He looked at his watch – 9:45. Three hours and twenty minutes into the flight, the letdown into Hawaiian airspace has started. In about 45 minutes the Hawk would start looking for his ride, what might be the ride of his life.

He rose up and looked back over the headrests.

She was gone.

The chignon was gone. In the seconds it took the attendant to joke about his broccoli, plus ten more seconds for his calculation of the 767's glide ratio, and a quick peek out the window to see if Mauna Kea was visible yet, the damn Falcon had gone.

She hadn't gone aft to the restrooms – he'd have noticed her if she had walked aft. She must have gone forward, into first-class, but that area had a cloth sash across the aisle to discourage entry.

A cloth sash? These people go through Schlage deadbolts like poop through a tin horn. How would a cloth sash stop her? She's forward, you're not. Go back to a crossword puzzle.

He unbuckled and stood up for the first time during the flight, feigning a stretch, which actually felt pretty good. Looking to the seat where she had been, he could tell that unless she was overtly ducking down and hiding, she was gone. The aisle was open to the restrooms, and he took a walk.

He returned to his seat and buckled up. He was totally frustrated, as if learning whether the winsome stranger's eyes were light grey or tartan plaid would make any significant contribution to a litany of continuing enigmas.

❖   ❖   ❖

And while with silent, lifting mind I've trod
  The high untrespassed sanctity of space…
    …put out my hand, and touched the face of God.

The level of activity picked up in the plane's cabin. Passengers, making a horseback guess that they'd be taxiing up to the terminal gate in twenty minutes or so, were starting to gather up their truck from their seat back pockets and load it into their carry-ons, and those with children were readying the kids to disembark. A few little guys, unaware that a forced yawn would pop the pressure from their ears, were whimpering.

And the attendants were gathering up the last of the coffee cups and lunch trays, and stowing pillows in the overhead compartments. The seat belt lights had been turned on. He looked out the window. The blue Pacific now formed a clear line where it met the skies on the horizon, and Mauna Kea poked above the haze as it always did when they brought the Orions into the Navy's Barbers Point station near Pearl Harbor.

The captain keyed his microphone, pausing the Webley Edwards slack-key guitar Hawaiian music that had been playing over the cabin's PA system for the past hour. Brent expected the usual Chuck Yeager drawl about the events that would take place in the next few minutes and the balmy temperature at the Honolulu airport.

"Ladies and gentlemen, this is Captain Kittell. On behalf of the flight crew I'd like to thank you for choosing us to fly you to the fiftieth state.

"We request at this time that passenger Hawk turn on his or her attendant call-lamp under the overhead compartments. We are holding a message for passenger Hawk. Please turn on your attendant call lamp."

Brent could see passengers looking forward and aft for passenger Hawk, and he joined them, wondering what kind of message could possibly be this urgent and command the cooperation of a flight crew, already busy working through traffic into the arrival corridor of an international airport.

None of the under-compartment lamps was lit. The attendants leaned over, searching for someone reaching up to press the lamp on.

That's me.

He sat, not wanting the flight to end this way, a flight somehow devoid, thus far, of the zombies that had been toying with him for three days.

He reached up and pressed the button, lighting the lamp and sounding a tone heard through most of the cabin.

An attendant, not the pretty one who yielded the lunch, stopped next to him.

"Mr. Hawk?"

Brent looked up at her with the look an adolescent gives the nurse calling his name in the dentist's office.

"Yes?"

"Mr. Hawk, would you please come with me to the aft compartment? We have a telephone there."

He followed her. He heard motors begin to extend the flaps from the wings.

She led him to the end of the aisle in an area used for food preparation enroute. She picked up a wall-mounted phone and spoke into it.

"Mr. Hawk is on the line."

She handed him the phone. A female voice, in the clipped tones of an air traffic controller, told him that she was patching a call from the airline's home office telephone switchboard onto their company surface-to-air UHF frequency. The next voice, she told him, would be the caller, and to talk in a normal voice, and warned him that the frequency was not discrete. He held on the line. The attendant watched him with a concerned look on her face.

A long tone started, then stopped, and a male voice came on the line.

"Mr. Hawk, you are in grave danger. This phone is not secure. The instructions will be brief and will not be repeated.

"When you are met at the airport there may be two or more parties holding signs with your name. Travel only with the party who displays a torn five-dollar bill. That bill will match the other part of the bill which is now in the front pages of a pocket book in your possession. That is all."

The line then emitted a continuous tone. He handed the phone to the attendant who touched a button and announced that the circuit was clear.

Brent asked the attendant if he could sit for a minute, and she unfolded the crew jump-seat. "You'll have to return to your seat in about five minutes, Mr. Hawk. Can I get you some water?"

He nodded.

A few minutes passed, and he returned to his seat, buckled the lap belt, and looked out the window. The plane was now obviously shedding altitude, and some buildings on Waikiki Beach were identifiable. The plane shuddered as the landing gear dropped into place. The flaps were almost fully extended; the plane would shortly turn onto final approach.

You are in grave danger.

Calls are not easily placed to passengers aboard an airliner in flight. Someone very powerful was at the helm of this operation.

Falcon? No – she was on the plane. But she had to be a player in the cast.

Katy's words echoed: *Don't get between Doeman and that skinny blonde. And don't get mixed up in a female catfight – that's what this has turned into, and you'll lose.*

He remembered the rest of the instructions: *in the front pages of a pocket book in your possession.*

The crossword book was still in the compartment in front of him. The flaps had extended fully, and the plane slowed again. Tied-down small private airplanes lined the runway now passing rapidly beneath him, with the airliners of many nations queued up at the terminal.

He opened the book. The remnant of a five-dollar bill, torn almost diagonally in half, fell from the book into his lap.

It wasn't there when he left to answer the radiophone.

Christ, I could have looked down the aisle and seen anybody near my seat while I was on that phone.

The only passengers with line-of-sight to his seat were across two aisles. Their attention was turned toward the window on the right side of the plane, an island paradise unfolding beneath them.

A slight puff of rubber smoke flew back as the tires met the runway. Brent could see the reversing deflectors under the engine snap open as the crew ran the power back up, slowing the big plane in time to turn onto the high-speed turnout to the terminal.

Brent saw the deflectors open with his eyes and heard the engines spool up with his ears. But the capacity of his mind to process visual and aural input was now impaired. A week of shocks to his emotions had triggered a cumulative effect, and what might have been a minor enigma on Tuesday might today, following the sighting of the woman he called *Falcon* on the plane with him, be the straw that would break him. Unlike anything else that happened during the week, the on-board phone call, an exigency he had never even heard of before, and the torn bill appearing right under his nose had unraveled him physically and emotionally. He was close to breaking; he knew it, and it scared him. He had lost control.

The 767 crawled to the gate, the whine of the engines suddenly quieted, and the air-stair mated with the main cabin door to allow 223 passengers to disembark and begin their vacations. Passenger #224 sat alone on the plane, his head back against the headrest and his eyes staring at the overhead compartment. The nearest attendant was a dozen rows behind him and unable to see him. He put the torn bill in his pocket.

He pulled his satchel from beneath the seat and walked forward toward the door. The plane was now vacant save for some janitors who had come aboard and the flight crew still in the cockpit, their door latched open. On a better day he'd have told the crew of his Navy P-3 time and asked for a check ride on the color monitor displays glowing on the dash panel. And in the kindred spirit that binds all airmen together, they would probably have invited him in.

But on this late morning the first officer looked at Brent as he turned to leave the airliner, assessed his apple-green countenance, and became mildly apologetic. "Hope our descent wasn't too fast, but it looks like it might have been. Honolulu Approach dropped us faster than we'd have liked to, and I'm afraid it was kind of hard on you folks who haven't flown too often. Have a nice vacation."

Brent thanked him weakly and walked through the air-stair. The two-story window in the terminal building framed his first view of the blue ocean and the island, Diamond Head in the background. He was starting to feel better.

He fingered the torn bill in his trouser pocket and recalled the words of the resident Island heartthrob, Thomas Sullivan Magnum, P.I.

Just another day in Paradise...

CHAPTER SEVENTEEN

Friday noon: A lift from the airport...

The expansive Delta concourse was almost uninhabited during this lull between arrivals and departures. A few ground attendants were huddled around the counter of gate 21 where Brent had disembarked, engaging in some light conversation and relaxing following the onslaught of 224 souls from the 767 parked just outside the window behind the counter. One was sliding new flight numbers onto a display to indicate a 3:15 PM departure to LAX.

Brent was in Hawaii, two million Americans would give their all to be standing where he was standing, yet the only thought he could muster now was how nice it would be to be back in his old seat 33A when that big baby was refueled and pushed back, taxied onto the active, run up and slipped from the surly bonds of paradise. He had friends in LA – it might take a six-pack or two to explain to them the circuitous week-long route he took to have arrived there, and they still probably wouldn't believe him. The San Diego freeway ran right in front of LAX, maybe they could just give him a lift down the 405, hop off on the 20 to Costa Mesa, and drop him off at Balboa. It would only be 50 miles out of their way, but Patsy would just love to see him following their two days apart.

Sure she would. That's what I'll do.

He picked up his bag and started the long walk toward the *Baggage and Ground Transportation* area indicated by the arrow over his head. He glanced over his shoulder. Save for the airline and airport workers in the gate lounges he was passing, the aisle was empty.

He thought to himself, why am I being met by a person holding a sign? Surely, with all their space age toys they could have taken a photo of me and transmitted it to whoever is giving me the ride.

Maybe a code-name like *Hawk* does nothing to establish identity.

A photo of me could be intercepted, and they'd all know what I look like. But the *Hawk* code could be changed by a phone call if the plan was penetrated. Within Doeman's ranks my strings are being pulled by those who know me as Hawk, and the others can't manipulate me. That's got to be it...

He looked over his shoulder as he came to the concourse's intersection with the main terminal. A hundred passengers were lined up at five carry-on luggage X-ray machines. Only a plain-looking woman in a blue and white seersucker jacket and skirt that he'd seen back at the gate was walking along behind him, but he hadn't picked up a "tail" like he thought he might.

If the Scorpion were sending me to Hawaii he'd know where I was from the minute I got off the damn plane.

That's it! There's a faction-within-a-faction, not to be confused with the catfight between Doeman and the Falcon, who apparently serve totally separate masters. Not to say that they're good or bad – anybody who believes in their own principles is good, and those who don't are bad. Simple as that. Where that leaves the Falcon remains to be seen. In this game of nerves, jerseys with numbers wouldn't be a bad idea.

Then we have the five-dollar bill angle. Whoever cooked that stunt up knows the *Hawk* code-name but has moved a notch up in the hierarchy. Three signs from three drivers may appear with the *Hawk* code in the taxi zone, but only one will have the torn five-dollar bill that matches his.

Still thinking to himself he reasoned that that side has demonstrated some juice too – they phoned me in an airliner in flight.

You are in grave danger.

How could I be in grave danger? I don't have the money yet, so I can't get conked over the head for it. Where the buyers bought the four houses, if they buy them at all – and given all the recent surveillance, bugging, and dumpster-raiding, by now is probably the second-best known fact in Rio Verde. Right behind the first-place *Doeman-and-Douglas* show of Wednesday night.

And after the past three days, Jeff Terrell's wife's paranoia, and Susie Santini's departure from Sunset Escrow notwithstanding, Brent was starting to wonder how this could imperil him so greatly anyway. So what's the danger, really?

He sat down on a bench for a short break. He'd been in Hawaii for ten minutes and wouldn't mind watching at least one well-filled-out little sundress pass by. He took off his sport coat and hung it on the end of the bench.

Across the concourse the woman in seersucker stopped at an espresso stand. Brent didn't notice her.

❖   ❖   ❖

He lazily watched the tourists in the busy airport, the tanned bodies standing in the luggage X-ray lines on the way out to the gates and the Mainland, and the paler faces of those, like himself, on the way to the hotels and the beaches.

The rest felt good. He had been on the move since he woke up this morning – getting to the school to meet the shuttle, driving the thing to the airport, and checking in at the airline gate. Then four uninterrupted hours in a machine full of vibrations and bells and strangers' voices, standing up only once to see if the Falcon was hiding from him, and then walking aft to the restroom. He sat on the bench, people-watching for ten minutes. He smiled to himself as he envisioned a crowd of people bearing Hawk signs, all standing in the parking lot right now wondering where the hell he was.

And he thought about that. Were he a courier sent to pick up B Hawk, and were he to see another courier with the same sign, he might be inclined to wonder if there were enough hawks to go around.

This spy business has its own rules of etiquette. Scorpion, take note.

But he had a job to do, and the hesitation he had known about this journey since Doeman sprung it on him yesterday had give way to the anticipation of suspense and adventure that he had yearned for for his entire adult life. The events in the next few hours could make the Realtor's evening with the DEA agents in the hotel in West Palm Beach look mundane.

Of course, that guy wore a bullet-proof vest and had seven narcs with riot guns backing him up in the next room...

He scooped up his sport coat and his bag and walked again. A sign pointing down and to the right directed arriving passengers to the baggage claim area. He was probably the only passenger to arrive in Honolulu today or any day with only carry-on luggage, and he walked past the crowded baggage carousels.

The air conditioning had felt good in the terminal, and as he walked toward the automatic outside door it slid open, and he felt the natural island air. The outside air was neither hot nor cool by any means, but temperate and pleasantly humid, well short of the mugginess he had known in the Far East. He had been here many times before, and it was always this first scent of the Islands that he enjoyed the most – the fragrances of a dozen different tropical flowers and shrubs, here cultivated in profusion in a huge landscaped area just outside the terminal door. In spite of the dubious nature of his trip it was good to be back.

The party could start any time. He had arrived at the airport and left the terminal. He was outside in the ground transportation area. Taxis and limousines, many with the crests of popular hotels on their doors, and minibuses from a half-dozen rental car agencies lined the curbs under the canopy half-open to the blue sky. The limousines congregated in an area a hundred feet away. He looked for a driver holding a sign lettered Hawk.

Instinctively he pulled his Navy-issue sunglasses from his shirt pocket and slipped them on, partly to knock down the bright sunlight, but now also to allow him to scan the crowd from behind the black lenses without the crowd being too sure who he was eyeballing. As he walked toward the parked limousines he could see a score of drivers standing by parked limos in a variety of costumes, most island-inspired, a few more sedate from the major hotels, but none in the black suits accepted in the more cosmopolitan cities as the livery of a chauffeur.

Brent looked at the names on the signs that many of them were holding, a menu of surnames drawn from an international phone book, a few in brush-stroked Chinese characters. He also watched the eyes of many of the drivers and the tourists standing in the area ostensibly awaiting a cab or a rental-car shuttle. One or more of them could also be interested in the arrival of the visitor from Rio Verde.

How many people on this island know what I look like?

One man caught his eye, a youngish Oriental, Japanese, he thought, short, about Doeman's height. He was standing across the driveway from most of the passengers, paying little attention to anything in particular. It was his clothing, and the physique he had hung them on, that drew Brent's attention.

He was wearing a sleeveless black T-shirt with black knee-length pants, tight at the waist, which Brent estimated to be about a 34, loose through the thighs, and drawing tight again just below the knee. The cut of the garments was somewhere between martial arts apparel and the style popularized by the California surfers. The bamboo tabiis on his feet, an Oriental calligraphy embroidered on the back of his shirt, and the braided queue of a samurai warrior swung the pendulum toward the martial arts influence. The rest of his scalp was shaved and as deeply tanned as the rest of his body. The long black goatee was a dramatic touch.

His arms were massive, the size of Brent's thighs, on shoulders consistent with his biceps. And his calves below the pants were proportionally as large. A tattoo of linked chain girded his left bicep at its midpoint in an inch-wide band, and a bird with golden-feathered plumage decorated his right arm. He wore many bracelets on each thick wrist and a jade hoop earring in his left ear.

And even though he was wearing tiny round gold-framed sunglasses, Brent could tell he had a glare in his eye, the kind of glare you don't have to see through the glasses. His glare was one you could *feel* across a dark parking lot on a moonless night.

The man was as menacing as any person Brent had ever encountered, and he didn't look to be even working at it. He was just standing there passing time. He wondered what it would be like to wake up some morning – this morning would have been nice – with that look in his eye, those arms, the tattoos and the earring and go forth to the four o'clock meeting with Doeman's bosses and tell them just how the cow was going to eat the cabbage.

Brent looked back at the limo drivers.

A nondescript woman had joined the group of drivers with a sign on a stick with a passenger's name, looking at the crowd of passengers spilling from the terminal door. She stood out from the crowd, separated by her light blue jacket and skirt more consistent with Mainland attire and not the usual garb of a limousine driver. She was relatively pale, definitely not a resident of the islands, and carried a good-size purse on a strap slung over her shoulder. Brent had seen policewomen carrying purses this big, usually to enclose a pistol. While this woman didn't fit the police stereotype, a gun in her purse was still a possibility. But she didn't fit into any of his past 48 hours of mega-scenarios.

He had to move to see her sign, obscured behind those of several other drivers. A step or two to the left and he could see the name:

Hawk

She looked around the crowd. Brent thought back to his walk from the terminal gate to the main foyer of the airport. He looked again at her blazer. It was seersucker.

She had followed him – why he noticed the seersucker he couldn't remember, except that he liked the summer fabric and had a couple of seersucker sport coats. She stood looking at the crowd, knowing damn well who he was. He let the charade continue for a moment while he collected his thoughts, careful not to let his glance fall on the sign again or meet with hers. He was probably being watched by others.

He fingered the torn half-bill in his pocket. At what point would she reveal her half, if she had it? She didn't look like the type to be mixed up in this kind of sordid endeavor.

But neither did Doeman.

No other *Hawk* signs appeared. Nor did she reach in her purse or a pocket for a bill.

He bit the bullet and stepped forward out of the small crowd of people that he'd been with. He reached into his pocket and pulled out his torn bill, holding it low like one might hold a tip for a maître d', and looked at her. He caught her eye, and their eyes remained locked through both their sunglasses. He raised the hand with the torn bill slightly, now holding it more obviously like a Kleenex. She didn't move.

Now what do I do?

He looked away and watched an MD-11 that was climbing out for points unknown, wishing to some degree that he was aboard it, wherever it was going. Brent had quit smoking years before, but he thought that this would be a time when the Scorpion would have lit a smoke. He waited for a few minutes glancing around to see if she had a partner in league with her, and speculated for the first time in 24 hours about whether this could turn into a forced abduction, the pencil-pusher being dragged kicking and punching into a waiting car.

She held her ground, not moving or looking back at him, content to stare into the crowd for this *Hawk* fellow she was booked to pick up.

Brent decided to approach her, holding the bill more openly, looking for a response. She had the only sign – the voice on the radiophone had said *There may be two or more parties holding signs with your name.* OK, so there weren't. Maybe this was a false alarm, or she didn't get the message. He picked up his bag and started to walk toward her, slowly. And he thought while he walked of the other warnings on the radiophone.

You are in grave danger.

Travel only with a party who displays a torn five-dollar bill.

And his own thoughts:

Someone very powerful is at the helm of this operation.

His pace slowed. Someone had moved heaven and earth to place a call to an airliner.

Falcon was aboard the airliner.

Katy's words in the diner:

The stringbean's probably the only one on your side.

Brent stopped after five paces toward the driver with his sign. Something was wrong with this picture. He felt a tap on his shoulder and turned around.

The terrifying countenance of the muscular warrior-in-black was standing behind him and spoke sternly in a low voice devoid of accent,

"Mr. Hawk….?"

Brent turned to face him, and the specter of this person, obviously even shorter than Doeman now when standing four feet away, loomed even larger as a threat. The tan seemed darker, the extremities more well-developed, and the resonance of the voice, although only two words were spoken, sent chills down Brent's spine. He was standing with his feet well apart, his arms crossed, holding something in his right hand hidden by the left bicep with the tattooed chain encircling it. Brent could tell at this range that it depicted beads of jade connected with gold link. The tattoo was nothing short of a work of art.

"Yes?" Brent looked at him, the glaring eyes hidden behind the little round shades.

"I believe this fell out of your case when you were sitting in the terminal lobby." He handed Brent a pocket book. Brent took it as his crossword puzzle book and started to slide it into his bag.

"Oh, thank you ver…." Brent saw the book's cover and yanked it back out. The warrior smirked.

BFD 4/94 had been inked in, in Brent's own scrawl.

It was *his* Grisham.

"How did…?" No. No point in asking how this man came to be in possession of a book that disappeared three days and 2,000 miles ago. Nor did he ask the next logical questions: *Why are you giving me this book? There's a message – what is it?*

If anything made any sense, the book was taken by the two in the white van cleaning his carpet, who were not on Doeman's team. This man, therefore, was Doeman's enemy. Or at least her opposition.

The meeting was arranged by Doeman; therefore this man is not taking me to the meeting. Assuming I go with him. Also assuming he asks me to go anywhere, which he hasn't.

If anything makes any sense, that postulation and conclusion do.

Brent spoke: "Thank you."

"You're more than welcome." The warrior crossed his arms over his chest. Brent looked at his right bicep. The detail on the tattoo he had seen from a distance was astounding at close range. On an average man artwork this expansive would have had to be applied to the back or the chest. It was a bird in flight, soaring with wings outspread, delicate feathers extending from the back of the golden wings to muffle the sound of the bird's inexorable approach to his prey. The bird's eyes were orange with the characteristic vertical iris of a nocturnal hunter, and mean, not unlike the warrior's. Smaller white feathers protected the bird's yellow talons from the hapless prey's teeth, and the bird's white head on the anterior curve of the warrior's tanned arm led into the orange hooked beak of a raptor.

Christ.

Brent stopped and looked at the warrior's face and saw the slight hint of a smile.

A raptor.

A *hawk*.

The warrior did not move. Brent thought for a moment. He'd concluded that this person was among Jane's opposition. But she herself came up with the *Hawk* appellation, and used it on his airline ticket. The tattoo was either a remarkable fluke, or Jane, herself, had turned on her bosses and was now in league with the Falcon.

"You will come with me, please, now," the warrior spoke, the *please* a mere formality. Brent resisted, picking up his bag and stepping back several paces, looking for an exit route. The warrior could surely decapitate him with his bare hands if he could catch him, but Brent, knowing that he didn't have much to lose, was willing to take the chance that the guy didn't have a great set of wheels for a 50-yard sprint.

The warrior saw this all in Brent's response and quickly reached into a deep cargo pocket on his thigh and pulled out the crumpled half of a five-dollar bill and handed it to Brent.

Brent straightened it and pulled his partial bill from his trouser pocket and spread it open.

He then held the two hemispheres of Honest Abe's bifurcated skull together. They mated. The warrior took them from him and put the pieces back into his pocket. The warrior nodded at the driver in a parked limousine, and it pulled into a space near them. The warrior opened the passenger-side rear door and motioned for Brent to get in. As he did he looked over his shoulder for the woman in the seersucker outfit. She was gone. The limo pulled away from the curb rapidly and changed lanes into the route that would take them out of the airport complex.

❖　　❖　　❖

Travel only with a party who displays a torn five-dollar bill.

So far, so good. The well-traveled bill was again intact. Interesting. The bill had to be torn by someone on the Mainland, prior to departure. This wasn't dreamed up in Hawaii by some of Doeman's or the Falcon's big brass after the plane had departed.

Stretch might haul your tail out of it before you get hurt.

Katy's words. Prophetic? Maybe. Doeman knew the *Hawk* routine, probably before the Falcon did. That elevated the probability that the two were now joined in cahoots against Doeman's clients.

Former clients.

Brent thought of the old bromide that *When you're up to your ass in alligators, it's difficult to remember that the objective was to drain the swamp.* In this case the swamp was represented by a bunch of terrorists who wanted a roof over their heads. That's how it started Monday anyway. Now less was making any sense hour by hour. Brent was at a loss to understand the players' relationship to each other.

Just don't get caught between Doeman and that skinny blonde. If us girls are reading it right, they've got their own score to settle, and the government and witness things have long since been left in the dust. This is a female catfight now.

Brent glanced around the old Caddy limousine. He thought it was about a '70, knew it was silver and had been pretty well used during its lifetime. Cars don't hold up real well in Hawaii. He hadn't seen a hotel name or crest on the doors or back window, nor a commercial license plate like a vehicle-for-hire uses, but then he didn't have a lot of time to absorb its grandeur from the outside before Fu Manchu virtually stuffed him into it.

The interior was huge; from the rear seat where he was directed, to the rear-facing seat at the forward bulkhead of the passenger compartment where the warrior sat, staring at him, unblinking. Two forward-facing jump seats were available. They were folded down into two little humps on the floor. The driver and front seat passengers sat in front of the bulkhead, the compartments separated by near-opaque glass panes which could slide apart like the sliding back windows in pickup trucks. They were closed now. Brent knew there must be a driver up there, only because the vehicle was staying on the road in spite of its high rate of speed, which suggested the presence of a driver. He thought he could see a silhouetted head move occasionally on the passenger side but couldn't clearly tell and didn't really give a damn.

The warrior saw the mental gyrations that must have been going on in Brent's mind. He spoke again in a voice Brent could barely hear across the long compartment:

"You are safe. You must practice relaxation techniques now. Nothing will go wrong while you are with me. Good things are planned for you."

Stretch might haul your tail out of it before you get hurt.

He had been in the car for an hour, most of which time he had been awake, a small part asleep and the rest a-something-in-between, trying to evade the stare of his bespectacled host who had moved not a big muscle since the car pulled out of the airport onto a freeway nor after the roads became narrower and slower. Brent attempted conversation a time or two, to no avail. Other than his few words of reassurance, the guy was a sphinx.

The view could have been pleasant; the road they were traveling certainly was. The urban area around the airport and downtown Honolulu had transformed into a rural ocean view with rolling hills and agrarian scenes not unlike Rio Verde's on one side of the road, and a series of small homes and condominiums and an occasional neighborhood market passing on the ocean side. But the limo's windows were almost as opaque as the divider between driver and the driven, and the luster of the island greenery was almost totally obscured. He'd hate to ride in this buggy after dark.

The rear window was somewhat clearer, and Brent was able to see out of it by looking directly ahead at the dark divider window that worked as an oversize rear-view mirror. He watched the rural island panorama as it receded into the distance, not a bad vantage point once he became used to watching a mirror-image.

After about 10 miles, a van, and to no great surprise for Brent, a white van joined them through the last two turns the limo had to make to get onto a road along the coast that would have afforded an absolutely spectacular view had he not been seeing it from the inside of a Noxema bottle.

The van flashed its headlights twice, and the limousine pulled over to the side of the road, the van pulling off to the limo's right and stopping alongside it, just far enough away to get the limo's passenger door open.

The limo driver and the passenger, if any, stayed in their seats while the warrior opened the limo's passenger-side rear door, and then stepped out onto the red soil on the shoulder.

"You wait here," he glared at Brent.

No problem. Couldn't agree more.

The van was so close to the limousine that Brent couldn't tell what was happening. He knew it was too early for the meeting by about two and a half hours, and he knew he didn't want to get saddled with a satchel full of money yet, and he knew for damn sure that he didn't want to get into that windowless van on this deserted rural road.

And he recalled the warrior's calming words, struggling to believe them. And now beginning to.

He heard the sliding door on the other side of the van open, then voices coming from inside it. After a few minutes he heard the door slide closed.

The van accelerated as fast as it could short of raising a cloud of red dust. As soon as its rear tires touched the pavement, the driver floor-boarded it. Brent watched it as it fishtailed off down the road.

But he should have been looking out the open rear door of the limousine. A figure had been standing next to it as the van sped away. It was wearing a long violet muumuu and a straw hat with a wide violet band drawn through the hat's brim and tied below her chin. The sunglasses were huge, and with the pulled-down hat brim covered most of the face.

Brent didn't see her until she was almost all of the way into the limousine, pulling the door closed behind her as she fell onto the floor. The Caddy pulled out onto the road as fast as a three-ton limo with a twenty-year-old engine could accelerate.

He looked at the bright floral lump on the limo's floor, his innate ability to sort out visual input and correlate it to the world around him having been decimated in the past few days. He was in what a clinician might call a state of shock as he looked at her but nothing registered. It was a woman – only that much cognizance was left in him.

Patsy pulled off the hat with one hand and shook her light auburn hair until it tumbled over her shoulders. With the other hand she yanked off the sunglasses, then crawled the two feet back to where Brent sat, pushed his knees apart, and still kneeling, fell against him, then put her arms around him and whispered into his ear:

"Happy birthday, Skipper!"

CHAPTER EIGHTEEN

Brent's Dénouement: A Killing in Real Estate...

Brent put his arms around Patsy, one hand high on her neck, the other low across her waist, and held her tightly, less a hug inspired by love and affection than one of fear, an innate human reaction like the strength imparted to a child holding a parent as if it would make everything OK when things go bump in the night. The limo continued its trip down the narrow road along the coast for many minutes while Patsy, still kneeling on the floor, rested against his chest, her head on his shoulder. Neither spoke.

She finally looked up at him and could sense the confusion and a trace of residual terror in his eyes, both open, staring at the headliner of the car. His breath was coming in long cycles, and she could tell his mind was racing. She finally broke the silence.

"It's over."

He recalled the warrior's words: *Good things are going to happen to you.*

But he also recalled the ecstasy and relief that he enjoyed so briefly yesterday afternoon when he awoke from his nap and thought the whole Doeman thing had been a dream. Then he recalled his frustration when he realized that the past few days hadn't been a dream, and that he was still in the same pickle he had been in before he fell asleep.

But over the past three days, he had become increasingly skeptical of every innocuous occurrence that befell him, and instinctively sought the darkest explanation conceivable. He was holding his best friend, the one who could have given him the most strength to endure the week, yet he felt a fleeting distrust for her too.

Patsy's involved with Doeman or Falcon somehow. Is she going to the meeting too? Is she a part of this now? What can I safely tell her?

She pulled herself to her feet and swung around to sit close next to him. He lifted his right arm over her shoulder and pulled her tight, although not the death-grip that he'd held for their first few miles together. He looked at his watch. 2:10. The meeting was in less than two hours.

"It's over," she said. "We're on Hawaiian time now – none whatsoever. You have nowhere to be today. The week is over."

She sat up and away from him for a moment and pulled her legs up on the seat facing him.

"Katy was right," she said. "We took this thing too far."

He looked at her.

This thing?

"What do you *mean?*" he asked. "What do you know about this week?" He took both her hands and asked her again, "Do you know anything about what's been going on?"

"Yep. I was there on day one, Monday. You've got a week to hear about it, and it might take me that long to unravel it. But you're OK. Get it through your head – there's no meeting this afternoon, no spies, no carpet cleaners, no bugs in your wagon."

She moved up and sat on his lap, and he toppled over to his left until he sat half-against the door of the limo.

"But before you get to hear anything about the hole the Scorpion dug himself into, I want to find out if that little trollop taught you any new tricks behind the bed-and-breakfast Wednesday night!" She fell deeper into his arms.

Brent felt instantly better. Brent's extracurricular nocturnal activities in the shadows of the bed-and-breakfast on Wednesday night had formed the focus of her screaming, crying one-sided conversation yesterday, and her joking admission now that she was "in" on that peccadillo took some pressure off him. And the feel of her soft flesh and the nylon bikini bottom where his right hand rested under her muumuu further decreased some pent-up tension…

Whether the admission or the touch had created this instantaneous quantum loss of stress, he knew that the instinctive and habitual paranoia he had worked himself into would take a few more days to subside. But he also knew that he was starting out of the woods. Brent laughed out loud, a hardy, long laugh, as he realized that he had been the object of the greatest low-budget sting in the annals of modern man.

But he'd come this far – he could wait a few miles to hear about it. He had other matters to attend to at the moment, delivered to him by a white van and all topped with auburn hair and freckles.

The two lovers, each only a few years away from membership in the AARP, commenced to make up for lost time in a sequence of necking, petting, groping, and giggling that neither had engaged in in the back seat of a car since Gidget Goes Hawaiian played the drive-in back home in Rio Verde.

❖   ❖   ❖

The two came up for air in about five minutes, and Patsy reached into a beach bag that she had carried aboard earlier in her crash-landing into the limo as the van screeched away. She pulled from the bag a red plastic Thermos bottle, and digging deeper, two Styrofoam cups. She placed the cups in Brent's hands.

She sat back on the seat right next to him. He looked at her for the first time in several days. It occurred to him that the last time he saw her was Wednesday morning at the office meeting.

"Where are we going?" he asked.

"Down the road."

"Somehow I suspected that. What's in the Thermos?"

Within the Thermos was some sort of island Kickapoo-joy-juice, golden and cold as it flowed from the bottle. And welcome. Brent hadn't had anything to drink since the coffee on the airplane.

"How much further are we going?"

She looked out the window. "I'd guess about ten miles. Or do you spies use *kilometers*?"

"Cut the crap. Are you sure I don't have to be at a meeting at four o'clock?"

Brent was up to 80 percent sure that Doeman *et al* were fictional, but little leftover fears still plagued him.

"There's no meeting."

"OK, from the top, Patsy. You fruitcakes have taken ten years off my life. Who all was in on this?"

"Everybody in your life including your mother. From the top?"

"Yep. From day one." He sat back and enjoyed his fruit punch.

Patsy stared off into space for a few minutes. "I knew this moment would come, but so many things have happened that I don't know if I can keep them straight myself.

"For openers, my sister Shannon was in town with a friend of ours from LA for a travel agency computer software convention at the Best Western in Fairfax."

Brent recalled that Patsy had a younger sister whom he'd never met. And he remembered Patsy saying once that she worked for an airline in their computer scheduling and ticketing complex.

"And Irma Landau approached me a couple weeks ago, said the company's been making money hand-over-fist and wanted an idea about what to do for your bonus this year. And I reminded her that your birthday was a few weeks away, and that maybe we could tie the bonus and your birthday together for a big party or something."

His *birthday. Today!*

He'd completely spaced it.

Patsy had wished him a happy birthday when she fell into the limousine. In the confusion, he'd missed that entirely. It couldn't have had anything to do with the shock he felt at that instant, trading in a menacing late-model warrior for an older lass who's last words to him were that she'd like to kill him.

"How does this fit in with Doeman? Are you going to tell me about that, or dink around with your sister and Irma's life story?" Then he asked, "Or do you even know who *Doeman* is?"

"Of course I do. And keep your shirt on, I'm getting there. This thing didn't come together easy, and I'm not going to explain it in two sentences."

She looked at his rumpled oxford cloth office costume. "Actually you can take your shirt off, if you want. You look ridiculous. Where did you think you were going when you got dressed this morning, church?" Then she continued.

"I know everything you did this week, from Monday afternoon on. You've probably long since forgotten that you were going to try to play with Dave's head with one of your goofball Scorpion fantasies. I was having lunch with Shannon and our friend Monday and told them you wanted an IBM-lady or whoever she was supposed to be to come into the office and act like Pussy Galore out of Harvard Business School. My sister asked if you still thought you could be the next Ludlum or Forsythe if only you could learn how to type. Then we all thought of a dozen different ways that we could chase Dave's tail all over the valley."

Patsy's words Monday morning: "I'll call sis and we'll add some girl stuff that will even scare you."

Not what I had in mind…

Patsy went on. "Then I told them that the two old codgers that own the office, or at least their wives, wanted to do something for your bonus, and we came up with some ideas for that, and we talked about that for a while. We sat around for about an hour and a half after lunch, plotting a move against Dave. Both the girls were in town for the week on their companies' nickels, with four hours in class and the rest of each day to run around loose. Dave would have had no idea what would be happening to him. We would, but we needed a plot to tie it together.

"After about two pitchers of margaritas this beautiful truth came to us – the whole stunt would be totally lost on a jerk like Dave. We were coming up with some heavy stuff, but we would have needed some cooperation, like Felicia or Katy at the switchboard and almost the whole office staff. Most of these people could give a damn about Dave, and the fun would go out of it, and the thing would fizzle before it came to fruition."

Brent interceded, "Did you know what that fruition was going to be?"

"No, but we knew whatever it was was too good to waste on Nichols. So we thought, who is deserving of this much attention from his, or her, friends?

"And my name naturally came up."

Brent smiled. Baiting Nichols with the floor call seemed like a lot longer than four days ago.

"Who came up with the relocated witness premise?" Brent asked. "It was a good one."

Patsy looked out the window and at her watch as if she were looking for somewhere they were supposed to be. Brent, by force of a reflex he'd picked up in the past week, jumped out of his skin, looked out the back window, and looked at *his* watch.

"Little jumpy are we, Skipper? I'm just trying to figure out where we are. Yes, we are going somewhere. Most vehicles in motion are. And no one, to my knowledge, with bedroom eyes, a white van, or a sack full of money is going to be there waiting. I'll take it back about the bedroom eyes – *I'll* be there. Now relax."

She picked up the Thermos and refilled their cups. He allowed that a sandwich wouldn't go too badly right now either. She kept looking out the side window, almost an impossibility through the dark shading.

"Anyway, we went our separate ways after lunch Monday. But the work wasn't over for the day. We had a whole headful of ideas, no common thread, but we knew that even with what we already had that we could put you off your trolley. I called Katy, told her that you and I were going to dinner and to call a war council of the office for that night at Round Table. She did. Sis brought the preliminary ideas to the pizza parlor. Be pleased to know that while we dined at the Green Mill Inn, 16 of your fans from the office, plus both the receptionists, a few stray husbands and wives, and someone who thought it was an Amway meeting gave up their evening to plan the demise of the Scorpion. Oh, and Mrs. Landau was there. Pete and Holly sent their regrets, as they were quite busy showing a listing."

Brent smiled. Pete and Holly had no regrets that night.

"Irma Landau went to the *Round Table*? Did she wear her fur stole or just a summery little St. Laurent thing?"

"She wore jeans and bought the first pitchers, but it gets better."

He started to ask how it could get better than that, but she put her finger to her lips. He quieted. For a minute.

"You mean to tell me that everyone in the office was wise to this from Monday night on?"

"Everyone but Nichols. We figured that he'd screw it up somehow, and he's unconscious to whatever goes on anyway, so he kind of got left out."

Brent found himself silently recounting the chronology of the week, as Patsy sat forward, apparently still looking for some landmark or familiar point in the road. The rural setting with the older weathered homes and farms had started to give way to more upscale condominiums and apartment complexes on the ocean side of the road with imposing gated entrances and wide greenbelts separating them. A landing strip had been carved from the cane fields toward the mountains, a low two-story tower suggestive of a Japanese shrine controlling the flights of many larger turboprop aircraft and a few helicopters.

This was not the low-rent district.

Brent thought about home. He was in the islands – with a toothbrush, two cameras, and that's about all – running around the back side of Oahu to a meeting that wasn't going to be, his Explorer sitting out in a schoolyard 2,000 miles away, his ukulele going out of tune in the afternoon sun on his deck, no ticket home, and riding in somebody's aging limousine to God-knows-where.

And they've probably forgotten about me at work. Somebody else – Tom – can handle the tough questions and change the toner in the copier. By Monday they'll all have signs on their cars with their home numbers. And Katy will have stuffed animals all over the lobby, and the illiterate janitor will take the BB63 cap to his kid. They won't need me anymore. But what the hell, they didn't even like me before I left.

He thought about Doeman. What a piece of work – probably could be in the running for an Oscar. And the high-tech stuff. How did they get access to the sophisticated repeating four-letter-code pattern? And the barcode reader Doeman used Wednesday?

How the "assassins" got his unlisted phone numbers was no mystery now – half the office knew them. Ditto the keys to his townhouse and the Explorer – he had duplicates in his desk drawer and hanging on a nail in his carport.

"Who played the part of Doeman?" he asked Patsy who had sat back in her seat, close to him, as if she'd found her bearings.

"What did you think of her?" Patsy asked, glancing toward the driver. "Was she a pretty credible operative?"

Brent daydreamed off to dinner at The Shadows and the candlelight as Doeman wove her tale of her father while she rubbed his ankle with hers and held his hands tightly. He'd like to know who scripted that yarn.

"Yeah. Who'd you guys recruit to play her part? She was damn good."

"I understand that you came close to finding out just how good she really was. Maybe you should meet her again sometime, this time in broad daylight with little ol' Patsy chaperoning. Would you like that?"

Brent had to think twice about that. Some memories are better left alone to age like fine wine, with the knowledge that you can't go back. He may never see her again without smelling a phantom trace of gardenias and hearing a Scott Joplin slow drag. What made Wednesday night magical was the temporal nature of his attraction for Doeman – an affinity that could never exist past midnight.

Sure. Why don't you just tell little ol' Patsy why you'd rather pass on that reunion. She'll understand.

He finally answered, "Oh, maybe someday, but I don't know how it could ever come to be."

Patsy reached across him to push a button on the door, its nickel plating well worn with use. He heard a chime beyond the opaque glass obscuring the chauffeur's seat.

The sliding panels of glass separated slightly, then he saw four fingers with polished nails grab the right panel and pull it open, then reach across to push the left panel open. Two faces turned to smile at him, then finally laugh out loud, the face on the left then turned back to watch the road. He saw her eyes in the rear-view mirror. They were dark, with dark eyebrows, and they sparkled as she laughed. A gardenia was tucked into the right side of her collar-length black hair.

Doeman.

Was the gardenia planned with malice aforethought to expedite my trip to the booby hatch, or a mere fluke that she plucked off a tree just before she got in the limo with the warrior?

Data was beginning to filter through his retinas, slowly into his brain for processing, like a 1950s TV set when jet-black became black-and-grey, then lightened here and there to white after the set was turned on, revealing a picture over a few moments in time. On the figure sitting in the passenger seat he noticed first a blonde chignon, and as that vision was being processed he saw the eyes. No Elton John shades, no shadow of a stairwell in The Shadows to obscure them.

Light grey with a trace of sky-blue around the cornea.

Like ice on fire.

Falcon.

He had memorized the tip of her right ear this morning on the airplane, and the Polynesian-pattern fabric in the scrunchie that held the chignon in place. She had been on the plane, no doubt about it. The malaise he had felt all week returned momentarily.

Patsy was looking at him as he stared at her sister. She tightened her grip on his hands.

"It's OK."

The Falcon reached for the scrunchie and pulled it free, letting the hair fall over her narrow shoulders. She shook it. Her hair was longer than Patsy's, and lighter, but there was no doubt from their facial features that they were sisters.

Doeman spoke, "Your friend doesn't talk much, Patsy." She was relishing his state of shock, looking almost under the steering wheel as she aimed the big limo down the road. She started to slow it down.

Patsy turned to him. "Would you like to meet my friends? This is my sister, Shannon Benham, and I believe you've met our chauffeur, Rebecca

Fisher, whom you may call Becky as soon as you can break the Doeman or Jane habit, and a few other choice nicknames Katy said you had for her."

Brent crawled forward along the limo's floor and extended his hand to Becky who put her left hand back as she steered with her right. Their touch was genuine. The looks in their eyes, unseen by Patsy and Shannon, spoke volumes between Brent and Becky.

He turned to Shannon, and he shook her hand. He then sat back onto one of the humps of the closed jump seats on the floor.

"I guess all I can say is *well done*. Jane, you put on the performance of a lifetime."

All three laughed. "We have a lottery going on how long it will take you to quit calling me Jane."

From far back in the limo Patsy said, "Slow down. The park's around the next point." She looked at Brent. "Could we interest you in a burger and a beer? We're going to a park with a restaurant next door that claims to be the home of the best burgers on the island."

"You could. And at this moment it's probably home of the best restroom in the islands."

No argument was heard there. Three of the four people aboard had been cooped up in the limo since they left the airport two hours ago, Becky, who drove it to the terminal area, Shannon the Falcon who made a mad dash from Gate 21 where she had just landed from a transpacific flight, to beat Brent the courier who himself had just landed on the same flight but took his sweet time to get to the Caddy.

Becky, a.k.a. Doeman, wheeled the big limo into the parking lot adjacent to the park.

The four disembarked and walked across the grassy expanse of the public park sloping down toward the ocean two hundred yards away. Patsy stopped, looked at Brent in his Mainland trousers, and asked Becky for the keys to the trunk.

"I've looked at this nerd all I care to," she said.

She opened the limo's trunk, pulled out a plastic bag, and tossed it to Brent.

Within the bag were the shorts that he couldn't find last night and a decent shirt, not a scrub shirt but at least a loose one appropriate for the surroundings.

"Put these on and you'll be the better man for it." And *voilá*! Beneath them in the bag was his favorite Hobie swimsuit that he assumed was at Patsy's. His missing Grisham novel was safe in the limo, returned to him by the warrior. Hang around long enough and who knows what else would show up – his duckie slippers?

He returned before his hostesses, last heard giggling on the path to the powder room, and admired the setting. He found a table beneath a thatched cabaña outside the bamboo-framed restaurant, adorned with nautical trivia, fishnets and outrigger canoe paddles – the travel-brochure décor of the islands. Two hundred feet across the park was a palm-lined two-story garden condominium complex with its own sandy beach and volcanic rocks to swim out to. Brent looked at it and thought that after the week he just had, a few days here wouldn't be too hard to handle. The L&H crew had already forgotten him by now anyway.

The girls walked back to the table from the restaurant lobby, and he watched them. Shannon was taller than he thought the Falcon might be – he'd never really seen her up close, standing still. She was as tall as he was. In her shorts she formed a montage of the earlier times he'd seen her – the long powerful legs on the bike by the river path, the slim ankles crossed under the table in The Shadows, the rail-thin torso, and those eyes. The chignon was gone. Patsy had shed her muumuu. He heard them commenting about Shannon's trip this morning. They sat down just as the waitress walked to the table.

Brent looked up at her. "A Budweiser, if you please and a burger medium-well. And water for my horse. My wives will order for themselves, and see what the boys in the back room will have. You may have the bill sent to our room."

The waitress shook her head in mock disgust, and all three girls ordered. Shannon looked at the limo across the park, then at Becky. "Who's driving that jalopy home? One of us better stick with something beside Bud, or we'll wind up upside down in a pineapple field."

"It sounds like you're volunteering. I drove out, you drive home. Sounds fair to me."

Shannon ordered an O'Doul's – Killarney Kool-Aid, as Brent called it in Rio Verde. But he always kept a few in the refrigerator for such occasions.

Brent looked at them.

"I'm waiting." Whatever was in the Thermos had started to take effect, he finally had a pair of shorts on, and he felt as though he'd rejoined the human race. "I believe you have a story to continue. You alluded to persons whom I once trusted congregating at Round Table for a giant pepperoni-and-Douglas last Monday night."

His look turned to Patsy. She started:

"I wasn't there. But rumor has it that the central issue was to get you to Hawaii for your birthday, and of course me with you. We decided that much at lunch on Monday."

"And a Hallmark Snoopy card and two plane tickets would have been too mundane?"

"Yes. That would have been sufficient for a mere mortal. But the decision was reached by the Knights of the Round Table that the mighty Scorpion must get himself there. With our help."

Becky chimed in. "I *was* at the pizza parlor. The general assumption by all was that you have an inventive, evil, twisted, some said sick mind, and tend to turn chance occurrences into chaos for those around you. We just decided to create a few chance occurrences and spent the next six pitchers making a four-day timetable to drop a few hints and let you self-destruct."

"Did you know then how it was going to come together?" Brent asked.

"No," Becky continued. "But we *did* know at lunch Monday that we had to get cookin' if we were going to pull it off by Thursday night. We had four days. So I called your VoiceMail and made an appointment for one o'clock Tuesday. Then I went shopping for the most unattractive clothes I could find. I found the little denim number that was two sizes too big for me at a second-hand store downtown. My roommate at the motel was clued-in and she made the appointment from a script I left her. She's dying to know how this thing came off."

Brent digested that. "OK, the Knights of the Round Table soaked up suds Monday and refined the scenario. Who among them came up with the relocated witness thing? That's what made it fly."

Shannon answered, "Actually most of the knights went *every* night for a critique of the day's activities, except for *Jane Doeman* here, who got a square meal on Wednesday. Then she looked at Patsy. "What was the name of that woman who was convinced that the two guys in the end booth were planning on robbing the place with the machine guns in their briefcase?"

Patsy answered, "Marcia Terrell. Jeff's wife. She's a little paranoid."

Brent laughed. "Yeah, like Hannibal Lechter's a little horny. Marcia came up with that?"

He was surprised. "That's uncanny. I saw Jeff in the break room Tuesday and I asked *him* about the relocated witness he sold a house to."

"That's not uncanny, Brent, it's a plan coming together. It *was* a little opportune that you asked, but as Sis said, you have a mind that goes right for that stuff. Actually, Jeff was dialed in that night at Round Table, and you'd have heard about his witness and the people chasing him if you hadn't asked, or even if you hadn't gone back into the break room. He'd have tracked you down and fit it into some conversation before the day was over."

Brent was beginning to understand the extensive planning that went into this.

"Who's *Doeman*? Who thought of that name? Christ, it sounds like *Jane Doe*."

"That's exactly how I started my life of subterfuge over the margaritas. Then it dawned on us that Jane Doe might sound a little fishy. So I became *Doeman*. We were afraid it was still too obvious."

"And you called me Brett just to annoy me."

"Right."

"Of all the things in the world you could have asked me to do, why the CCIM commercial real estate hocus-pocus when you asked for the information on my VoiceMail Monday?"

"Because the office agreed that you'd rather take a beating than have to do anything involving commercial real estate. Tom coached me on the terms out of some book in your office. I didn't have a clue what he was talking about, but he made me sound like an expert. He's not too keen on that stuff himself."

An understatement. He hates that lingo worse than I do, and the only time he'd talk about it would be to make my life miserable.

The hamburgers arrived. Truly the finest hamburgers on Oahu.

"What I'm interested in hearing about was your lunch at the Blue Heron," Shannon interjected. "By the way, you can thank Katy for that contribution. She knows your love for healthy food is legendary."

Brent looked at the huge bacon cheeseburger with the fries spilling onto the wooden tray in front of him.

"Katy did that to me? I hate that place. *That's* why we went there?"

Becky flexed her heavy arms like Charles Atlas and pumped out a chest to match. "Do I look like a health-food freak? That's the worse meal I ever had. After you dropped me off I walked to Burger King."

We could have carpooled. Small world...

"Somebody in there called you 'Jane'. How'd that happen?"

"Prearranged. An advance party from the office asked the cook if he'd call me Jane. Ditto with the waiter. Belsky told him that I was coming with a guy who used to trap condors for a petting zoo."

Becky's pale cheeks turned a little red. "Did you like my grand entry into your Explorer?"

"I've had other clients approach it differently. Was the swan dive intentional?"

"Actually, no. I had planned on looking a little ungainly, but when my knee slipped off the seat, I had nowhere to fall but forward. I was mortified."

"You didn't bring that denim suit with you here, did you?"

"Don't get your hopes up. It's in your dumpster at the office. Maybe the two tall guys that were going through the trash will find it."

❖   ❖   ❖

The burger boards were bussed away.

"Where did you come up with that marvelous machine?" Brent said, admiring the big silver sled across the park in the lot.

"Thank you, Captain Durst," said Patsy. "It seems that wherever airline flight crews run out of hours and stop to rest, a hundred of them chip in a few bucks to buy the biggest car they can find for under $500 then put some plates and insurance on it. Pretty doesn't count for much; it just sits out day after day shuttling between the company hotel and the airport. Hap knew we were coming here, knew the car would be available during the day Friday, so he had one of his buddies leave us the key after they used it this morning."

Brent turned to Becky again. He still had a hundred questions. "What was the shorthand you were using?"

"I have no idea. I don't take shorthand."

"Felicia says it was Cyrillic."

They all laughed. "It might have been. Apparently, it let your brain go into overdrive. You thought I was writing in Cyrillic, empirical proof that I'm a spy that nobody's told the cold war is over, and I'm still running around at warp speed doing whatever spies do in Rio Verde. Pretty sinister stuff."

"Who generated the two pages of four-letter symbols? Felicia said you couldn't do that if you tried without making a few recognizable words."

They looked at each other and laughed. "What pages? Did you ever see any encoded print-runs?"

Brent thought about that.

"No." That news came from Felicia. He never actually saw the printout.

He stared at a big trimaran on a broad reach a quarter mile out from shore. It was so wide it barely heeled in the swelling sea. Beautiful boat...

What else had he been snaked into? He thought fondly of the pretty, loyal receptionists, two of his better allies against a cold, harsh, uncaring world.

We can call your house, but it won't prove much – the office phones all sound like two cans strung together with tinfoil.

But he never heard the phones himself. He had taken Katy's word for it.

"Does Felicia really have a buddy at wherever that place was?"

"She really does, at Loma Linda Hospital," Patsy answered. "It dawned on her Monday night that he had been in Army Intelligence, so she called him Tuesday morning and he came up with a dozen buzzwords guaranteed to hit a spy of the Scorpion's renown's hot-buttons. Doeman's sad tale at dinner of her father the gunrunner was his creation, kind of based on a true story, really. And he helped Katy with the good-spy-Falcon, bad-spy-Doeman theory, which really made no sense whatsoever except to say that Falcon was your ally and you were grasping for an ally."

Becky feigned a look of deep hurt. "By the way, how come I never got a code name, like *Falcon*?"

Brent laughed. "Actually, after you mooned me getting into the wagon, I considered the *Penguin* but *Superman* had already taken it. Maybe I should have called you *Luna*."

Brent was now running down a mental checklist of the props and events to pull off the sting.

"What was that barcode reader you were using on those listing sheets you brought during the showing?"

Becky thought, and then said, "Watch a UPS driver next time you get a package. They scan the barcode labels with that thing so they can keep track of packages as they deliver them. Sooner or later they can download it in to a computer over a phone line. You didn't take a real good look at the barcodes, did you? They were all identical, something to do with second-day air to LAX terminal. Bobby Cochran can tell you how it works."

Bobby Cochran. Felicia's husband. Route manager for UPS. Looks like the picture of Harry Belafonte on a late 1950s RCA Victor album jacket, Harry on a sailboat with a red shirt open to the waist. Bobby was in on this too?

"Bobby was in on this?"

"Original cast. Brought us the code reader and a roll of barcode labels. I turned your information inside out, stuck the codes everywhere, and put some Roman numerals on it. I had no idea what I'd done, but I brought it Wednesday afternoon when we looked at houses."

The carpet cleaners? Bobby and Shannon?

Shannon grinned. "Yup. The brown coveralls were from UPS' truck shop, and we rented a carpet washer at Safeway as a prop. We parked and hauled it in, then just killed some time, hoping your neighbors would see them and tell you. Aldo showed up so we let him in on it, but if he hadn't, somebody else would have."

"Why did you take the Grisham book?"

"Dumb luck," Shannon said. "I started reading it while Bobby worked on some office stuff and we listened to some CDs. I walked out with the book accidentally. I guess I unintentionally gave you something to think about. Finished it on the plane this morning, by the way. Thanks."

"And you were in the white van at the reservoir?"

"That's Bobby's van. I rode Patsy's bike around the path once while Bobby was unlocking the Explorer with Patsy's key, just so you'd see me and let your devious mind try to attach some profound meaning to my being there."

Becky added, "We knew you noticed her Tuesday morning from the feedback we got from Felicia. She said your eyes fell out of your head when Falcon sashayed into the lobby. We couldn't trust Shannon with any contact with you because she was afraid she'd start laughing. It was all we could do to hold the dinner at The Shadows together with her down there watching. That wasn't easy. We went out earlier in the day and scoped out a table for us where you could see her on the deck. I met her after dinner in the ladies room and she had cracked up, dying to know what we were talking about at dinner."

"You had that table picked out before we got there?"

"Didn't you see the hostess' face when you asked for the *Smith* party? She was in on it, and I thought she might have given it away when she looked at us. Then I almost lost it when she said *walk this way*. That line was right out of an old cult movie called *The Young Frankenstein*, when Cloris Leachman told Marty Feldm..."

She paused as Brent started laughing, "I've seen the movie. I thought the same thing while we were following her!"

"The other time we almost lost it was in the escrow office. We had it set up with them for when you came in for the earnest money funds transfer Thursday morning. Toni was laughing so hard, she was afraid to look up from her desk."

Brent flashed back to that. "Where was Susie Santini?"

Patsy answered, "In the back room, probably. We told her to lay low on Thursday. Toni had a Brent-watch going in case you walked up the street. They all dove into the back room so they wouldn't start laughing. Kitty Perez didn't make it – she was half-under the counter while you were talking to Laura Bigelow."

"And who might Laura Bigelow have been?"

"She might have been Toni's mother, retired from teaching speech and drama at Fairfax High for 30 years. This was the role of a lifetime. All her escrow talk was scripted. We figured that if we created her deaf enough that you wouldn't hang around trying to BS with her like you usually do with all the escrow officers."

"How come all the listings were REOs? That couldn't have been just the luck of the draw."

Patsy fielded that. "When we decided Doeman should go out looking at homes, somebody had the good sense to realize that we could get a lot of innocent sellers' hopes up, so we made them REO properties. We knew that if banks owned them and they were on lockboxes, that nobody would be sitting around waiting for an offer."

Brent looked at Becky. "Why did Doeman have a beer at that last listing? I thought her body was a temple."

"Surprised myself there, Brent. I was so damn thirsty I didn't even think – just blurted it out. They sure hit the spot, didn't they?"

Brent got up and stretched. The sun had moved west while they talked, and the cabaña's shade no longer fell on his chair.

Much of the week had fallen into place. It's a miracle any work at all got done at L&H. His mother, obviously included. The agents in the office giving him the cold-shoulder; hell, they were probably on the verge of cracking up laughing for three days. The night on the river with Doeman. How much of her tenderness was play-acting? Did it start as a charade and almost get out of hand in the shadows by the river? For her, as much as for him? If she *was* acting, she's in the wrong business with the travel agency. She could make it in Hollywood.

Brent found a certain dichotomy to the Scorpion, with international mercenaries hot on his heels four hours earlier, and now his biggest concerns were making sure they had a designated driver and whether he could find a clothing store that took plastic in case he wanted to change shorts.

Brent looked at Becky. "You mentioned your roommate at the Best Western. Did you check in to the bed-and-breakfast downtown just for this caper?'

"Did you ever see me *inside* the building?" she answered.

The figure in the hat turned toward him. She rose to walk from the park bench across the deep lawn in the yard.

And later,

She stood at the heavy mahogany door with her hand on the knob, framed by the big oval beveled window as he walked toward the Taurus.

Brent laughed as Becky watched him recreate Wednesday night in his mind.

He'd never seen her inside the bed-and-breakfast.

And he thought of the dumpster. "Who was in the dumpster, or was Mike Driscoll in on this too?"

"In like a burglar," Patsy replied. "We brought him in because he would be out on his beat at two-whatever-it-was in the morning, and the call would have to come then to make the VoiceMail time signature right."

"That was one of the times you put *Doeman* in a tailspin," Becky added. "We never anticipated that you would tell me that the dumpster was raided, and when you did we had to have a war council to see how to handle it. I obviously had to fake some great concern, bordering on aborting the home purchases. So a few of us met. Happily for Felicia you had cut her loose early and she had nothing to do before her flight, so she joined us."

"How many pitchers?"

"Only two. It was a short meeting."

"Why Orange County for Patsy, the condo in Balboa?"

"Because that's where all the rich studs live, and you were doing penance," Patsy responded. "Where did you want me to go and pout, Buffalo?"

"That's where we could have blown it, too. Poor Katy was horrified – the news Thursday night reported that John Wayne airport closed for fog for the first time in seven years, after she told you that I could see Santa Catalina from Balboa!"

"Felicia is only 20 miles away from Balboa, probably looking for you right now," Brent remembered.

"Felicia knows damn well where we are."

Shannon looked at her watch, then at Becky. "We have to get that limo back to the hotel by four. We better think about rolling, but I believe we still have some debriefing to do."

Patsy had walked to the car and pulled out a beach bag, and slowly walked back holding it high for the other ladies to see.

Brent interceded, "Not so fast. Tell me about the five-dollar bill on the airplane this morning."

"OK." Patsy took this question, trying to get all this over with for the ceremony to follow. "Becky and I flew in last night at six o'clock; Shannon was on standby for a crew jump-seat on the same flight, but a four-striper bumped her. She spent the night last night in the employee dorm and only by luck, if that's the word, wound up on your flight.

"She saw you boarding, and her wheels started turning. She found an empty seat in front of you where you had to notice her chignon, which she basically hates but it became her trademark for this week. Except for her ponytail Thursday when you saw her by accident in the borrowed Miata leaving my house. She can tell you what happened on the plane."

Shannon took over. "I ducked into the crew locker area when I saw you and put my hair into that damned bun. I couldn't go forward because I knew you'd see me, so I called the captain, whom I flew with years ago, and asked him for a favor. I wrote a script for his announcement, told him to make it just before landing, and he told me he didn't even want to know what I was doing, but he'd make the announcement."

Shannon continued, "Vince Baransek was the purser, the male voice you heard on the line after one of the new stews, I didn't get her name, gave you the lead-in in the flattest voice she could muster. Vince's words were also scripted, and Vince and the stew both agreed with the captain that they didn't know me either if the thing got out of hand. Vince was pretty convincing, wasn't he?"

You are in grave danger.

"I tore up a five-dollar bill while you were on the phone getting paler by the syllable and stuck half in your crossword book while you were talking. My God, I was looking right at you down the aisle, scared to death you'd see me and screw up a week's work. Then when the plane landed, I was the first one off and ran like hell to get the torn bill and your Grisham novel to Percy and to clue him in on what to do with them when he found you. Then I had to find *Doeman* and the limo in the parking lot and get them to the passenger pickup area."

"Who's Percy?"

"A hairdresser in a beauty shop a lot of us use across from Waikiki. He was the Japanese fellow who had the other half of the five-dollar bill and babysat you until Patsy came aboard. Have you forgotten Percy already?"

The warrior?

"The guy was a *hairdresser*?"

Brent thought of the arms as big as tree trunks and those miserable little beady goddam sunglasses. And the leer.

"I wouldn't let him touch my hair," he said.

"Don't worry; he wouldn't have it any other way. And yes, he was set up earlier in the week, and that's where we got the H*awk* alias for you. His tattoo is an island legend."

"The blue seersucker suit holding the H*awk* sign. Who was she?"

"Just a friend we met last night who was catching the three o'clock back to LAX." Becky answered. "She thought the whole thing sounded like fun, so we gave her a job to do."

"Two last questions: Why did Doeman look so good Wednesday night? That didn't fit. And who was with the Falcon that night in the shadow on the deck?"

Becky blushed. "I just felt so damn stupid-looking and frumpy with my butt up in the air for the whole barbershop to see Tuesday that I wanted to look like a lady at dinner, maybe for myself. It didn't fit with the plan, but I couldn't stand to look like Doeman at a nice dinner house."

Shannon chimed in, "My date was Tom Yarbrough. He's really a nice guy. Thinks highly of you, by the way."

Patsy pulled the beach bag onto the table. Then she quieted for a moment.

"You probably ought to know that we almost lost the whole thing at one point. Katy finally couldn't stand what all this was doing to you after it really got moving, so she sent you home for a nap on Thursday afternoon. A grand finale on the Mainland was planned Thursday evening with a kidnap involving a white van, but she said if we didn't tone it down and just let you lance at your own windmills, she'd spill the beans right then. By the way, I called her and told her to spread the word with the staff that Brent had survived and, finally, had actually laughed. "

Patsy suggested a five-minute recess so the girls could powder their noses. Brent beat them back to the table and was enjoying watching the surf.

They had pulled off a four-day, 2,000-mile stunt with two dozen people involved, and nobody was hurt.

It was masterful.

The girls returned to the table.

He asked, "How much did this little stunt cost you guys?" He was feeling a little guilty.

Patsy answered, "About 300 bucks worth of beer and pizza."

Shannon asked Brent if he got her five-dollar bill back from the warrior. He fumbled around in his pockets.

"I guess not," he admitted.

"Make it $305."

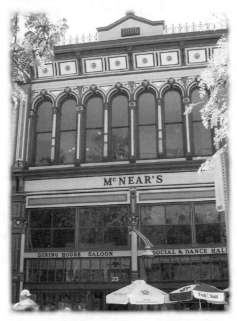

And lo, three came from the East bearing gifts...

Patsy reached into the nylon mesh beach bag that had been sitting on a table under a cabaña during the time it took Brent to wind down to the last of his questions, at least the last for now. All knew that when he finally lit back in Rio Verde he'd spend another week regaling his coworkers with a barrage of how dids? and what ifs?

She pulled out envelopes and packages directed to *Skipper* or the *Scorpion*.

"The occasion, which most of us have neglected in this spellbinding tale, is to celebrate your birthday. Your Hawaiian party has begun, the Rio Verde version will commence in your absence in two hours at the End of the Beginning." The hot mid-afternoon sun had moved enough to shine directly onto the table, and his hostesses had shed their beach cover-ups, leaving only bikini tops of varying hues and capacities. He approved of all the party decorations, large and small.

"To that end, your few remaining friends entrusted us to deliver some tokens of their love, appreciation, and tolerance toward you. We will start with this package, only if you can guess who sent it." She slid the first across the table, emerald-green wrapping with a thimble-sized gold 49'er helmet tied to the ribbon.

Brent feigned amazement. "Whoever could have sent this?" He slid his penknife under the taped fold on the end. A framed photo of Katy appeared, in her full cheerleading regalia, the 'Niners' offensive line huddled around her with a football they had autographed at her feet. This photo was a keeper, captioned *Happy Birthday, Brent* 1994 and destined for a special spot on his office wall. "Turn it over." Shannon was across the table and could see the back of the frame.

An envelope, small, with a note in Katy's handwriting was taped to it. *Ask for anything and you shall receive. Well, almost anything… Love, K.*

Inside the envelope was an invitation for two to a VIP box on the fifty, for the home opener against the Bills in three weeks. He felt something deeper in the box and kept digging, until he exposed the signed football shown in the photo. Another treasure for the office…

How he loved that girl. But of course, he couldn't let on…

A small box, now, for his attention. He slid off the paper and opened it. Aha. A new Garfield cup, to replace his old chipped and stained one. A card was inside:

I'll fill this every morning for a year, and you don't even have to call me sweetie!
And forget the gas in the Granada; it was worth it.
Love, *Felicia*
P.S. I *broke the code. It says* HAPP YBIR THDA YBRE NTXX

And now, an envelope. Curiously, this was to Brent and Patsy. He opened it. A key fell out onto the table, and a look of genuine surprise came over his face. Patsy smiled.

He looked up. "I'll read this.

"'Patsy and Skipper,

Landau hates that nickname…

'Thanks for a good job. North of the park where you are sitting now is a condominium with a pool, a beach, and the key to our old Toyota Tercel in the garage. Use them all. The key fits unit number eight. It's on the beach – we hope the sound of the surf won't keep you awake. See you a week from Monday, seven sharp. Thanks again.'"

Brent looked up, then back at the card. "It's signed, 'The two horses' asses.'"

Christ. Did I ever really call them that out loud or just think about it?

Penciled in under their signature, in different handwriting, *and their wives.*

Brent looked across the park at his new home for the week and pledged to take back almost every rotten thing he'd ever said about the founding fathers.

He thought of Horton Landau's idiotic invasion of his office meeting Wednesday morning, and questioned whether that pledge would hold. Then he looked again at the beachfront condo and its commodious chaise and a table for his morning coffee while he watched the grey whales sound out in the ocean, and the wahines comb the beach, or whatever wahines do in the morning.

OK, make it *every* rotten thing he had ever said.

Patsy slid the last package across the table toward him along with a huge card marked *Skipper* with somebody's stick drawing of a sinking sailboat with a battleship's smoking guns pointed at its wreckage.

He picked it up and gauged its size and heft.

Wonderful. Somebody gave me a toaster.

"Not so fast. Here's the card." He opened an oversize card. It was from the office staff. Each of those ingrates who had contributed to landing him into this enviable pickle had written a short note, and as he scanned them he could tell that most were uncharitable, the ladies taking various runs at him for his miserable treatment of their friend Patsy with that scarlet woman, and the men generally wanting to know what Doeman was like when he pulled her up to 30,000 feet and banged her throttles. Rafé's greeting was in Spanish, and even the janitor wished him *a happy berthday*. Mike Driscoll signed it with his badge number, indicating that he might have been slightly mistaken about the dumpster, sorry for the call, but happy birthday anyway.

Brent laughed out loud and put the card aside. He looked forward to reading each insulting greeting later.

He turned to the package. The girls were quiet. He could tell this was a dandy. He slid his knife under the gift-wrapping.

The box inside it was light grey, and he could see a multi-colored apple with a green stem and a bite taken out of it. He'd seen that trademark before on half the computers in the office. The wrapping obscured half of the bold black lettering on the box, all he could see was *ikTake* 1. He pulled the rest of the wrapping off and sucked in his breath. Just as he had done when he saw the blonde bun in the airliner, but this time for all the right reasons.

It was Doeman's digital camera.

The Apple *QuickTake* 100 digital camera that she carried Wednesday afternoon, the camera that he lusted after and was dying to pick up and sight through, but didn't want to give her the satisfaction of asking to borrow.

The camera he could take a picture with, and instantaneously enlarge it or shrink it or brighten it or put it onto his computer screen or send it to a friend or a client on a floppy disc.

He pulled the Styrofoam-packing halves apart and finally held it in his hands. He was somewhere between ecstatic laughter and tears. The girls just looked at him and smiled.

Patsy broke the silence. "Happy birthday, Skipper. I said it earlier, but I think you might have been preoccupied. That's from everyone in the office."

He just sat, laughing, starting to speak, then failing. And starting again. And failing again.

Shannon looked across the table at his watch as he aimed the camera toward the surf.

"We'd better leave you two alone. Have a great week."

Hugs were exchanged all around. Brent taking his last chance for a few birthday kisses, a pleasure afforded a gent of his stature and advancing years. He held Becky an extra moment, and just a little tighter than he did Shannon. He knew he'd never know if the walk in the shadows was an act, or two hearts at the precipice.

As Patsy and Shannon covered some last-minute sister stuff, Becky looked up at him and moved her lips in a low whisper that he barely heard.

Mahalo.

She turned and walked away, pulling Shannon along toward the limo. He watched.

You're welcome...

When they reached the limo, they both turned and waved, Becky slowly – with just the fingers of one hand.

❖   ❖   ❖

The limo drove back toward the big city. Patsy and Brent gathered up their gear and his gifts. The camera was on the sling around Brent's neck. He knew that Mainland cowboys take their hats off for only one reason, and suspected that their Hawaiian *kamaaina* counterparts probably do no differently. Brent's camera would only leave his neck for the same reason. He caught a sexy come-hither glint in Patsy's eyes.

The camera would probably be leaving his neck shortly.

Their condominium was spectacular, elegantly furnished in a Polynesian motif with an unimpeded view in both directions along the coastline. Patsy had stocked it when they landed last night with two steaks, among other things, and a miniature Jack Daniel's and a bottle of merlot she brought along from Rio Verde. White corn was a little hard to come by in the Islands. Enough of his clothes to get by for a few days and evenings, purloined out of his townhouse by Bobby and Shannon, were hanging in their closet. Brent spotted a gas-fired barbecue on the deck.

She rolled the sliding doors onto the lanai open allowing the sea breeze and the sound of the surf in. "It's modest, but we call it home until Sunday morning. Seven days is a good beginning."

Brent stood behind her and putting his hands on her slim waist, said, "Thanks. I could add a whole bunch, but it all comes back to that."

"You're welcome. The pleasure was ours."

"One other thing." He turned her to face him and said, "Something I said to Doeman during the week never came out this afternoon in the park."

"What was that?" she asked.

"You mentioned that seven days was a good beginning. Doeman – *dammit!* – Becky asked me at dinner Wednesday if I'd ever marry."

Yup. Got a lady all picked out, probably ask her to tie the knot by the end of the year.

Patsy grew light as a feather in his arms and drew in *her* breath.

She smiled, "Yeah, I think Becky might have mentioned that Thursday morning."

Brent looked her in the eye, "Well, we're going to have to talk about that this week."

"You're a romantic bastard, aren't you?!"

She held him close as she digested the truth that owing to the alterego of the Scorpion living within him, this moment may be as close as Brent will ever come to a proposal. After a moment she asked, "Want to see the rest of the condo? There's a dynamite view from the room at the end of the hall."

"Not so fast. I never got my present from *you*."

"Don't worry, Skipper. I wouldn't leave home without it."

And on those words of reassurance uttered as they walked down the hallway together, Brent's four o'clock meeting began...

Rio Verde, 4 months later...

Much to everyone's, and primarily **Brent's** surprise and amazement, **Patsy** broke off their engagement, leaving only a brief *Dear Brent* note bemoaning her second-fiddle status to the **Scorpion.**

❖　　❖　　❖

Rio Verde, 6 months later...

Katy reminded Brent that he had an in with a travel agent, namely Jane, er, Becky Fisher, who could help him arrange a surprise 50th anniversary trip for his mom and dad aboard the Concorde to Paris.

What better use for the money he'd earmarked for a honeymoon...?

❖　　❖　　❖

Rio Verde, two years later...

Kathleen O'Rourke married 'Niner rookie running back Seamus Geohegan, a second-round draft pick out of Notre Dame. They reside in a million-dollar home in Woodside, not far from Candlestick Park. She still journeys to Rio Verde every Friday for lunch.

Felicia Cochran left the firm to start a family with husband **Bobby** but remains as L&H's computer consultant. Her vaunted southpaw opponent has twice again blown her doors out in the national finals, but both were invited to a White House Excellence in Athletics banquet last year. She still drives the Granada.

Shannon Benham, a.k.a. the *Falcon,* and **Tom Yarbrough** bought a 36' Hans Christian and moor it on the Sequoia River where Brent must see it each morning on his way to work, but they have so far refused to let him sail it. Tom took Brent's place as manager of L&H; Shannon works out of their home on her computer linked to her company headquarters at International airport.

Horton Landau and **Oliver W. Holmes** sold the brokerage company to the agents, much to the chagrin of their wives, who then hired a secretarial service. The founders still play golf, frequently but separately, and visit the office, sparingly. Brent has kind words for both of them.

Rafé Morales' activities resulted in a state grant with matching federal funds for the creation of an ombudsman service, seminars and toll-free telephone assistance for Hispanic clients and state real estate licensees.

Pam Stone replaced Katy at the receptionist desk, following her graduation *summa cum laude* in microphysics from State University. She financed her education and the purchase of Patsy's home from the fees and royalties she received as a *Playboy* centerfold, featured in an eight-page foldout with the L&H lobby and break room as backdrops.

Pete Stephens and **Holly Harris** still work together as a highly successful real estate listing team. He has asked Brent to be his best man.

Lydia Wainscroft dumped her boring husband, let her flaxen tresses fall to her butt, quit the symphony and adapted her embouchure to a silver tuba she bought at the Rio Verde high school auction. She now spends several evenings a week alone on nearby Stinson Beach playing Andrew Lloyd Webber favorites into the setting sun.

Jeff Terrell left L&H and moved to Seaside, Oregon after his wife **Marcia** sold a novel about a mild-mannered real estate agent who got dragged into a web of international espionage by an unattractive caterpillar who later metamorphosed into a beautiful butterfly. They hangar their Learjet in nearby Astoria and visit Rio Verde occasionally.

Captain Hap (D*ead Stick*) Durst bought a franchise for coin Laundromats in the aft sections of wide-bodied aircraft on transoceanic flights to offer passengers a worthwhile alternative to in-flight movies. Heat for the dryers is bled from the final compressor stages of the planes' inboard engines, a process Hap received a lucrative patent for.

Tom Rathman, who Katy replaced in the closing seconds of Brent's daydream, joined the Los Angeles Raiders and made a four-yard plunge with time off the clock to win himself and coach Art Shell another Super Bowl ring.

Lawrence Taylor, who blew the tackle allowing Katy to score in that daydream, left the gridiron as one of the all-time greats in the NFL's history. His 56 jersey was retired a year later.

The **Blue Heron Health Food Café** was the site of the second-largest drug bust in the northern part of the state, resulting in indictments of all of the employees and most of its devotees. The building is now occupied by The Spotted Owl, an upscale hamburger-and-chicken-wing café and microbrewery.

The **M.S. Steamer Gold** was found in a marine salvor's yard across the bay, then refurbished and towed to its old berth at **McNear's Mill** in time for the mill's centennial celebration. It's now a floating museum and chamber of commerce.

Dave Nichols and **Patsy Benham Nichols** are the proud parents of three-month-old twins. Tom canned Dave from L&H just on general principles. Patsy considers her life now peacefully dull with only the never-ending demands of two infants replacing the unpredictable antics of the **Scorpion.**

The old chapel/office became the headquarters for The Douglas Property Management and Travel Agency, the popular new husband-and-wife firm in Rio Verde. The clock on the belfry still reads 7:16.

Brent still leaves the Villa Verde townhouse early each morning for their new office, as **Becky Fisher Douglas,** a.k.a. **Jane Doeman** waves goodbye to her husband, slowly, with just the fingers of one hand…

❖   ❖   ❖

Douglas Property Management & Travel Agency